Praise for *THE UNDOING*

"Beautifully imagined and beautifully written, hypnotically suspenseful and truly chilling...this is a very superior thriller."
—#1 *New York Times* bestselling author Lee Child

"Smart, gripping, and thoroughly absorbing. Dean's *The Undoing* had my brain twisted for hours."
—*New York Times* bestselling author Chelsea Cain

"Averil Dean's *The Undoing* is a tense, suspenseful tale that pulls the reader down a twisted path to the spine-tingling conclusion."
—*New York Times* bestselling author Heather Gudenkauf

"Dark and haunting...a beautifully disturbing character study. And the writing itself—this isn't simply good prose. The words are poetic and painful and unforgettable. *The Undoing* is a superb novel. Dean's career as a suspense writer is going to be great fun to watch."
—*New York Times* bestselling author J.T. Ellison

Praise for *ALICE CLOSE YOUR EYES*

"Chilling, riveting, intriguing, surprising and compelling, and I can't think of a debut that kept me turning pages faster or more breathlessly."
—M.J. Rose, international bestselling author of *Seduction*

"*Alice Close Your Eyes* is a crisply written, wickedly suspenseful debut...a dark, sensual nightmare.... Don't miss it."
—David Bell, author of *Cemetery Girl* and *Never Come Back*

"*Alice Close Your Eyes* will have readers on the edge of their seats. Promising newcomer Dean spins a web out of the deepest human obsessions...to reveal a haunting story."
—*Booklist*

"Dean's marvelous debut is dark, gritty and relentless... This psychological thriller borders on the erotic as it draws the reader into its web."
—*RT Book Reviews*, 4 stars

"A haunting, intense novel that is at once psychologically compelling and emotionally unsettling. Taut pacing and skilled storytelling support a breathtaking plot and characters that are heartbreaking and horrifying yet somehow still accessible and sympathetic. It's scorching, disturbing and tragic, but well-crafted and impressively written."
—*Kirkus Reviews*

"An absorbing, deeply disturbing, darkly erotic psychological thriller of tragedy and revenge. Fans of...Gillian Flynn (*Gone Girl*)...will love this disquieting novel."
—*Library Journal*, starred review

Also by Averil Dean

ALICE CLOSE YOUR EYES

THE UNDOING

AVERIL DEAN

A NOVEL

Recycling programs for this product may not exist in your area.

ISBN-13: 978-0-7783-1739-5

The Undoing

For questions and comments about the quality of this book, please contact us at CustomerService@Harlequin.com.

www.MIRABooks.com

Printed in U.S.A.

First printing: January 2016
10 9 8 7 6 5 4 3 2 1

For Andy

THE UNDOING

"Be that word our sign in parting, bird or fiend," I shrieked, upstarting:
"Get thee back into the tempest and the Night's Plutonian shore!
Leave no black plume as a token of that lie thy soul hath spoken!
Leave my loneliness unbroken!—quit the bust above my door!
Take thy beak from out my heart, and take thy form from off my door!"
Quoth the Raven, "Nevermore."

Edgar Allan Poe

AUGUST 2014

JULIAN MOSS UNFOLDED the note and pressed it over his face with both hands. With his fingertips he molded the paper to his eyelids. His thumbs pushed the edges to his cheeks. The paper smelled like money now, like old leather and sweat. He wished he had a mirror so he could see whether the ink had transferred to his face, the opening line like a blue tattoo across his forehead:

Julian~
I know what you did.

He eased forward, the note dangling from his fingers. Gravel crunched under his boot and skidded over the ledge, clattered on the rocky outcropping at his feet, then plummeted in silence to the river far below.

A long-ago conversation trailed through his mind: his father's voice, describing a friend who had dived from the penthouse suite of a Seattle high-rise. The guy had gone there with a real estate agent as if he were looking to buy the place, making polite conversation throughout the showing, checking the taps, full of jokes about the owner's choice of flooring and all the mirrors in the master bath. When it came time to leave, the agent glanced back and saw his client's feet disappear over the railing.

A quick death, according to Julian's father. From that height it would have been like dropping a water balloon.

Not that it would be that way for Julian. The ravine was not that deep, and the slope dropped off in a series of rocky shelves. There would be no spectacular burst at the end, no terrible, literal emptying of his head. For him it would be more concussive, like a pumpkin tossed down a flight of concrete stairs.

The agent said he'd heard his client laughing, right at the end. Julian could understand the guy's state of mind. He felt the same giddiness, a lightening of the senses, as if the air itself were pulling him skyward, the pine trees standing like spectators with their arms out ready to clap.

His eye was caught by a yellow wink of light at his wrist. His watch. He imagined his mother, signing for his possessions at the county morgue, finding the watch among them. Knowing or coming to know what it meant.

A dizzying relief poured through him at having remembered in time. He unclasped the band and pulled off the watch. The hands had long since stopped turning. A diamond had come loose from the face and rattled around behind the glass like the bead in a Cracker Jack toy. Easing back from the ledge, he wound up and threw the watch as far as it would go. The band turned itself inside out as it went, flashing and wriggling in the air. It sailed across the ravine and disappeared into the scrub on the other side.

His arm seemed lighter without it. A faint stripe showed at his wrist, the skin there tender and pale where the sun hadn't reached and where the dark hair of his forearm had worn away. Strange to think how much the watch had meant to him once.

The heft of it, the shine. How was it that he'd never realized how heavy the thing was? For the first time in years, he felt the weight of both arms equally, one no lighter than the other, neither side dragging him down.

A fine feeling, balance. He wished he'd tried it sooner.

He steadied himself with one hand around the branch overhead. The rough bark was gummed with sap, releasing the astringent scent of pine into the morning air. To his right, at the tip of a crescent-shaped shelf of rock, a veil of white smoke lifted into the sky. Through the haze he could see the skeletal outline of the Blackbird Hotel. Its spine and ribs stood in jagged black lines against the sky, and at the far end, the old stone chimney teetered unsupported, leaking smoke from both ends. As he watched, an arc of water rose over the ruins, undulating gently as the fire hose swept back and forth. A subtle rainbow formed in the mist, appearing from the ground, then fading, unfinished, just before the apex.

He raised his eyes and looked out the mouth of the ravine, past the smoldering hotel to the bank of the mountain range beyond. Wide swaths of the hillside had been cleared and were thick with late summer grass that gleamed in the sunshine like new-fallen snow. The lifts were still now, spidery black cables trailing post to post up the hill in shallow arcs, the chairs swaying gently in the breeze. He imagined himself hurtling downward, the air whistling in his ears, the far-off roar of the crowd tugging at the tips of his skis. A rise in the snow, liftoff, his body tucked up tight as the chatter of the skis was silenced.

It had been years since he'd felt the wind that way, self-generated, in evidence of his own physical power. Already he could feel his body weight, the inexorable tug of gravity against the soles of his feet, the mindless acceleration. He wondered whether his father's friend had laughed all the way down for the sheer joy of falling.

The note fluttered in his hand as if calling for attention.

He let it slip from his fingers. The paper drifted down and caught on a thorny bush, opening and closing in the breeze like the beak of a duck. He could see the words inside—*I know what you did*—abruptly superimposed with the memory of Eric's voice in that dead-on mimic, quacking like Donald Duck.

Julian laughed, a wide, billowing sound that swelled around his ears and made him sway on his perch like a bird in high wind. The wave of hilarity lifted him to his toes, drew his head and shoulders steadily back. But once started, the laughter wouldn't stop. It began to grind through his torso, shred his throat, until he was drawn stiff as a bow on the edge of the ravine and racked with pain. He loosened his grip on the branch and opened his hand, let the bark scrape over his palm and all the way down his fingers. Then he let go.

His hands filled with air, a gentle kiss over the sting.

Oh, Celia.

How she would love to see him now.

ONE DAY EARLIER

THE TOWN OF Jawbone Ridge started life around a copper mine. No more than a diggers' camp at first, a ramshackle collection of pine-log boxes that flanked the road, which snaked through the treacherous San Juan Mountains to feed the community and shift the copper ore. The camp was soon fortified by a mercantile and a saloon, legitimized by two brick hotels and a post office, and for a time the people thrived. But eventually the price of copper plummeted and the miners moved on, leaving the hollowed-out detritus behind them.

The slope was steep on that side of Deer Creek, and a century's worth of Colorado snow had exhausted the town, which was gradually losing its grip on the mountainside, collapsing down the embankment to the riverbed below. The surviving buildings had gone swaybacked and frail, propped up on nests of two-by-fours and tied to the trees around them like elderly relatives on life support.

The slow spectacle was a draw for visitors to nearby Telluride, who skied in to the Ridge for lunch and dumbstruck pictures—*Can you even believe this place is still standing?*—and returned along the network of ski lifts to the cloud-laced peak, then down again on Telluride's side of the mountain, trailing perhaps a new set of poles or a scarf with the town's tagline in bloodred letters, listing sideways as if toppling down the fleece: *The Crookedest Town in the West.*

It was a living. Barely. A few overbuilt homes were nestled among the aspen, the ultimate in inaccessibility, but for the most part the charm of Jawbone Ridge was lost on the masses. The town's precarious situation made visitors uneasy and anxious to get away. The ground there felt uncertain, and the year-round residents had a strange way of moving, never stepping too hard on the frozen ground, their eyes sliding warily uphill as if waiting for the mountain to let go and finally finish them off.

At the far end of town, the road curved sharply along the edge of the ravine, then split off and turned abruptly uphill. The windshield of Julian's car filled for a moment with pine boughs against a flat blue sky—then, as the road leveled off, the scene was replaced as if by magic with the roof, walls, windows and doors of a dark, narrow building.

Julian turned the car aside on the gravel lot and killed the engine.

Next to him, a woman's voice filtered back into his mind.

"…two years ago. And it was beautiful weather. We didn't even want to stop. We were the last ones on the gondola, and by the time we got to the top I had to pee so bad I didn't think I'd make it to the bathroom."

Emma giggled, a soft purring sound. She stretched widely, seeming to notice for the first time that they had arrived. She pressed her hand to the window, fingers spread like a spindly starfish.

"What is this place?" she said.

After the blocky cabins and rugged lines of Jawbone Ridge, the hotel next to them was strangely proportioned, crouching on the edge of the ravine as if driven there by the cluster of buildings below. A tall, crooked little place, with two steep arches flanking the portico and a roof like a hat smashed down over the top. The age-blackened walls imposed a sort of gravitas, and the leaded windows a sense of romance, but the hotel gave Julian the impression of a child at the edge of the playground who has not been asked to play.

Dark, neglected, unloved and unremembered.

No. Not true. Celia had loved the Blackbird. And Julian sure as hell remembered.

He popped the trunk and pulled out their bags: his, in sleek charcoal gray, hers a candy-apple red, studded around the handle with rhinestones that bit into his palm. A damned silly color for a suitcase and exactly the sort of thing Emma would choose. She had a passion for bling and kept herself well glazed: lip gloss, diamond earrings, a satin headband to hold back her wheat-blond hair. The effect was so convincing that he had only noticed her weak chin yesterday morning when she got out of the shower, her hair slicked back and face bare of makeup. This girl hadn't even been given orthodontics, and here he'd taken her for money, for one of his own. Now he noticed the overbite all the time and held it as a sullen resentment against her, as though somehow she'd deceived him.

She was smiling up at him now, her rabbity head tilted to one side.

"Used to be part of the copper town." Julian nodded toward the sign in black and red above the door: BLACKBIRD HOTEL. "Built by the mine owner so he'd have someplace to stay when he was in town, above the stink of it all. It's changed hands many times since then, been modernized and all that."

He faced the hotel with their bags in his hands.

An unexpected thrill of anticipation expanded in his chest. Any second now, Celia would open the door, or lean out an upstairs window, her hair lifting out like a banner, that slow smile on her face to show she'd been waiting for him. The sensation was so strong that for a moment he found himself searching the windows for movement, straining to hear her voice.

A second later, the excitement subsided. She wasn't here. She never would be again.

Emma was waiting for him. She seemed to occupy too small a space in the scene, as if he were seeing her through the wrong end of a telescope.

"Are we going inside?" she said.

Too late now to change his mind. A cold knot of dread replaced the warmth of his original response. The Blackbird didn't want him here any more than Celia had.

They crossed the rutted gravel lot and mounted the front steps. Julian opened the heavy wooden door and held it with his foot as Emma went inside. A bell hanging from the brass knob jingled as the door swung shut behind them.

Beyond the tiny vestibule, the room opened with surprising expansiveness to a tall, narrow space with a massive stone fireplace towering like a sentinel on the opposite end of the room. To their left was a winding staircase with a curved wooden banister, soaring up to the second floor. At its foot, a heavy door stood half-open; through the doorway, he could see a couple of hammered copper pots hanging from a rack and the edge of the long kitchen table. Celia had sanded that table to a beautiful sheen and finished it in a rich chestnut brown. She used to rub it down with an oiled rag after every meal; you'd catch the scent of it sometimes while you were eating, a faint bite of lemon where the warm plates sat.

As he watched, the kitchen door opened farther. A woman came halfway through the doorway and stopped. She was wearing a dark T-shirt and a pair of designer jeans so tight they had set into a series of horizontal creases up her thighs. On the front of her shirt was a screen-print image of the Blackbird Hotel, in white lines like a child's drawing on a chalkboard.

Julian caught his breath.

Again he felt vaguely disoriented, thrown back in time. Yet Kate Vaughn was unmistakably part of the present. Her brown hair was lighter now, longer and fashionably streaked, but she looked much older than when he'd last seen her five years before. The babyish roundness of her face had gone, leaving a sharper line at her cheekbones and chin. It was the face of a beautiful woman now, evolved and polished. Cute little Katie, he used to call her. But it seemed that girl, like so many other things, was gone.

He thought at first that she was going to come forward and embrace him. She took one step, then hesitated as if she'd changed her mind.

"Julian," she said.

"Hello, Kate."

"How are you?"

"Surprised, at the moment. I didn't realize you'd be here."

He understood the lay of the land immediately. Kate's family must have bought the only remaining property on the Ridge. Presumably to indulge her, to assuage any lingering grief; the Blackbird was far too small to make more than a very modest profit. Nothing like the Vaughns' resort hotel in Telluride or the two in Vail and Crested Butte. Kate had probably finagled this tiny property out of her father like a kid with her heart set on a fancy tree house.

He'd met Justin Vaughn once or twice. A sweet, shrewd guy with three daughters and a knack for keeping them happy. Kate was the youngest by fifteen years, and she could wrap her father around her little finger simply by adding an extra syllable to his name: *Dad-dy, can you lend me the car? Dad-dy, will you buy me a hotel of my own, the Blackbird Hotel, we can't let them tear it down…*

"Oh, you two know each other?" Emma said, affecting an air of cool disinterest.

"We used to," Kate said. "In the biblical sense. Kate Vaughn."

Emma's face was blank as she took Kate's outstretched hand. "You went to church together?"

Kate's mouth twitched at the corner, a dimple winking in her cheek. The moment swelled as Julian realized he should introduce them and couldn't, because he didn't know Emma's last name and wasn't entirely sure of her first one. Emma could be Ella, or Anna, or Abby, or Eve. He had resorted to an assortment of pseudo-endearments over the past few days, waiting for her to repeat her name—which, maddeningly, she never did.

Kate turned to Julian.

"You heard about the reopening, I take it? Did you get our email? I blasted it to everyone in my contacts."

He nodded. It had given him a shock to see the Blackbird's photograph appear on the screen. He'd shut the window down immediately, unable to open it again for more than a week. When he finally gathered the courage, he pored over every page and all the fine print on the hotel website.

THE HISTORIC BLACKBIRD HOTEL
GRAND OPENING
JAWBONE RIDGE, COLORADO

Nowhere had the flyer mentioned the Blackbird was now one of the Vaughn family properties.

"I didn't realize—" he said again.

"Yeah, that's my dad's thing. I think he doesn't want people to realize it belongs to us. Not our finest business investment, by a long shot. He probably wants to save face if the whole thing folds or falls off the cliff or something."

She walked over to a small desk, where a computer sat next to a stack of unopened mail. Insects buzzed from outside the half-open windows.

"So, what's up? Do you need a room?"

"No," said Julian.

"Yes," said Emma at the same time.

"We just wanted to see the place," he said. "We don't need a room. Probably stay at the Adelaide."

It was a foolish thing to say, with two suitcases at his feet and this fluffy blonde hotel accessory clinging to his elbow. But seeing Kate here unnerved him, gave his anger a point around which to coalesce.

"It looks good," he said, glancing around. "Very...tasteful."

A deep flush rose up her neck. "Yes, well, I'm not sure the whole bohemian thing would have worked out that well in the long run."

"I think it would have worked fine."

"Do you? Would you have me leave it as a shrine?"

"I would have had you leave it alone."

"Ah. And is that what you're doing? Leaving it alone?"

Julian pressed his lips together.

"They were going to tear it down," Kate said. "I'm trying to save it. I would have thought you'd approve. They were your friends, too."

"What friends?" Emma said.

"You didn't tell her about the murders?" Kate said.

"She doesn't need to hear about that," Julian said.

"Murders!" Emma said. "Of course I need to hear about it. When was this?"

"What's it been now, Julian?" Kate said. "Five years?"

A slow prickle crept up Julian's back, under the collar of his cotton shirt. His ears seemed to fill with sound, a low, almost electrical hum that muffled the sound of her voice.

Five years. An anniversary, a number that meant something, that indicated something might happen again. Five. Dangerous, sharp-sounding, like a blade or the edge of a stony cliff.

"Five," he said, carefully.

"Wait, you were here?" Emma said.

"We were both here," Kate said. "Staying in the hotel, that is. We didn't witness the crime or anything."

A sour taste convulsed Julian's mouth. *No,* he wanted to say, *I didn't see a thing; it's nothing to do with me.* But the words were swimming in water and he couldn't get them out.

"Oh," Emma said. "So who was murdered?"

Kate slid behind the desk and switched on the computer. "My friends. My three best friends."

Emma was taken aback. "Oh. I'm sorry, I thought…if you don't want to talk about it…"

"Celia Dark. Celia's stepbrother, Rory McFarland, and her boyfriend, Eric Dillon."

The computer chattered to life, an alien presence in the gothic gloom.

"We don't need to go into it." Julian's temple ached from gritting his teeth.

"I don't mind." Kate smiled and gave Emma a little half shrug. "It was a long time ago. And anyway, there's no escaping the topic here on the Ridge. It was all anybody talked about for months. You couldn't get away from it, not if you lived here."

Julian walked to the other end of the room, where the boxy new furniture was arranged around the fireplace. It looked nothing like it had five years before, nothing like the way he remembered it.

After the murders, Kate had sent snapshots of the common

room and kitchen, along with a bundle of newspaper clippings she'd carefully packed and mailed to his mother's address in New York. Block headlines at first with thick chunks of text, then smaller, sketchier pieces, featuring standard-issue high school pictures of the three victims and a bigger photo of the Blackbird Hotel. The news petered out at last to a single column of newsprint from the obituaries page: Eric Dillon, Rory McFarland. Their faces grinned out at him, blurred as if by smoke, the ink like soot on his hands.

There was no obituary for Celia. Julian never knew whether the paper hadn't run one or whether Kate had simply forgotten to include it with the others.

"So did they catch the murderer?"

"There was no one to catch."

"You mean, one of them killed the others?"

"Maybe. It's hard to tell for sure. We know that Celia's stepbrother, Rory, was killed first. He was in the kitchen, shot once in the chest. The room was in a shambles—broken dishes everywhere, chairs overturned. Apparently he and Eric had been fighting. There was a broken bone in Rory's hand and two in Eric's face, blood everywhere. Which was exactly what you'd expect from any fight Rory was involved in. The police assumed at first that Eric had left the fight and came back with a gun to finish it. But that didn't seem to make sense when they looked at everything else."

"Why's that?" Emma asked.

"Because Celia was the one left holding the gun."

It occurred to Julian that Kate must have told this story a hundred times. It had the rhythm of a recitation, a prayer-like cadence. He wondered what it was like here on the Ridge, afterward, what the locals made of it. He had almost no memory of the town itself. Its residents were part of the peripheral setting in his mind rather than personalities in their own right. Reddened, snow-scrubbed faces, thick hands, everyone booted and stomping in doorways, swallowed up by their winter clothes. No one outside the Blackbird had penetrated his consciousness far enough to leave more than a faint impression.

He went to the window. From the sun-dried slopes, crossed with lift lines and dotted with dusty snowplows, the mountains stretched north for hundreds of miles. Though the hills and valleys were covered with trees, they felt barren to Julian, motionless and devoid of life. He wished he'd come back in the wintertime, to see the mountains caked with snow and everyone outside enjoying it.

Kate went on.

"So they thought maybe she was trying to stop the fight and shot Rory by accident, then blamed Eric for what happened and killed him, too."

"And where was she?" Emma said. "Your friend?"

"Upstairs, in her bed. Shot through the heart. The gun was still in her hand." Kate's gaze fixed on him. "Julian's gun, actually."

Emma looked at Julian doubtfully, and Kate laughed.

"He was with me at the time," she said. "That's my story, and I'm sticking to it."

"So it was all an accident, in a way," Emma said. "Why do people always fight when they go on vacation?"

"Oh, they weren't on vacation." The computer had booted up, and Kate sat down in front of it. "They owned this place, the three of them together. They were in the process of renovating to turn it into a B&B. There was a little tray of spackling paste in the kitchen, still wet. Celia had been prepping the walls for a coat of paint when the trouble started."

"What were they fighting about? Money?" Emma looked disappointed, as if the ghost story had let her down.

"That's a good question. The only question that matters,

really. But it wasn't money. They weren't like that. No one could understand what had changed, why they suddenly imploded that way. It didn't make sense."

A memory crept into Julian's mind: a dead sparrow in the grass, its legs curled like dried twigs, and the revulsion on Celia's face as she looked at it. Celia hated death. She was terrified by it. Yet she'd taken her own life and the lives of her two best friends. She loved them and she killed them and she killed herself. What they were fighting about didn't explain a thing.

Across the room, a jingle. Kate was trying to give them a room key.

"No," he said. "I told you—we're going to the Adelaide."

"Oh, but I want to stay here," Emma said. "Maybe we'll see a ghost."

Kate handed her the key. Emma turned to him, grinning, dangling the key chain over her thumb.

"Why did you buy this place?" he said. "What was the point?"

Kate sat back, light from the computer washing over her face.

"I don't know, Julian. I guess I just couldn't let it go."

He held his face impassive, but his throat was tight with grief and something akin to fear. He picked up their bags. They seemed much lighter now than they had ten minutes ago; he could barely feel them.

As they reached the foot of the winding staircase, Emma paused to look back.

"What were they like?" she said.

"Oh," Kate said, as if this was something she'd never considered. "They were…"

Silence crept into the room. From far away, Julian could hear the echo of laughter, the bright crackle of the fire, a murmur of music and voices.

Dead. All dead, and they had taken him with them.

Kate turned her head toward the kitchen, the half-open door. Her answer came just as Emma started up the stairs, leaving only Julian to hear.

"They were really young."

Kate stayed at her desk as Julian and his girlfriend disappeared into the upstairs hallway. She could hear the girl's voice, still chattering, exclaiming over the old hotel, and Julian's grumbled responses. A door opened and closed, leaving Kate alone in the silence.

For a few minutes she sat where she was, staring out the window. A blue jay hopped along the gnarled branch of a spruce tree, tipping its head to get a look at her. She imagined herself from the bird's point of view, framed by the windowpanes, alone at her desk, how she'd still be here when the bird looked down from high above.

I'm lonely, she thought, surprised.

She opened the right-hand drawer of the desk. Under some folders and a stack of bills, she found a photograph, still in its heart-shaped frame. Eric had taken that picture. She remembered looking back at him, with the whole snowy mountain laid out at their feet and Julian's arm snug around her shoulders. Both of them grinning so hard at some joke of Eric's, Celia and Rory flanking the camera, doubled over with laughter. She wished she could remember what they all had found so funny, two months before the laughter died.

She had hardly recognized Julian today, he'd changed so much. Even his voice, once smooth and self-assured, now had climbed in pitch and developed a petulant whine like a child's. And his face, though still tanned as it was in the photograph, seemed sallow and pinched, with a furrow between his brows and a strange new habit of dragging his gaze around the room as if the sight of it exhausted him.

She wondered what Julian had been doing over the past five years. The last time she saw him was the night of the murders, when he had taken her home with some vague promise to check on her the next day. But he never did that. Like the others, he was simply gone.

She had heard about him from time to time: Julian was in Australia, New Zealand, Indonesia. Hot places, sunny and flat. An odd itinerary for a skier.

She had nearly forgotten him until last winter, when she'd run into Zig Campanelli at a bar in Telluride. Zig was Julian's best friend—if Julian had one of those. They had known each other since they were teenagers. It would have seemed strange not to ask after him, and after a few minutes she did. But even Zig seemed puzzled by the changes in Julian.

"He's not skiing anymore," Zig said. "Hasn't for years. I don't know whether he busted something important or got bored or what. Last time I heard from him, he was in Bali, said he was sick of the snow. That's all I could get out of him. He sounded…"

"What?"

But Zig only shook his head.

"This is it," Emma said. She shut the door behind them and leaned back with an ecstatic sigh. "This is where she died. I can feel it."

The buzz in Julian's ears had built to a dull roar. Who was this girl to say she felt something from Celia? As if she knew anything at all about what had happened, had even a sliver of an idea what it was all about. He ground his teeth in anger.

Shut up. Stupid girl.

What had he been thinking to bring her here? Here, of all

places. She was nobody special, a friend of a friend, the tail end of a long chain of acquaintances that had started, as far as he could remember, with his buddy Zig Campanelli. The two of them had worked together for a time at ESPN and maintained a sporadic friendship over the years, which was built more on a mutual need for points of contact than true affection.

Zig had a way of introducing Julian that set them both up for admirers.

"This is my good friend Julian Moss," he'd say. "Used to make a living carving up the ski slopes, kicking my ass most of the time. Swept the championships more than once, went to the Games and came home with a bronze in downhill. Then somebody noticed he's not all that bad-looking, under the helmet." Here he'd give Julian a friendly little clap on the shoulder. "My boss gave him a job anchoring the championships at ESPN. And the rest, as they say, is history."

And he'd saunter off, drink in hand, leaving Julian with another chance to parlay that biography into something truly worthwhile.

Julian hadn't seen Zig in years, but, like the Olympic medal, he was the gift that kept on giving. When Julian had surfaced again in Colorado three weeks before, there wasn't a scene in which he wouldn't have known someone who knew someone else.

In fact it was Emma, her girlfriends giggling and clutching at each other in the background, who had approached him. They must have talked at some point, to some end, but if so the conversation had been so perfunctory that he couldn't remember a word of it. She was in his bed the next morning. He had fucked her and she was willing to be fucked again and was not inclined to complain about the fact that his head was not with her for a moment. He was a status lay for her. The thrill, if there was one, was in his name.

It was a fair trade. When he asked her later that day to come up here with him, she agreed happily, possibly imagining herself as Julian Moss's girlfriend, a further bump in status. She could write about it on Facebook, or send a Tweet, or whatever was the latest venue for the humblebrag: *Driving up to Telluride with Julian. First time in an F-Type, OMG!!!*

She was entitled to that. It was his end of the trade. He was aware that the ache in his jaw was not Emma's fault. She couldn't help the nasal drone of her voice or the fact that it bored into his ear like a hungry beetle. It was irrational to blame her when she was clearly doing her best. But every time he looked at her vapid face—features so like Celia's but put together all wrong—he wanted to take her by the shoulders and shake until something came loose.

He set down the suitcases and walked slowly back to her. Emma gazed up with a fatuous smile as if she thought she was too goddamned irresistible for words. He unbuttoned her shirt. She was wearing some sort of push-up bra, with a hard lace-encrusted pad that scratched his palm.

Celia had never worn anything under her shirt. The shallow swell of her breast made barely a ripple in her clothing, so he supposed she didn't need one. But he'd once caught a peek through the armhole of a loose-fitting blouse, where her ribs laddered up the side of her bare chest, and he'd sprung so fast he had to leave the room.

"Take your pants off," he said to Emma. She wriggled out of her jeans and stood against the wall with her hip cocked, grinning as if she expected him to take her picture.

He put his hand between her legs. Right away she started to sigh and coo, wriggled into his hand with that eager camera-smile on her face, cupping her breasts in her hands so that the ridge of her implants stood out beneath her skin.

An easy girl. The kind of girl he used to enjoy. He'd tell

her what to do and she'd go along, eager to please, those vacant, colorless eyes blinking up at him while she sucked him off like she'd seen the pretty girls do on cable TV. She might throw in some move of her own, some tease of her fingers across his balls or a knuckle to the perineum, something she'd read about in *Cosmo* and could claim for her own. Probably she'd swallow when he came, going *mmmm* like his semen was the best thing since mint chocolate chip. And it would be good for the moment. But in a week or a month, she would recede with the rest of them, who existed in his memory like the cities in a traveler's diary, dreamlike and insubstantial but determinedly annotated:

—the dreadlocked woman whose breasts dripped like ripe fruit into his open mouth (Burning Man, milk lady)

—the French virgin with skin so dark she seemed to melt into the shadows, disembodied, her scent mingling with the briny perfume of the sea (Samudra Beach, Venus blunt—holy fuck what was *in* that?)

—that sloe-eyed whore who gave him head in Amsterdam, whose little-girl voice had sent him running, terrified, back to the rose-tinted sidewalks and right the hell out of town (blue pigtails, Daddy issues)

Et cetera, et cetera.

And now Emma. He searched her face for something to remember her by. A few freckles on her nose, glitter in her mascara and nail polish. He kept glancing away, then quickly back, as if he could startle her face into his memory by sneaking up on it.

After a moment she pulled away, frowning. "Are you okay?"

He tried to smile.

"I'll be more okay if you get on your knees."

She grinned, confidence restored. Everything would be

okay, her expression implied, once he'd done her. And she might be right about that.

Assuming, of course, that he could get it up. At the moment he felt nothing, nothing at all. His body was curiously soft, vacant as Emma's blond head, the blood floating down his arms and legs without the faintest inclination to gather and pool into a hard-on. Even when she unzipped his jeans and took him in her hand...

Nothing.

Maybe it was the Blackbird. Being in Celia's room, with this girl who could be described on paper in similar terms but was as unlike Celia in personality as it was possible to be. The woman he remembered, eccentric as she was on the surface, was even more so underneath. There was a quiet force to Celia, a sense of the unknowable. She was real, warm, terrifyingly alive.

Only she wasn't anymore. Now she was only bones, or maybe ash. He wished he'd thought to ask Kate what they'd done with Celia's body. He could have visited the cemetery to see her name carved in stone. He could have learned her middle name, her birthday. He could finally have brought her flowers.

None of these ruminations was going to solve the immediate problem. He stepped back, zipped up his jeans and pulled Emma to her feet.

"Sorry," he said.

"What happened? You were really into it yesterday."

"Into it. Yeah."

"We were doing good. I mean, that thing you did in the elevator..."

"Yeah, you liked that?"

"I liked that we might get caught." She eased forward, one hand on the front of his jeans. "I wanted to, kind of. I like being watched. It feels like that here, doesn't it? Like the ghosts might be watching..."

"Nobody's watching," he snapped.

"There could be. You were here then. You met them. Maybe they know you're back—maybe they can see us. I'm pretty intuitive, my mom always said so. Maybe I can call them."

He caught her hand and pushed it away. "You might be the least intuitive person I have ever met."

"What is that supposed to mean?"

Her head tilted to one side. Though there was a fighting spirit in the words themselves, her eyes were big and soft, head tilted again in that befuddled way, as if she couldn't quite believe he meant to insult her.

Julian felt a rush of words surge up his throat, unstoppable and bitter as bile.

"It means that I couldn't be less 'into it' if you paid me. If you were swinging a dick. If yours were the last pair of plastic tits on planet Earth and if yours was the last ass I could ever grab and if you were the owner of the last hole between the last pair of legs, I still would not be 'into it.'"

Her face crumpled, as suddenly and completely as a child's. Tears welled up at the rims of her wide-open eyes and rolled in wavy gray lines down her cheeks, bearing specks of glitter in their wake.

Julian raised his eyes to the ceiling.

"Why did you even bring me here?" she said.

He dug his car keys from the pocket of his jeans and held them out to her.

"No idea," he said. "Go home. You can take my car."

"I—I can't drive your c-car. Where would I leave—" She teetered around the room, pulling on her clothes, hopping into a boot.

"It doesn't matter. Go home."

"How can I—"

"Get out," he roared, and she snatched the keys from his hand and darted out the door. He heard her feet pounding down the hallway, and she was gone.

Julian stood for a minute looking down at the bed. He smoothed the covers, straightened the pillows and tucked the bedspread underneath. This wasn't Celia's bed, he realized now. Her room had looked much different from this, filled with candles and books, and her mattress sat right on the floor without a frame and with only an old door for a headboard. She had a piece of fine silk hung on the wall, embroidered with brightly colored birds sporting long tails that curled like bouquets of flowers at the ends. He had asked where she found it.

"A friend gave it to me," she said. "This nice old guy who used to come in for coffee every afternoon—black, no sugar, no nothing. He liked to talk. He told me stories about the Blackbird, people he remembered from when he was young."

That was her. That was Celia all over. He imagined her nodding gently, encouraging the old man's nostalgia, revealing nothing about herself.

His throat ached. He couldn't lie here in Celia's room, where she'd lived and fucked and wept and died. The walls still smelled like her, that peculiar warm scent of her, that smoky vanilla mixture of sex and incense and Celia's own sweet skin.

He went out to the hallway, down the row of doors. Four on each side, counting the one he'd closed behind him. A tiny hotel by anyone's standards, but Celia had dreamed of it since she was a little girl. She and Rory and Eric had played here as children during the years when the hotel stood vacant, and Celia had fallen in love. He imagined her wandering down this hallway, her tawny hair made dark by the shadows, fingers trailing along the walls. She would have skipped down the curved staircase, her little feet pattering on the floor. She would have been humming, craning her neck at the pine trees outside the leaded windows. Would have laid her hand on this very banister and felt the smooth wood warm to her touch.

Later, after Eric had bought the place, they had stripped the pine floors and waxed them to a lustrous amber glow. Celia brought in low couches lined with pillows and blankets in rich colors and contrasting patterns and arranged them around the river-stone fireplace with a copper-sheathed coffee table at the center—a contribution from Rory, a nod to the hotel's mining days. Everywhere there were candles and old brass lamps, dropping pools of golden light that flickered and danced when anyone walked by, and from the ceiling hung a chandelier made of elk antlers. But the brightest light came from the fireplace itself, and this was where they gathered every night after dinner, cradling cups of mulled wine or cold mugs of beer. Rory always sat nearest the fire, stirring at it lazily with a long green stick. Then Kate in the chair next to him, and Julian directly across. Celia would stretch out on the divan, facing the hearth, her long legs draped across Eric's lap, her eyes sparkling with firelight.

Sometimes, rarely, Eric would bring Celia her guitar and she'd play them a song. She had a book of old children's poems and had composed some simple melodies around them.

> My age is three hundred and seventy-two,
> And I think, with the deepest regret,
> How I used to pick up and voraciously chew
> The dear little boys whom I met.
>
> I've eaten them raw, in their holiday suits;
> I've eaten them curried with rice;
> I've eaten them baked, in their jackets and boots,
> And found them exceedingly nice.

But now that my jaws are too weak for such fare,
I think it exceedingly rude
To do such a thing, when I'm quite well aware
Little boys do not like to be chewed.

She was not particularly musical and the chords were uncertain, but her voice carried with it a sort of enchantment that held him frozen and breathless, hardly daring to blink. She had a slow, throaty drawl, a holdover from her father's Cajun heritage, and she'd set the melody to a gentle waltz rhythm that rocked her body in small circles as she played. He remembered thinking that she should have been somebody's muse, an artist's lover, but had the misfortune to be born and raised among athletes.

He would have watched her for hours. But she'd see something in his face and she'd hesitate, pressing her fingers flat over the strings to silence them.

The fireplace was dark now, and the room had been redecorated. The velvet divan had been replaced by a leather sofa, so slick and firm that he almost slid out of it when he sat down. The side tables were ye olde lodge style, made of logs and twigs; a pristine iron coffee table had been sanded around the edges to make it look worn. Celia's collection of local art had been replaced by matted nature prints in thick frames, and next to the door, a brass plaque declaimed NO SMOKING in neat black letters. No copper bin full of logs, no scent of pine sap in the air—and, cruelest of all, the hearth had been fitted with an electric fire and a pile of fake ceramic logs.

Julian crossed his arms to warm himself. He hadn't realized the hotel would be so different. In a thousand years he wouldn't have guessed that it now belonged to Kate Vaughn.

I couldn't let it go, she'd said, and that much he did understand. This had been a magical place with Celia in it. But the hotel was dead now. Celia had gone cold inside these walls and she was gone.

Julian leaned his head back on the unforgiving sofa and closed his eyes.

In the morning, he walked to the gas station, the only one in Jawbone Ridge. He bought a red plastic gas can and filled it at the pump.

A pickup truck had stopped beside him. The driver, a young man with sleep-flattened hair, asked if Julian needed a ride.

"No, thanks," Julian said. "I don't have far to go."

Back up the hill. His feet pounded a rhythm on the gravel, the weight of his body seeming to be all in his feet while his head and torso floated helium-light up the curve of the road. To his right, the mountain rose in scrubby lumps of rock and patches of grass, where a season's worth of pine seedlings bristled in soft pale green swaths across the earth. The ground fell steeply away left of the road, then rose again in bounding ridges along the banks of Deer Creek. He could hear the water moving—not in a rush of snowmelt, but with the runoff from an overnight storm, the water flowing rapidly in humps of white and brown.

He rounded the last bend in the road and started up the long, steep drive to the vacant Blackbird Hotel.

The first time he'd come here, it was with Celia alone. He had been familiar with nearby Telluride, having trained and competed there several times over the years, but had never found a reason to go around Bald Mountain and turn up the side road for Jawbone Ridge. But when he started seeing Kate, and spending time with her circle of friends, he began to be curious about the place. He wanted to see for himself what was going on inside the Blackbird Hotel.

Celia was sweet that day, eager as a child. She showed him

through the rooms, each one littered with sawhorses, hand tools and buckets of paint. An unwieldy industrial sander was sitting in front of the fireplace. Wrappers from someone's lunch lay crumpled on an overturned pail by the window. But as she described their plans in detail, Julian began to see it come alive.

"I like this place," he said, looking around. "Good bones."

Her face lit up.

"It'll be beautiful when we're finished," she said. Then laughed, ducking her head. "Or, not beautiful exactly, but handsome. Proud of itself, you know? The poor thing's been sitting up here alone for as long as I can remember. I want to fill it up."

"You talk about the hotel like it's a person," he said.

She ran her hand down the sanded banister.

"Not a person, exactly. But personal."

Afterward they went outside to sit on a slatted pine bench overlooking the river. A breeze moved through the aspen, rustling their coin-bright leaves, and from overhead they could hear the wind sighing through the pines and the occasional caw of a hidden crow. For a while, Celia was silent. Then she said she liked the sun.

"You're not very tan, though," he said.

"No. I only get freckles."

Her skin was lovely in the clear light—a smooth, velvety white like the petals of a speckled flower.

"You bought this place together?" he said. "You and Eric and Rory?"

"On paper, yes. But it's Eric's money. His dad died a couple of years back and left him what he had."

"You all went to the same school, I think Rory said."

"He and Eric were in the year ahead of me."

"Did you enjoy school?"

She considered a moment before replying.

"No."

"Why not?"

Again she paused, thinking it over. "It's too hard to know what the teachers want you to say."

"They want you to say what you think."

"Do they?"

She was quick with that, her eyes wide-open. For the first time, he began to see the guile of this girl.

"Sometimes," he said.

They sat for a while in companionable silence. Celia didn't rush to fill it. She was quick to catch a mood, poured herself into it like water.

"Have you always lived here?" he said.

"Since I was four, when my dad and Rory's mom got married. He came out here on a contract to do some construction work on a new hotel—actually it was the Adelaide, one of the Vaughn properties. Didn't you say you were staying there?"

Julian nodded.

"Beautiful, isn't it? One of the best views around, I've always thought."

"You like it up here?" Julian said. "You're happy?"

"Yes."

It struck him then how rare it was to receive monosyllabic responses. Most people would say, "I love the mountains" or "It's home" or "The skiing is amazing." This girl was content to simply say "Yes." But her replies had weight, a forceful impact. She really meant yes; it was a firm and definite assent. She gazed down at the water, nodding gently.

Her placidity surprised him. With her wild tangle of hair and gypsy's clothing, he would have suspected a more nomadic spirit. But Celia never expressed—to Julian, at least—a desire to travel. She sat next to him in the sunshine with her hands folded in her lap, that sweet faraway expression on her face, as if she'd left her body unattended while her mind was elsewhere.

Impossible even now to imagine a girl like that with a gun in her hands.

Julian's gun.

He passed now through the hollow vestibule, up the curving staircase to Celia's room. His footsteps made a slow heartbeat of sound as he came through the door, which in turn gave a tiny scream on its hinges, but when he paused at the foot of the bed—silence.

He opened his suitcase, felt around under his clothes and pulled out an old book of poems. The pages fell open to the verse that had been running through his mind since they'd arrived last night in his car. He read through the poem to the last stanza, the only one he couldn't remember:

And so I contentedly live upon eels,
And try to do nothing amiss,
And I pass all the time I can spare from my meals
In innocent slumber—like this.

He ran his hands over the pages, the delicate drawings. Then he ripped the pages from the book, tossed the cover on the bed and twisted the papers tightly into the shape of a cone. He set this aside, uncapped the gas can and doused the bed. He splashed gasoline on the walls, opened the window, soaked the curtains and the carpet. The rest of the gasoline he carried down the hall. He turned the can upside down as he descended the staircase, leaving a small pool of fuel on the old floorboards at the bottom and another on the smooth leather cushions of the sofa. The fumes rose to his face, toxic and fragrant as perfume. He tossed the gas can aside and went back upstairs.

He retrieved the paper cone, pulled a lighter from his pocket and flicked it at the tip of the pages. Flames licked at the edge of the paper and bloomed from the cone, a fiery bouquet. At a touch, the fire sprang across the covers in looping lines that melted into a pool of blue-tipped flames. He backed away slowly, the heat rising over his skin in breathy gusts.

The tune continued to trail through his mind, fragmented and disconnected: *Oh, I used to pick up and voraciously chew, the dear little boys whom I met…*

From the end of the hall, he heard the room ignite in a groaning rush. A few seconds later, the first flames leaped through the open door. He dropped the fiery cone at the foot of the stairs and watched as the fire retraced his steps, up the curve of the staircase and into the hall.

He went outside and stood looking up at the old hotel. The window at the end was bright orange, the first long flames licking at the window frame as the smoke began to roll in thick clouds from the front door. An image of himself filled his mind. Walking through the burning doors, up the staircase, down the fiery hallway to Celia's room. He would lie down in a bed of flames and rise again like the Blackbird, like a phoenix straight to the sky, absolved and reborn.

But even at this distance, the smoke was acrid and sharp in his lungs. People didn't burn to death quietly; they went screaming and flailing.

He thought of Rory and Eric, who had died here with Celia. Their faces had dissolved in his memory, features interchanging in his mind's eye. He'd almost forgotten now what their voices sounded like, couldn't always be sure which conversation had taken place with Rory and which with Eric. They had become a single entity, two halves of a whole. They had lived and died and were remembered as they had lived: together.

Rory and Eric would approve of what he'd done. The Blackbird belonged to Celia. Julian was returning it to her, sending it heavenward on a cloud of billowing smoke.

It was the only apology he could think to offer.

JANUARY 11, 2009

CELIA WAS BURNING. From the minute he walked into the room and settled his gaze on her, from the first sunshiny flash of teeth in his smooth, tanned face, the squeak of floorboards under his weight, getting closer. From even before that. Years before that. This longing had simmered in her belly since childhood, when she would admire the straight line of his shoulders and the thrilling vertical channel between the muscles of his abdomen, and feel some unnamed stirring that made her long for the bright swing of his attention, as if without it she were standing underdressed in a storm. Now the fire raged between them in waves of all-consuming heat. It was him inside her, both of them in the heart of the Blackbird, a crackling hot inferno that exploded down her thighs and raced beneath her skin and tore through her throat like a flame.

In the hour before her death, Celia had never felt more alive.

If Celia ever had to explain what it was like to be living out her childhood dream, she would talk about the walls. Miles and miles of walls, the Blackbird had, and every one of them covered with wallpaper or cheap vinyl paneling, or spiderwebbed with tiny cracks, or pockmarked with holes in the plaster or the doors. Sometimes, as here in the kitchen, all of the above. She imagined the listener—a sympathetic motherly type like Mrs. Kirby at the post office—who would someday come to stay in one of the rooms they were renovating. *You wouldn't believe such a small hotel would have so many walls*, Celia would say. *I never thought we'd see the end of them.*

Some of the rooms had been too much for her. In Two, she'd seen right away that the wallpaper was not going to budge and had papered over it with nubby grass cloth the color of summer wheat. That was Rory's room, calmly masculine, with a punched tin lamp and curtains made from lengths of painter's cloth, a pinstripe in chocolate brown that Celia had sewn around the edges.

"I'm still gonna throw my socks on the floor." Rory had run his hand over the walnut dresser and the Hopi blanket across the foot of the bed.

"You can lead a boy to a hamper," said Eric, whose room even in high school was aggressively neat, "but you can't make him use it."

In Eight, where Julian Moss was staying, joined some nights by Kate, Celia had started strong but been foiled halfway through. Some of the wallpaper glue had hardened over time to the color and consistency of amber, and no amount of chemicals or steam would remove it. She was forced to leave the clover-green wallpaper in ragged vertical patches, but had discovered by trial and error that she could glaze those walls with a tinted wax and leave them as they were, with the pine boards showing through the strips of paper. The effect was strangely pleasing. She hung a huge copper clock over the headboard and some unframed oils on the walls and moved on to other projects.

The kitchen, though, was special. It was Celia's space, her private sanctuary, a big shabby square room with open shelves above and cavernous cupboards below, and for this room nothing would do but walls of robin's egg blue. She had stripped every last shred of the wallpaper here—a tedious, finicky job that took a solid week—and now the cans of paint stood ready on the floor, the dishes and crockery shifted to the countertops in order to clear the space. Tomorrow she would open the first can of paint and roll it over the naked wall, a luxurious task she had long anticipated.

She scooped up a dollop of spackling paste and pressed it into a nail hole next to the pantry door frame, smoothing it over with the end of the putty knife. She stood back to inspect her work, pushing a strand of hair from her forehead with the back of her hand.

Miles of walls. I had help, of course. I had Rory and Eric.

Always when she thought of her stepbrother and his best friend, their names went in that order. Said quickly, the syllables blended into one word: Roreneric. You couldn't say them the other way around. She wasn't sure why.

Rory and Eric could do anything. Together they'd repaired the roof, sealed the windows, replaced the gutters and the faucets, refinished the floors. Huge, impossible jobs, but they tackled them together, cheerful and undaunted. Celia would hear Eric's tuneless voice ringing through the old hotel, the beat of his music thundering from the stereo: *Do ya, do ya want my love, baby, do ya do ya want my love…* A crazy falsetto, cracking over the high notes, punctuated by Rory's rumbling baritone urging him to keep his day job. Eric would laugh, cranking up the volume just to piss him off. They filled the empty rooms with the sound of power tools, hammers, the clatter of boards and nails, heavy thumps of their boots on the floor. The most beautiful sounds in the world.

Rory and Eric. Their names formed an impression in her mind that was less about the way they looked than about the way they felt, their dual presence like a pair of moons swirling elliptically around her: one near, the other far, then switching, accelerating, swinging away and moving heavily back. She felt the weight of them physically, a cosmic tug that kept her always wobbling slightly off balance.

No one who knew them casually could believe they'd be such good friends. Eric seemed like the antithesis to Rory's golden-brown solidity. His pale skin was the canvas for a collection of tattoos, an ongoing attempt to illustrate his identity in a way that Rory had never needed to do. Eric was dark, pierced, mercurial, with an IQ approaching genius and a blatant reluctance to use it, as if he were too smart even to think up the things that would challenge him, too smart to keep his own brain ticking. He could easily have become frustrated with Rory, who had struggled for years with undiagnosed dyslexia and hadn't read a book cover to cover in his life. But Rory was not unintelligent, and he had a commonsense canniness Eric lacked. When Eric wandered off course, Rory provided ballast.

Celia set down the spackling paste tray and made a wide stretch. A hot ache pressed at the back of her eyes. She had lain awake the night before, her thoughts all scraps and snippets: a flash of someone's face, a fragment of conversation, memories like the pieces of several different puzzles all laid out on a table, impossible to assemble. At dawn she rose and went up the narrow back stairs, through the dollhouse door to the attic—a long, slanted room with one dingy window at either end and a century's worth of accumulated junk, once so thick you had to turn sideways even to get through the door. Over the months they had sifted through it, had carried down pieces of furniture, paintings with cracked frames or rips in the canvas, boxes of books and musty old clothes, an enormous elk's head mounted on a wooden plaque. Eric had hung this in the kitchen, as a joke, because Celia didn't eat meat—which had upset her at first because she didn't realize it *was* a joke and thought he meant for it to stay. But he took one look at her face and laughed, kissed her head and hauled the poor thing down to the truck with the other flea market items.

From the mudroom, she heard the door open and close, a thud of boots on the floor and the nylon whisk of someone's coat. A moment later, Rory came through the kitchen door, pulling off his cap as he ducked beneath the lintel. The ends of his hair were dusted with snow, his eyebrows threaded with ice. His bootless feet in purple socks made no sound, but the floorboards creaked a little under his weight.

He looked around the room, hands slung low on his narrow hips.

"Looks like a bomb went off in here," he said.

Celia held up the tray. "I'm spackling. It's a dirty job, et cetera..."

Rory hunted briefly for a glass, settled for a coffee cup and went to fill it at the kitchen sink. He drank off the water in five or six long swallows, his head tipping slowly back, then refilled the cup and stood with his hip leaning against the counter.

"Finally got the shed organized," he said. "And I hung the new door. You would not have appreciated the spider situation out there."

"Body count?"

"Twenty-six."

"Yikes."

Rory grinned. Nothing fazed him. Spiders, leaks in the roof, faulty plumbing, snarls of electrical wire. He tackled every job with the same easygoing confidence; it was all in a day's work, whatever the day might bring. He had a way of jollying Celia and Eric along, his blue eyes crinkling around the corners, mouth curving open around the white gleam of his teeth.

Captain America, Eric called him. Here to save the day.

And Rory did seem unambiguously heroic at times. He radiated good intention and that comforting solidity a strong person brings into the room. It was almost impossible to imagine a situation Rory would not be able to handle, or that anything awful could happen while he was around. He made everything seem simple.

Celia waited while he drained his cup for a second time and set it in the sink. Now would be the time to bring up the topic of Julian. Knowing Rory—and her own inability to articulate the problem—this conversation could take a while. "I'm glad you're here, because I want to talk to you."

He came through the pantry doorway. She felt him approach and knew without turning her head that his mood had shifted. His cool cheek pressed against her temple.

"You can talk, but I'll hear you much better in twenty minutes."

He took the tray from her hands and set it aside, slid his hand around her head to turn her face to his. His mouth opened over hers, cold inside as if he'd been eating snow. His teeth felt sleek and hard under her tongue.

She shivered. "You're freezing."

"Warm me up, then."

"Here? Don't we know better than that?"

"Yeah, we definitely do," he said.

She expected him to lead her out of the pantry and up the winding stairs. But he slipped his hand around her wrist, thumb to forefinger like a bracelet.

"They won't be back for a while," he said. "We have time."

He pulled her against him so she could feel his erection at the small of her back. He traced the line of her neck with his lips and teeth, buried his nose in the hair behind her ear. His hands began a slow descent down the front of her body, then up again, under her sweater, a ticklish chill across her ribs. His palms were rough and calloused, so big that with both his hands over her breasts it felt as if she'd added a layer of chilled fresh clothing.

She sighed and turned her cheek to his lips. Easier—much easier—to set aside the conversation about Julian and just go along. Later she would tell him everything and they would figure out together what to do. It could wait a few minutes longer.

He reached down and unbuttoned her jeans. Hand-me-downs from Kate, painting clothes, so baggy that they dropped to her hips before Rory had even touched the zipper.

"Don't turn around," he said.

The lifts had been running sporadically all afternoon, stopping and restarting as inexperienced skiers skidded over the ice trying to round the tight corner at the end of the ramp. A wall of clouds poured like wet concrete across the sky and hardened around the mountaintop, leaking tiny pellets of hail that stung Eric's cheeks and clattered over the vinyl seat of the chairlift.

He shouldn't have come out today. It was Julian really who wanted to ski. He said that Kate was getting clingy and he needed a third wheel.

"I keep thinking I've got to cut her loose, but I'm not ready to have that conversation. I need a reason to procrastinate. You know how it is."

Eric wasn't eager for the day. There were a hundred projects waiting for attention at the Blackbird, and he'd barely gotten home after almost a month away. He'd felt guilty about it this morning, but Celia had only kissed his cheek and told him to go, have fun, nothing was so urgent that it couldn't wait another day.

He had explained his reluctance to Julian as they sat in the mudroom pulling on their boots.

"Stay if you want, man," Julian said. "But if she's telling you to go..."

Outside they could hear the thud of Rory's ax chopping wood. From the kitchen, the splash of running water and the clatter of dishes. Eric hesitated, elbows on his knees. Julian had paid for his trip to Alaska, for the cabin and the helicopter and the tickets and the food. It seemed ungrateful after only a few days back not to do him this one favor in return.

His thoughts spun in circles: go, don't go, a dozen chattering reasons for and against. Impossible to think through the noise.

Julian got to his feet and pulled his cap down over his ears.

"In my experience, if a woman really wants to put you to work, you'll know it. Today you're getting a pass. I'd take it if I were you."

He opened the door in invitation. A gust of frigid air blew into the room.

"Arctic," Eric said. "Go ahead. I think I'm gonna add another layer."

"Sure you are."

"Give me five minutes. I'll meet you at the bottom of Prospect."

Julian went out, shaking his head.

Eric sat for a minute after he left, listening as he said goodbye to Rory. When the sound of chopping resumed, he kicked off his boots and went into the kitchen, where Celia was drying the last of the breakfast dishes. She was wearing a cotton nightgown and an ancient, enormous cardigan of moss-green wool. Her hair trailed down her back in a day-old braid.

He stole up behind her and slipped his hand under the sweater to cup her breast.

"Come upstairs," he said.

The side of her cheek curved upward as she turned off the faucet.

"I've got exactly one hundred and forty-two things to do today," she said.

"Hundred and forty-three."

He kissed her warm ear. She tucked up her shoulder and turned to face him, smiling, but with one hand flat to his chest.

"Later, okay?"

"That's what you said last night."

She wobbled her head, acknowledging this.

"Are we fighting?" he said.

"No."

"Then come upstairs and prove it."

A flash of impatience crossed her face, so quickly he couldn't be sure it had been there at all. She had pressed a kiss to his cheek and shooed him along, and he'd let himself be sent away because of the kiss and the smile—but now, on the stalled ski lift, it was that swift exasperation he couldn't get out of his mind.

He tried to remember the tools of self-control: *Think before acting. Count to a hundred, or five hundred. Talk it out. Call for help if you think it's going sideways.*

He peeled off a glove with his teeth and pulled out his cell phone. He dialed Celia's number. It rang four times and went to voice mail. And not even her voice, but the canned response the cell came with.

He shoved the phone back into his pocket.

One, one thousand, two, one thousand, three, one thousand, four…

The lift hummed to a start. It traveled a few yards, then

stopped again with a jerk that set the chairs swinging. Eric could just make out the lift operator in his box at the top of the run—only forty yards to go, but it may as well have been a mile.

"Goddamn it," he muttered.

Julian sat back comfortably, his arm around Kate's snow-dusted shoulders. If Eric was there to circumvent trouble with Kate, he was doing a fine job; she had been bubbly and easy-going all day, in spite of the weather.

"No point stressing, man," Julian said. "You have somewhere else to be?"

Eric ground back the answer with his teeth. Though they'd been sedentary for almost an hour, his heartbeat was tripping like a snare drum. His eyes burned with cold, with the chain of sleepless nights that had started in Alaska and continued at the Blackbird Hotel.

From his breast pocket he pulled out a flask of whiskey, unscrewed it and took a burning slug. Julian and Kate waved it off, so he took a couple more swallows himself, then more after that since the flask was nearly empty.

The exchange with Celia nagged at him, became tangled in the threads of previous conversations, as if the words had come untethered from their context. He couldn't remember who said what, or when, or whether certain comments were a response to something someone else had said. He couldn't put the pieces together. He couldn't think. That was the problem—he couldn't *think*. His mind was a freight train, fast and unsteerable, pushed by its own weight and momentum with Eric like a panicked conductor trying to keep the fucker from jumping the tracks.

He stared into the whiteness, rocking back and forth with the energy leaping in his chest.

That impatience on her face. She wanted him to go, didn't

she? Wanted to be rid of him. He remembered standing in the hallway—was that last night or the night before? He couldn't be sure. But definitely he remembered standing in the hallway with his hand on the doorknob, and finding it locked.

At least…he thought he remembered.

He blinked into the snowstorm. On every side, the snowflakes whirled and dissolved into a fine white mist, like a cloud.

I'm losing it, he thought helplessly.

Kate was chattering on the seat beside him. Her voice was painfully bright, a needle in his ear.

"I'll bet Celia was glad to see you," she said.

"Got that right." Julian laughed. "I thought there was an avalanche last night, but it turned out to be Celia's headboard banging on the wall."

Eric's racing mind skidded to a halt. A hard tremor shook his body, locked his jaw.

Last night.

Time had gotten slippery again. He couldn't remember whether it was last night or some other when he'd awakened to find himself on the couch downstairs, blinking into the dying embers of the fire. He'd gotten very drunk—he remembered that. All of them sitting around the hearth, and Celia plucking out a melody on her guitar while Julian lounged back in his chair, laughing with Rory and Kate. Eric had watched with a drink in hand, but he'd kept himself distant. Once he'd met Celia's eye and she'd smiled—a blank kind of smile like she meant it for someone else and Eric just happened to be in the way.

He must have fallen asleep soon after. Someone—Celia, of course—had covered him with a blanket, and they all went upstairs and left him alone beside the cooling hearth.

He'd never gone upstairs last night.

If it *was* last night.

He glanced over the edge of the chair at the crazy swirling flakes. Surely there weren't enough snowflakes in the sky to fall this way for so long; they must be cycling around, like the inside of a snow globe, the same flakes falling and rising again—how could you tell?

He dragged his mind back to Celia, trying to focus through the haze. But her face appeared again with that fleeting glance of impatience, that thousand-yard smile, turned away and with her eyes shut tight as he fucked her, like she was imagining someone else in his place. The memories rose like specters in the storm.

Panic rose to bursting in his chest. He had to see her.

Right now.

"There's no place like home." Kate was laughing. Shrill peals of hilarity, driving the needle into his brain.

As if she knew.

As if they both knew. And thought it was funny.

Maybe everyone was in on the joke. Maybe Celia was making a fool of him. Celia and Rory both, making fun, making other people laugh at him.

Eric pressed his hands over his ears, rocking back and forth. The chair swung wildly through the snow. Overhead, the cable creaked in protest.

He had to see Celia. Now, right now, right fucking *now.*

He could just make out the surface of the run thirty feet below the lift. The snow was falling up, burning cold against his face.

He swung himself out of the chair, dangling over the snow by one hand. As he dropped to the ground, he heard voices from the white mist overhead, disembodied, calling his name.

Julian heard Eric land with a muffled thud on the snow. The kid didn't pause to pop into his rear binding, just slid into the whiteout without a backward glance. The snow folded behind him like a curtain.

"Something tells me that wasn't Eric in Celia's bed last night," he said.

Kate turned to him. Her eyes were hidden behind silvered goggles that reflected his own image back to him, warped as a funhouse mirror.

"As if you didn't know," she said.

Always afterward, with the blaze of orgasm retreating into embers, Rory expected relief. Temporary, maybe, and only physical, but there should have been some period of minutes or hours when his skin felt tougher, when his mind stopped chasing itself in circles and found a reason to rest.

"Insanity," Eric once said, "is doing the same thing over and over and expecting a different result. Or maybe that's stupidity. They're not that far apart..."

Not that he was talking about Rory when he said it.

Under his palm, he could feel Celia's heartbeat, quick as a bird's wing, her slender collarbone at his fingertips. He nuzzled into the downy hair behind her ear. The scent of her flooded his nose.

Minutes passed with neither of them moving. Celia would always wait, as long as he wanted, letting him soften and slide away before she'd ever make a move to free herself. He traced her spine, his fingertips rasping gently against her skin. His jaw had left pink stains on her shoulders and neck, but his fingers were too rough to soothe them away. He used his wrists and the backs of his hands.

She was waiting, patiently, not complaining about the hard floor or the chill in the air, or the work she needed to get back to, or the way he'd been just now—too hard and fast, too eager to get inside her and not at all eager to leave. She didn't talk about Eric, but Rory wondered if she'd been with him, too, that morning, whether she was exhausted trying to keep up with them. Exhausted by the secrets they were keeping.

Eric was their friend, after all. The three of them had been together since they were children. He remembered the first time they came here, hearing Celia run up and down the hall overhead and Eric's footsteps racing up the steps to join her. Rory had stood in almost exactly this spot, plucking at the peeling wallpaper and failing utterly to understand what Celia saw in the place.

To her it was magic. She said no one would ever leave a place like this.

It didn't seem that way to Rory. Not at the time and not now. The only magical part of the Blackbird was the girl who lived in it.

He helped Celia to her feet. She lifted her face and kissed him. It was a woman's kiss, openmouthed and generous. Her lips were cool and fresh; her arms twined delicately around his neck. It was like being kissed by a flower.

It almost decided him. The words crowded up to the base of his throat.

He couldn't say it. He had to say it.

The decent thing would be to leave Jawbone Ridge. Just get in his truck and keep driving. In the summer, on his way back to town, spent and filthy from his job with the forestry service, he'd sit behind the wheel at the foot of the mountains and think, *Turn around. Go the other way.* But somehow he never could do it.

He should never have let it come to this. He should have stopped, could have stopped a hundred times. They could have gone on being family to each other, the way his mother always intended. He could have found someone else.

But those possibilities were behind them. This was where

they were, and he wanted Celia with a single-mindedness that wiped away any mental image of his life but the one that included her. His desire had become laced with a possessive greed, so powerful that he'd lain awake night after night, twisted in the sheets, pulling at his dick like he could milk out some peace of mind, some resolution at the thought of Celia in the room next door, asleep in his best friend's arms. He'd allowed the jealousy to grow, sick with shame at his own weakness. It was unfair to change the rules, he told himself. This was how they'd always played it. He understood that. He tried to accept his role in her life. In the beginning he'd even encouraged it.

"This is a small town," he'd told her. "People think of us as siblings. They won't tolerate it. Go and be with Eric. No one has to know about…this."

"We won't be able to hide it," she had said.

But he had overridden her, patronized her. So sure always that he knew what was best for Celia.

Now he had to admit that she was right. He couldn't hide it. Every time he glanced in her direction, it was like looking through a mask, a parody of brotherly affection. He had to keep his eyes on her face, forget the live feeling of her nipple in his palm, the texture of her skin, the damp heat of her mouth. He had to watch with gritted teeth as Eric teased her, kissed her publicly, while Rory could only wait and scheme and smile, smile, smile.

What Celia felt about it he never could guess. On the surface she seemed unchanged, but he gathered small evidences in the things she said, in an indecipherable expression or sidelong glance, in the way she clung to him and cried his name. (Had she held him that way the last time? Had she come as hard? Did she want him more or less than before?) He examined every word and gesture, aware with each passing day that the unfairness of the situation had begun to rankle: he was tired of being the odd man out. He wanted to know where he stood.

He wanted her to break a promise. It was selfish and unreasonable and unlikely. Celia didn't break her promises.

He'd rehearsed this moment so many times in his head, piecing together what sounded like a convincing string of words until he said them aloud, alone in his room, the reproachful hotel groaning and snapping around him as if it knew he was scheming to steal its mistress away.

Fuck the Blackbird. Fuck Jawbone Ridge and brotherhood and promises. He had to put it out there. He needed her to himself.

The words that had long been boiling in his chest surged upward. As they spilled from his mouth, Eric walked through the door.

ONE DAY EARLIER

KATE OPENED THE top drawer of Julian's dresser. It was half-full of socks and folded-up boxers. The next drawer had things in it, too, but probably there was room to combine them. Kate hadn't been home in more than a week, and her clothing had begun to accumulate. She'd been using hangers, tossing laundry into her duffel. Waiting for Julian to offer some space for her to settle in. But he was absentminded that way.

She gathered up his clothes and began to shift them to the right-hand drawer.

He wouldn't mind. They had been dating for months now; they were a couple. Everywhere Kate went, people asked, "Where's Julian?" and their heads would swivel around, scanning the room. She'd roll her eyes and say that they were not joined at the hip, but secretly she'd feel a warm little glow at the association. Julian was somebody, not like most of the men from Telluride. He came from generations of money, but when she asked him where it all started, he was vague. Investments, he said, not looking at her, bored as if she'd blundered into some obvious question he'd answered a hundred times before.

That was the problem with Julian. It was so easy to irritate him and set his attention wandering.

It hadn't always been this way. When they first met, it seemed that Julian wanted nothing more than to make her happy. She wanted the same, or thought she did. They treated each other cordially. Never argued or took a stand on principle, never made demands, as if they were both afraid one really ugly fight would tear the whole thing apart. They built a careful stockpile of goodwill, as if saving it up against some future calamity.

It used to be fun, being with Julian. Sophisticated fun. She was always aware of her age and his, like when they stood side by side in the bathroom mirror, or when he pulled out his wallet and paid the tab in cash, always in cash, his long fingers beautifully manicured with nails like polished rock. His age was one of the things that made him interesting. His age, and his name.

After all, this was Julian Moss, who'd brought home the bronze on what turned out to be a fractured tibia, only five-hundredths of a second out of the lead. Julian Moss, whose calf swelled so badly afterward that he wasn't able to put on a boot and had to sit out the rest of the Games from the broadcast booth, the start of a new career.

Julian was wonderful. Everybody thought so. He'd put his fingers to his temple and lean in confidentially, as if the conversation you were having was the most important one he'd had in years. He gave you a full-on spotlight of attention, dark brows furrowed, his eyes moving slowly over your face as if memorizing it as part of some crucial inventory.

In return, he expected to be listened to. Early on he had told her, with that slow, half-pleading smile of his, "I like my own way, you know, Katie."

Well, that was all right. She always tried to give in, agreeing automatically and without complaint. And for a while that seemed to work.

Sweet little Katie, he called her. That's what she tried to be.

But lately he seemed to feel they had enough goodwill to last them. He began to spend it on cheap shots, unguarded glances, eye rolls that stopped just shy of full circle so that she could never be sure whether he meant them in anger or loving impatience. His lips had taken on a permanent sneer of amusement—or disdain, it was hard to tell. He said cryptic things that he refused to explain, as if it didn't matter what Kate read into them, only what he meant to himself. His moves in the bedroom were less playful, and he seemed constantly distracted, like Kate was in the way. Yet he used to be a considerate lover. Even the first time, hushed and hurried in a frigid stairwell, he had taken the time to make her come. He was experienced, patient, dominant. He'd bought her lingerie and sex toys, said it was all a game he wanted to play with her, that some women took it too seriously but he was glad to see that Kate was not one of them.

Now nothing she did was right. Last night was awful. Awful! The things he wanted her to do…

Tears of self-pity sprang to her eyes. She wiped them away with the heel of her hand.

It could be nothing. Could even be the start of something good. Maybe this was a last line of defense in what Kate's mother called "terminal bachelorhood." Maybe Julian just needed a little push, something from Kate to let him know that she would agree to whatever he had in mind. She told him, offhandedly, in the course of conversation, that she loved to travel, though she was perfectly content here in Telluride. She thought marriage was great but was also up for cohabitation. She didn't mind his age. She liked children, though she didn't think her life would be incomplete without them. Loved sex but was happy to give an unrequited blow job. She laughed at his jokes; she sang his praises.

Really, thinking about it, she was perfect for Julian Moss. Why, then, did she get the feeling he was slipping away?

As she got to the back of the drawer and the last handful of clothing, she stopped, staring at what she'd found.

She stood that way for several seconds, her pulse pounding in her throat. Then stiffly, methodically, she began to put his clothes back into the drawer, exactly as she'd found them. She let herself out of the room and closed the door behind her.

The lights kept flickering on and off.

Celia lifted her face and let the hot water stream down her neck, rinsing away the soap and shampoo. She screwed her eyes tight shut. She didn't want to think about what new problem might have arisen with the wiring in the past thirty minutes, what new task she'd have to lay on Rory and Eric. She laid her hands against the walls as if the Blackbird might be soothed and stop its twitching.

The lights flickered again, and the room fell into darkness.

"Really?" she said.

She'd been looking forward to a few extra minutes to work out the strain in her shoulders and legs, the knotted bruise-like ache in her thumb that flared at the end of any long day spent with a paintbrush in her hand. But the old claw-foot tub was oddly shaped, treacherous even with the lights on, and the steam felt dense and pressurized in a darkness as complete as this.

She turned the faucets and pushed back the shower curtain. Water streamed with a metallic patter around her feet as she reached blindly for a towel.

The lights came back. Celia flinched in surprise and nearly fell, grabbing at the towel rack to steady herself.

Eric had come into the bathroom. He was leaning against

the chipped tile counter, one hand in his pocket and the other on the light switch.

"Jesus," she said. "You scared me."

"Sorry."

She stepped over the edge of the tub, wrapped the towel around her body and tucked it under her arm. Eric took a second towel from the rack and started to dry her hair, gathering it in one hand to squeeze the water to the tip. His face in the mirror was thin and haggard, a specter moving through patches of fog. Over his fingers, the four tattooed letters he'd gotten years before: L-O-V-E, now sideways and reversed by the mirror. Ǝ-V-O-⅃.

A moment later his reflection was swallowed completely by the steam.

She turned to face him.

"Tell me what's wrong," she said.

His eyes shifted to meet hers—wide, beautiful black eyes, the whites as pure and smooth as milk. He opened his mouth and closed it again, deciding what to say. There were harsh lines like cuts running down between his eyebrows.

"Eric—"

"Tell me something. I want you to tell me something and be honest."

She nodded. The steam burned at the back of her throat.

"I want to know if you're happy here," he said. "With… with all of this."

"Of course I am. This is what I always wanted."

"What you always wanted. I thought you promised me an honest answer."

"Maybe it's a little more—"

"A lot more. What I'm asking is whether you're happy."

"I am."

The steam had gathered along his eyebrows and beaded at the tips of his lashes. He tilted his head.

"I can't tell," he said. "I just never can tell whether you're telling me the truth."

"Do you want that to be a lie?"

"Maybe."

"It isn't."

"Whatever you say." He plucked a strand of wet hair from her face. "I notice you don't wonder why I'm asking. Don't you want to know whether I'm happy?"

A suffocating weight pushed at her chest. She wished they could go outside, where the air was thin and light.

"I…I thought…"

Eric ducked his head to get closer to hers.

"You thought what? That if you're happy, everyone else is, too?"

"No, no—"

"Yes, yes. I think it hurts your tender little heart to imagine anything else. Easier not to look too close. That's what I think."

"That's not fair."

"No. Maybe not." He laid the towel aside and reached for her hand. His thumb traced a small nervous pattern on the inside of her wrist. "But you have to see that this place is no good for us. I think we should leave. Just leave, right now. Tonight."

A lump of panic rose in her chest.

"What are you talking about?"

"I just think, all of this, it's too much."

"You're tired," she said. "We're all tired. We knew it would be this way at first. Probably jet-lagged, too…"

She drew her hand away, fussed over an open drawer and

found a bottle of sleeping pills. She shook out two tablets. But Eric curled her fingers with his palm and held them closed.

"I don't need another pill," he said. His words, which had started uncertainly, tumbled out. "I need you. I need it to be just you and me. We can go someplace warm, someplace with palm trees and sand, where we can listen to the ocean every day, lay under the stars every night. We can get one of those big hammocks, baby, we can live someplace new, and you wouldn't have to work so hard, and there wouldn't be so much goddamn snow..."

His voice raced on, a current of words sweeping him far away from her. She looked at him, light-headed, as if some crucial underpinning had come loose; they could be sliding right now, down the Ridge as so many others had done before. She gripped the edge of the sink.

"I like the snow," she said.

He drew back as if she'd struck him.

A slow anger bloomed in her chest. How like Eric to throw down something this impulsive and expect everyone else to follow.

"You want us to leave here after all this work?" she said. "Leave the hotel half-finished. Just walk away, with no reason and no explanation—"

"Oh, I've got my reasons."

"No," she said.

He dropped her hand. The sleeping pills clattered to the floor. He backed away a step.

"You won't come," he said.

"How can you even ask? This is our home. This is what we've always talked about. You and me and Rory. How can you think of leaving him behind?"

"Easily."

"Look, I don't know what's going on between you two—"

"Because you don't want to know."

"Because I don't need to know. It's not my business. If you and Rory had a fight, go to him and work it out, because I sure as hell am not going to leave in the middle of the night and go off to sip mai tais on the beach with you."

"I see," he said. "You choose him over me."

Celia sighed. She reached up to stroke the hard line of his jaw, as though it might soften if she were patient enough to smooth it away.

"I choose us," she said. "The Blackbird. Like it always has been."

He shook her off, his mouth set in an unhappy line. His gaze traveled down her body, and he reached for the towel she had tucked closed against her chest.

She caught it first. Her fist curled across the knot of terry-cloth.

"Let's rest tonight," she said.

He laughed bitterly, peeling off his shirt as he turned to start the shower.

"And so it begins," he said.

Celia changed her clothes, pulled her damp hair over her shoulder and opened the door. Julian was standing just outside the bedroom door, in the dim hallway. His shoulders blocked the light from the staircase and cast his face in shadow, but even so she could see the smile creep across his lips as he bent toward her.

"Trouble in paradise?" he said.

His voice was low and rich with amusement, as though they were sharing an inside joke at the back of a crowded room. He propped his hand on the wall behind her head. She couldn't look him in the eye without stepping aside or craning her neck; either choice felt like a concession, so she willed herself not to move, not to lift her face to him. She stared past the shadowy bump of his collarbone at the wall sconce near the end of the hallway.

"Let me by, Julian."

He leaned in closer, lowered his head to speak from just above her ear. His breath was warm on her temple.

"What are you going to do when they leave you—tell me that. Do you even know?"

A shiver crawled up her neck. *Don't speak. He doesn't know us; he doesn't know what we're about.* But the question in her mind bubbled through the tarry silence and burst from her lips before she could stop it.

"Why do you hate me, Julian?"

For a moment she imagined a flash of surprise in his expression.

"I've been nice to you," she said.

The surprise, if it had been there, was gone. His face hardened. He pushed back from the wall and turned away.

"You haven't been," he said. "You haven't been nice at all."

TWO DAYS EARLIER

"CLOSE YOUR EYES."

"I'm a grown man, Katie."

"What does that have to do with it?"

"Only that years of experience have made me wary of surprises."

"You shouldn't be wary of this one, because it's excellent."

"Hmm. What are you up to now?"

"Five foot three."

"Seriously. What."

Kate sighed as Julian leaned back in his chair. His friends had turned back to their drinks and conversation, lost under a low din of chatter and the chink of plates and cutlery from the open kitchen behind them. She had tracked them down to Paco's, finally, where they sat amid a detritus of ski clothes and half-eaten lunch.

"Come with me—I'll show you."

"I'm eating," he said. "And we haven't paid the bill yet."

"You can come right back."

He took an enormous bite of pulled-pork sandwich and pointed at the plate of fries.

"This is meant to be a hot meal," he said.

"Okay, okay. But hurry up."

He raised his eyes to the ceiling. Not quite an eye roll, but almost.

He didn't know what she'd gotten him, though. Once he saw it, he'd understand why she was so excited to show it to him. She helped herself to his Coke, tapping her foot while he finished the last bites of his lunch. He wasn't in any hurry at all. With every bite he looked up as if to point out the fact that she was watching him eat.

"You're driving me crazy," she said around a mouthful of fries.

"That makes two of us."

"Don't you even want to know what it is?"

"What what is?"

"The surprise, for fuck's sake, Julian. Try to follow the plot."

He wiped his hands on a paper napkin, which tore as he used it, leaving shreds of paper all over his fingers. He summoned the waiter by holding up his sticky hands. "Cheap-ass paper napkin. Bring me a real one, will you, please? Like, out of cloth?" And to Kate, "Okay, honey, lay it on me."

"You have to close your eyes first."

"I'm not doing that." When the napkin came, he wiped his hands, tossed some bills on the table and zipped his wallet back into the breast pocket of his jacket.

"Jesus. Fine. Come on then."

She took his hand and led him outside, leaving everyone else behind with their coffees. Through both sets of double doors, down the icy steps and into the snow. At high noon the sky was so flatly blue that it looked like plastic. All the shadows stood narrow and hard under the glare of the sun, the pine trees spiked and dripping.

When they reached the corner of the lodge, Kate stopped.

"Ta-da!"

Parked beside the building was a brand-new snowmobile. Glossy red, sleek as an apple, with a fine spray of snow over its bonnet. Kate held out the keys.

"Happy birthday," she said, an unstoppable grin spreading into her cheeks.

Julian's face didn't change at all. He didn't take the keys.

"You are unsurpriseable," she said.

"Ye-ah."

"You don't like it?"

"Oh, I like it. It's just…a lot of present, Katie."

"Well, it's your birthday—"

"How did you know about that? Nobody else does."

"Well, somebody does, obviously." She tried to smile.

"Nobody."

She felt her face redden. This wasn't the way it was supposed to go.

"Have you been snooping around my stuff?" he said. "My wallet, maybe?"

"No, of course not."

"Then how did you know."

"Your mother told me, last month."

"My mother told you."

"Yeah."

"You don't even know my mother."

"Well, I do now, a little."

"How did you even get her number?"

"From my phone, of course. When you borrowed it to call her a couple of months ago." No need to explain how she had dialed and hung up twice before she found the voice to introduce herself and strike up a conversation. And how awkward it had been, as if Kate was the first person the woman had talked to in years. She kept asking whether Julian knew

Kate was calling, in a hopeful voice like the phone call would have meant more if he had instigated it.

Which it would have, of course, but why point it out? Why treat Kate as though she were being dishonest when she was only trying to do something nice for Julian?

"Let me get this straight," Julian said. "You called my mother, weaseled my birthday out of her—"

"Saw it was coming up and scored you a prezzy! I know—clever me, right? It's really sweet, too. I rode it up here to meet you. I thought we could play on it this afternoon."

He stood back, eyeing the snowmobile as if it were still on the lot and he couldn't decide whether to take it home.

"Come on—let's go for a spin," she said.

"I'd love to, but I have plans for the day."

"Just with Zig."

"I have plans, Kate."

"Why are you being such a dick right now? This is a present that I bought you for your birthday. It's supposed to be fun."

He looked at her as if bewildered by the concept.

"But, I mean, what am I supposed to do with it? I don't live here. I don't have any place to store it."

"You can leave it in our garage. There's plenty of room."

"Then really it's yours, isn't it?"

"No, of course not."

"But I'd have to ask to take it out, right? Someone would have to let me in to get it?"

"Sure, but—"

"So then it's yours."

"Well, you don't have to keep it at our place, obviously. Stash it wherever you want. I'll ship it for you, if there's somewhere else you need to be."

She was offended now, and Julian sighed.

"That's not the point. And I do appreciate the thought,

truly. But let's just call it a loan. We can go out on it tomorrow, okay? I promise. Not today."

"You have plans."

He stepped closer and chucked her under the chin with his forefinger, smiling indulgently as if he'd just granted her a huge favor.

"I'm not trying to be a dick. It's just too much right now."

"Yeah," she said. "Sure."

But her throat was tight and the back of her mouth stung with bitterness.

"Come on," he said. "Let's go back inside. I'll get you a hot chocolate and schnapps."

She reached for his hand as they went back up the steps. But he had already tucked it into his pocket.

THREE DAYS EARLIER

SNOW EVERYWHERE. SNOW on the mountains, poured thick as cream over the rivers and meadows. Snow on the rooftops, and in round downy pillows on the boughs of the pines. Snow in the air, lifted and churning, and pushed along the high street, where the town's battered green snowplow angled its wide shovel and scraped it to the shoulder, piled up in knobby humps ten feet high, leaving stripes of tawny gravel down the center of the road.

Jawbone Ridge looked its best under heavy snow. The leaning town seemed cushioned, the spidery supports lost in the snowbanks and the windows grouted with white.

Since Rory was working the slopes, Celia had borrowed his truck to pick up Eric and Julian from the airport. As they turned up the high street, she shifted into first gear and let the engine lumber up the mountain with her foot barely touching the gas, and as always the sturdy truck delivered them through town and up the treacherous slope without a slip. The Blackbird waited, huddled against the steely sky. Snow had collected in a smooth white cap over the roof, and the eaves were lined with fat icicles that had dripped to the crusted snow to form muddy craters along the walls.

They collected their gear and went inside, where the embers of a fire were crackling on the kitchen hearth and the table was already laid for dinner. Celia had strung Christmas lights in all the rooms, tiny twinklers in bright colors that lined the windows and trailed across the mantel. A spice cake rested on a rack next to the old range, ready to be iced.

She felt a rush of affection for the old hotel. So crooked and forbidding outside, so warm and friendly within. Like a curmudgeonly old man with a sentimental heart.

"Home sweet home." Julian leaned over the cake, inhaling. "It sure smells better than Zig's cabin. Eau de socks. What's for dinner?"

"Lasagna," she said. Eric's favorite. But he didn't seem to hear. He had been quiet all the way back from the airport and was gazing around the room as if he'd never seen it before.

"Nice," Julian said. "Well, I told Kate I'd go down to the Adelaide and meet her for a drink."

"Bring her back with you. We'll eat around seven."

After Julian left, Celia followed Eric up the stairs to their room at the end of the hall. As soon as they were inside, Eric shut the door behind them and tossed his bags on the floor.

"You've been busy," he said.

He circled the room, picking things up, putting them down. He sniffed at the candles, tweaked the white fairy lights on her dresser, ruffled the pages of the book she'd left beside the bed.

"A Fair Maiden," he said. "Still working the JCO list, I see."

"It's a long list."

"Mmm-hmm. All those dark and devious little girls. I can see why you'd be drawn to them."

He held the book in his palm and let it fall open to the pages she'd opened most often herself. She felt the heat wash over her face as his eyes moved down the page.

"You probably think Katya's the victim, here, don't you,"

he said. "Got no sympathy for Mr. Kidder and how he must have felt about that spade tattoo on her thigh? Poor old freak thought he was laying a track through virgin snow."

He snapped the book closed and looked up, smiling. Not the kind of smile she could answer with one of her own.

As she opened her mouth to speak, he caught her around the waist and backed her slowly against the door.

"You need me to tell you what to do right now?" he said.

His voice shook with tension. Already he was a mile down the tracks on his own train of thought. She knew from long experience that they should talk about whatever was bothering him. She should soothe him down, make the necessary appointments, get him on the phone with the doctor and back to the clinic for an evaluation. Those were the things she knew she ought to do immediately, out of love, out of a wish for him to be calm and happy. But a selfish need had stolen her resolve. Her heart had risen to her throat, where it tripped and rolled and snagged her breath.

He was in the zone.

He might say anything. Do anything. He was beautiful and dangerous, his energy snapping all over her skin.

"You're using me," he said, "to do your thinking."

It was unanswerable. She couldn't begin to decipher what he meant, and for now she didn't care. Out of long habit, she dropped her own monosyllabic responses—the ones most likely to soothe, least likely to be misinterpreted.

"You don't want to figure it out. You don't want to make any decisions."

"No."

"You're a coward, Celia."

"Yes."

His eyes flicked down her body. "You're such a girl."

He meant to insult her, but Celia was not offended. She

looked up at him, waiting. A tight, almost painful excitement was building behind her sternum, in her stomach, twisting her breasts as if he'd already plucked them between his teeth.

Say it. Whatever you want, say it, take it, whatever you want from me, anything at all.

"You really need me to tell you? Do it."

A quick sigh hissed past her lips. The quivering energy in his voice shimmered in the space between them and raced across her skin. She peeled off her sweater, her shirt, her jeans, her socks. She stood against the door like a criminal, dressed in only a pair of white underwear and a long black feather that hung from a cotton cord around her neck. Her braid fell heavily between her shoulder blades, its tip swaying across the small of her back.

"I've been thinking about you," he said in a thick voice. His eyes shifted from her mouth, down her body. "I've been… worrying."

He covered her breast with his hand. His fingers trembled against her skin. His jaw flexed and snapped shut with an audible clack.

"You're the one who left," she said. "I've been right here."

"With Rory."

"Who didn't leave."

He lifted his chin, staring down at her through the dark fringe of his eyelashes. "Put your hand between your legs."

It was a dare, almost, the way he said it. Or a test. Excitement quivered down her spine. She slipped her fingers inside her underwear. The heat began to churn in her belly even as her skin pebbled with cold.

Eric wrapped her braid around his hand, tugged her head back and kissed her. His mouth rushed over hers with a delicious unpredictability, slanting to get deep inside, then backing away to bite her lips and run his tongue along the edge of her teeth. His kiss was erratic, needy, his breath pouring into her mouth.

"Say you missed me."

"I did."

"Say it."

"I missed you."

He nudged her hand away and replaced it with his.

"You still want me."

"Yes."

He laid his forehead against hers. His voice dropped to a whisper as if he was talking to himself: "How do I know that, how do I know." But his mouth was on her neck, his nose in her hair. He took one long shuddering breath; then he was dragging her underwear down her hips, shrugging out of his clothes until he was dressed only in the blue-black tracery of his tattoos. His lips left a cool trail down her neck as he lifted her against the wall, pulled her down on top of him.

"You don't want anyone else."

"Shh…"

"Say it, say it."

"Ror—" Her brother's name was halfway out her mouth before she could stop it. She'd meant to say, *Eric, stop. Eric, don't worry. I'm here, I'm right here, just the way you left me.* But it was too late. He'd heard, and he knew her far too well to misunderstand.

An exasperated groan tore through his throat.

"Goddamn it, Celia."

His fingers tightened around her thighs. He swung away from the wall and carried her down to the bed. For a moment he held them still. The room was filled with the sound of their breath: his, deep and hollow and raspy, her own as shallow and quick as a child's. He laced her fingers in his, the right hand, then the left, and lifted them over her head. He looked down at her and their interlinked fingers, distraught. As if she'd been the one to leave, who had to be restrained from leaving again.

"I was lost, fucking lost, oh, God..."

Slowly he began to slide, all the way out and all the way back. She wrapped her legs around his narrow waist and pulled him closer.

"I've been here," she wanted to say. "I've been here all along."

Afterward, he held her beneath him, his nose in her hair. Celia kissed his damp shoulder and licked the salt from his skin. Over the whir of her own overheated blood, she could hear the cottony thud of his heartbeat hammering against her ribs.

"Tell me what's wrong," she said.

His lungs swelled, and he released a long sigh that cooled her skin.

"I wish..."

But the wish seemed to evaporate into the silence. He shook his head in the crook of her neck and rolled away. He sat up and rubbed at his eyes.

The afternoon light was fading; the room had gone dim. Celia found a lighter and held the flame to each of the seven votive candles clustered in a tray of river rocks beside the bed. The shadows leaped and danced across the wall.

"You have any blaze?" Eric said.

She didn't answer immediately. Unconsciously she must have been waiting for something like this, because, though his request was unusual, it didn't come as a surprise.

"Hey?" he said.

"Yeah, I've got some."

She and Rory had been smoking steadily, daily, in the

empty hotel during the weeks Eric and Julian were gone. Stoned, they had worked for hours without stopping, in a soft delirium that made the labor seem effortless and unphysical. At night they would drift together, charmed and befuddled, until the buzz was burned away by a sexual heat too intense to sustain it. For them, weed was the sweetest of tonics. But Celia made no move now to dig the tin from her dresser drawer.

"Well, break it out," Eric said.

"You know Dr. Paul said that stuff is—"

"Fuck Paul."

"—poison for you."

"Poison. Drama queen."

"It's not my word."

"I don't remember him putting it that way."

Celia gathered up her clothes and began to pull them on.

"It's just weed," Eric said. "We used to smoke together all the time."

"We didn't know any better. We didn't know what it was doing to you."

He sat up on the bed, propped his elbows on his knees and his head between his hands. He looked beautiful in the candlelight, dark and sensual and needy.

"My head is just..." He curled his fingers, then jerked them away from his ears, a big explosion. "I need to calm the fuck down."

Celia knelt in front of him and pulled his chilled hands into hers.

"Where are your meds?"

"I'm out."

"How are you out? I filled your prescription right before you left."

"I mean I'm out. I'm done with that shit. It doesn't help me, just makes me docile and stupid as fuck."

"No, it doesn't."

"How would you know? You don't know what it's like inside my head."

"I know you."

"Yeah? Sometimes I wonder."

Celia opened his hands and pressed her face between them, a kiss in each palm. She ran her thumb along the tattoo of her name on his wrist. "You're tired. Lie down for a bit before dinner. Tomorrow I'll call Dr. Paul's office and get you in."

"Fuck Paul..."

He lifted his chin and looked her in the eye. His irises were so dark that she couldn't find the pupils.

"Do you remember Mr. Sully?" he said.

Celia frowned, puzzled. "The bowling guy?"

When Celia was fourteen, Red Sully, of Sully's Sinks and Drywall, had learned that his wife was cheating on him and had beaten her to death in their home, using the bowling trophy that he, his wife and her lover had won together the week before at a tournament in Montrose. As children, Celia and Eric were sickened but also consumed by the dark humor of the crime. Eric had acted it out as Celia fell about in guilty laughter: *I got your strike, baby! Right here!*

"I've been wondering about that," he said. "Who do you think was the better bowler? Husband or lover?"

"I don't know. Probably the lover."

Eric nodded slowly. "Yeah, I think you're right. The bowling score probably sent the poor bastard over the edge."

Dinner at the Blackbird was served in the kitchen at the long wooden table, which had been there so long its legs had sunk into the floor, as if the pine planks were soft as dough. Every afternoon, Celia made a huge pot of chili or stew, using whatever vegetable happened to be in season or was lingering in the refrigerator from the previous night's dinner. Sometimes she made enchiladas or tamales, or lined up individual crocks of timbales and served them with whole roasted sweet potatoes and a pot of honey butter. She aimed to have something ready in the kitchen by six o'clock, when the lifts had closed and the skiers had made their way back up the hill with their gear, had changed clothes and poured themselves a glass of wine. But she knew from experience that it was better to have something that could be eaten at room temperature or kept warm on the back burner so people could come and go.

Kate was disdainful of the amount of time Celia spent in the kitchen.

"What was the point of that bra burning back in the day, if all you want to do is wait on a pack of ungrateful men?"

"I've never owned a bra," Celia said. "And they're not ungrateful."

"Maybe not, but I've never seen Eric with a spatula in his hand."

Celia had never seen Kate with a spatula, either. Usually, as now, she held a wineglass and sat at the kitchen table with the bottle near to hand. But Celia never asked for help. Cooking was a meditation for her, and she much preferred to do it on her own.

"You never will see it," Celia said. "He's a terrible cook."

"Because you spoil him."

"He spoils me, too. We do what we're good at. It doesn't need to come out even every day."

"If you say so. One giant step backward if you ask me."

"Why? This is what I want to do."

Kate shook her head.

Celia gave up trying to convince her. People either saw or didn't see, and she'd never been much good at arguing a point.

In any case, she'd never seen the kitchen as a likely battleground for the war of the sexes. Her father had been a wonderful cook. He taught her to make gumbo and jambalaya and big pans of spicy étouffée. One of her earliest memories was of his knife flashing up and down over the cutting board as he reduced a pepper and an onion to glistening confetti, then let her stir it into the pan with a long wooden spoon.

"Careful, chère, you don' wanna barbecue your fingers," he'd say.

But it was too late; she'd touched the side of her hand to the hot pan and started to cry.

"Oh, now," he crooned. "Now, now, now, let's see what the trouble here is."

He sat her on the counter and inspected the wound.

"Hoo-eee, that's a nasty one, pop chock. Give 'er here."

He held her hand in his under cool running water. As her tears dried, she could hear her father's thick mutterings in fragments at her ear: *Big dumb couyon…she too little and that pan too hot…ain' got the sense God gave ya…*

He bandaged the burn and set her up on the counter, far from the stove. She wanted to tell him it was her fault. She'd been clumsy; he was not to blame. But the words wouldn't come. Instead she scooted, a little at a time, until she was near the heat once more.

He shook his head and shifted a knife to the other side of the stove. "Gonna spend all my days getting sharp things outta your way. I see it clear."

But it hadn't worked out that way.

"So it's killing me, man," Rory said to Eric. "How was Alaska?"

Celia took her seat at the table and poured herself a glass of red wine. She sat gazing into it, already flushed and woozy from what she'd had with Kate. She could hardly make it through a day anymore without being helped along by weed or wine. She'd worried over it once to Eric, but he had only shrugged: *Do what you need to do, baby. Ain't no use feeling the pain.*

"Good," Eric said.

Rory tore off a heel of bread while he waited for the lasagna to come around. "Good? You just skied the Chugach, and you're telling me it was good?"

"That's what I'm telling you."

"Come on, man. I can take it."

"Nothing to tell. Alaska is outstanding. We skied and ate and partied, and now we're home."

"And the Isthmus? What was that like?"

"I didn't ski it."

"Oh. Why's that?"

Eric shrugged, moving the food around on his plate. From outside came the rumble of a truck engine and the clashing of gears as it negotiated the switchback turn up the mountain.

Julian broke in from across the table, his cheek round with a bite of bread. "It was gnarly. You'd have to be psychotic to ski that mother this season."

"You must have been bummed, huh? You've been wanting to hit that all year."

Julian swallowed, and his eyes slid sideways to Eric.

"What I said was, *I* didn't ski it." Eric spoke without looking up.

Celia frowned. These cryptic silences were unlike Eric—unlike all of them, for that matter. She glanced at Rory. He met her eye and gave a tiny shake of his head.

"Well," Kate said brightly. "What else happened today?"

"I heard about the Catapult," Julian said to Rory.

"What about it?" Kate said.

"Snowboarder went down," Rory said. "Banged up her knee."

"Jesus, don't be modest when there are women in the room," Julian said. "Have I taught you nothing?" He turned to Kate. "This girl went over the side edge of the run, you know, that rocky part between the trees left of Three? Bumbled right through the markers and landed ass-up in the worst possible place, dangling half off the cliff. Freaky place to land, really. The guys had to get out the ropes and climbing gear to pull her out."

Kate's eyes were wide. "Wait, that's like fifty feet down right there. How the hell did she manage to get into such a mess?"

"No idea," Rory said. "I left it to Gary to give her the safety lecture."

"So how did you get her out?"

Rory poured himself another glass of wine as he explained, with hand gestures and repeated proddings from Kate—who was further along in the night's wine consumption than the rest of them—how the complicated rescue was accomplished. Celia smiled and nodded along, but her gaze kept slipping sideways to the end of the table, where Eric sat quietly listening, his eyes expressionless and fixed on Rory.

"That took a lot of courage," Julian said. "You're a brave man, my friend. I don't think I could have done it."

"I was scared shitless, if you want to know the truth."

"Courage isn't the absence of fear, but the mastery of it." Julian raised his glass. "There's your Moss-ism for the day. Here's to you, man."

Eric raised his glass with the rest of them, but his expression remained flat.

"To Rory," he said. "Master of fear."

★ ★ ★

After dinner, Eric went upstairs to make some phone calls. Celia cleared the table, shooing Rory away with Julian and Kate—an action she immediately regretted.

Fragments drifted in from the conversation at the fireplace.

"…not for the faint of heart," Julian was saying. "I think you would have liked it, though. You'd have torn it up."

Celia couldn't hear Rory's reply, only his tone. He was as puzzled as she was about Eric's tepid response to Alaska.

"He doesn't have your cojones," Kate said.

"He did fine," Julian said. "He just lacks confidence. It slows him down, makes him question his decisions. And I think the avalanche freaked him…"

"Avalanche?" Kate said.

Celia eased closer to the door in order to hear Julian's reply.

"…milk run at the Lady, when Eric picked out a side line to the one the rest of us were skiing. I got to the bottom, and there's Eric schussing down the mountain, this huge cloud of snow behind him, you could hear it groaning…oh, I know, the kid is fast…yeah, totally fine, but his eyes were big as saucers…freaked me out, too, which probably didn't help…"

Celia heard the rumble of Rory's voice.

"…a better boarder than I will ever be. Must be something else…"

"I don't know, man. I've seen a lot of skiers in my day, and I've come to think physical courage is a good measure of the man. You have that…"

Celia finished the dishes and stood at the doorway. Rory's face glowed with firelight, and, though he was shaking his head, it was clear that he was flattered by Julian's appraisal. Possibly even agreed with it.

She went into the room, wiping her hands, a slow anger

building inside her. The pleased expression slipped from Rory's face. His smile became uncertain, a little embarrassed.

"Come sit down," he said.

"Actually, I was thinking I might go around to the Adelaide for a swim," she said. "Why don't you come with me? I'm sure Kate and Julian would appreciate some time to themselves."

"I'd sink to the bottom," Rory said, patting his stomach.

"I'll go with you," Kate said. "They'll still be here swapping ski stories when we get back."

Celia hesitated. Julian looked at her with an amused half smile on his face, as if he knew she didn't want to leave him alone with Rory.

You can't play this game, his expression said. *You don't even know the rules.*

"Oh, thank God it's empty," Kate said as they kicked the snow off their boots and opened the glass door to the pool house of the Adelaide Lodge. "Last week this place was crawling with kids. They were screaming so loud I'm amazed they didn't shatter the roof."

As they stepped inside, the humid air swallowed up the steam from their breath and filled Celia's lungs like a warm broth. A thin vapor rose from the smooth surface of the pool. She tossed her towel over the back of a terrycloth-cushioned chair. Its heavy iron legs screeched against the pool deck as she pulled it away from the table and sat down to unlace her boots.

Like all four of the Vaughns' hotels, this one gave off an air of solid luxury. Everything was solid, hushed, each piece fitting puzzle-like, neatly in its place. The glass walls of the pool room were trimmed in cedar, the corners softened with topiary and small pines, draped in frosted white fairy lights Kate's mother had found in France and converted to use with American electrical outlets.

Celia often wondered what Kate thought of the Blackbird. In all the months of work, she'd never offered more than generic enthusiasm, an admiration for their efforts and vision but little in the way of specific encouragement. Celia was careful not to ask for more. Coming from money like this, Kate surely saw the Blackbird as a joke, an oddity, with its eight small rooms and secondhand furnishings and awkward stance at the edge of the ridge. She'd never said so. She'd never said much at all. But the absence of her opinion spoke for itself, and led Celia's mind back to the remarks Kate would sometimes make while they were out shopping. She'd pick up a piece of jewelry or a pair of boots, inspecting it inside and out.

"You can tell the quality of a piece by the parts that aren't supposed to show. These jeans are overpriced. See the way the seams are finished? Total junk."

There was an unconscious arrogance in her voice, a teacherish way of picking things apart—often within earshot of the salesperson, which never failed to send Celia into a hot and agonized embarrassment.

No unfinished seams in a Vaughn hotel. Though rugged and unostentatious, a guest only had to open a door or pick up a downy pillow to get a sense of the craftsmanship and money behind it.

They peeled off their clothes down to their swimsuits and padded over to the hot tub. Kate turned on the jets to set the water churning. Celia descended the steps and let the warmth engulf her, all the way to the top of her head, the bubbles rolling over her body with a rumble that filled her ears. She came up smiling, rubbing the water from her face.

"Put your head in," she said. "The bubbles sound like thunder."

Kate settled against the side of the tub. "I can't. I'd lose my eyelashes."

“I’m about to lose my bathing suit,” Celia said. “I should give it back to you. It needs some stuffing on top.” She plucked at the triangles of blue-black fabric over her breasts.

“If only we could do a body meld,” she said. “We’d be perfect. What I wouldn’t give for your legs.”

“What I wouldn’t give for your teeth.”

“All your stuff can be bought, though,” Kate said. “Tits and teeth. Two minor corrections, and you’re a supermodel. I can’t think why you never wore braces, Cee.”

Celia hesitated. It seemed disloyal to explain that there hadn’t been the money for braces when she was a kid. In Kate’s world, if you needed something, you bought it. It was a form of innocence to believe life was as simple as that.

“I’m cultivating a look,” she said.

“Russian immigrant? You’ve got the cheekbones and the wardrobe. Work on the accent, and we can sell you off as a mail-order bride.”

Celia put on a voice. “Hey, beeg daddy. You vant I should keep you varm?”

“Good lord, that was like the bride of Dracula.”

“Target market—bloodsucking Wall Street executives.”

Kate laughed and settled deeper into the water, lifting her hair over the edge of the hot tub to keep it dry.

“So what was up with Eric tonight?” she said. “I thought he’d be falling all over himself with stories.”

“I don’t know,” Celia said. “Did Julian say anything to you about the trip?”

“He hasn’t shut up about it. He said it was amazing, talked a lot about his friends—who seem fairly uninspiring, if you ask me, but they go way back, so I guess they like to sit around and talk about the old days or whatever. He said the avies were running a bit and they lost some days to the weather, but other than that it was good.”

"Anything about Eric?"

"Not really. Julian talks about Julian. You know how he is."

"Sort of. He's more Rory and Eric's friend."

"Or they're his..."

Kate's eyes were half-closed. Her voice had dimmed and gone sleepy, but Celia could see a bright crescent gleaming between her lashes.

"You don't think it goes both ways?" Celia said.

"Mmm..."

"He's given us a lot of money."

"Not that much. It only seems..."

She didn't finish, but Celia understood: it only seemed like a lot to her and Rory. To Kate and Julian and maybe even Eric, the money was nothing at all.

"I get the feeling you're trying to tell me something," Celia said.

"Hey, you brought it up."

"But you like him, though? He's good to you?"

"Sure he is."

"Does he ever talk about the future? Getting married, anything like that?"

Kate suddenly sat up and opened her eyes.

"Why all these questions about Julian? You want him, too, I suppose?"

Celia stared at her friend. "What? No, I'm just trying to figure him out. It's not like that at all. Wait, where are you going?"

Kate was getting out of the hot tub, flipping the water from her hair.

"I have to go," she said. "I need to get up early tomorrow."

She toweled off and pulled on her sweater and jeans.

"We just got here."

"Well, I'm done."

"Katie—"

"It's fine, Cee. Forget it. I'll see you later, okay?"

She zipped up her boots and disappeared through the double doors to the hotel lobby, leaving her towel in a damp heap on the chair.

The door shut behind her. Celia subsided into the water, shaking her head. Strange the way two people could be in the same conversation following separate lines of thought altogether.

She pulled herself from the hot tub and stepped into the pool. The underwater lamp was covered by a rotating filter that turned the water from blue to green, to violet, pink and finally a thin bloody red. The temperature was a shock after the sultry heat of the hot tub. She dived off the steps into the chilling pink light, arms outstretched, a chain of bubbles drifting down her stomach, braid dragging along behind her like a rope, tugging at the back of her head. She reached the end of the pool, flipped around and pushed off again, now through a sea-green light, her legs pulsing up and down like a mermaid's tail.

At the far end of the pool, she paused to catch her breath, holding the edge of the deck as she dipped her head backward into the water. Ears covered, her breath was amplified by the underwater silence, sweeping in and out of her lungs like the surf on an empty beach. As she was about to push off again, she noticed a dark shape in the doorway across the room.

Rory, she thought. Her spirit lifted. He'd come for a swim after all.

She pulled herself upright and propped her elbow on the pool deck. Though the man's face was in shadow, she was almost sure it was him. She called his name and beckoned with one hand. Her voice echoed in the empty room, but the man across the pool didn't move. Something in his stillness unnerved her. She wondered how long he'd been standing there, watching.

"Rory?"

The man rocked back on his heels as if considering whether to come farther into the room. Then he stepped forward, into a circle of canned overhead light.

Julian.

Celia subsided into the water.

"Kate just left," she said. "You can probably catch her if you hurry."

He smiled, strolling to the edge of the pool. He turned her chair and sat down, leaning into the cushions with his legs stretched out.

The seconds ticked by. She waited for him to speak. Possibly he expected her to start the conversation. If so, he'd be waiting a long while.

She dove into the water and swam to the other side of the pool. Then turned and went the other way. Back and forth, glancing up through the water as she passed to see whether he was still there. And he always was, every time she checked, a dark unmoving blur at the side of the pool.

Go away. Go away, go away, go away.

She kept swimming. Back and forth, again and again, waiting for him to take the hint and leave. It began to feel like some sort of test, a message being communicated between them with every lap. He had the advantage, sitting comfortably by the side of the pool, while Celia grew more exhausted with every stroke. She began to struggle through the water, as though she were dragging the whole day behind her: Eric and Rory, the never-ending walls of the Blackbird, the fight with Kate—and now this. Julian. Fatigue began to consume her. Her arms grew too heavy to lift, and the angry strength in her legs had ebbed away.

Finally she stopped, gasping for breath, her back to Julian and one hand clutching weakly at the lip of the pool.

He hadn't budged. He was still there beside her clothes, with her towel draped across his knees as if to receive a small wet child.

"Tired yet?" he said.

She couldn't answer. Her eyes burned and itched—she rubbed at them with the heel of her hand.

"What are you doing here?" she said without turning around.

"I came looking for Kate," he said.

But he made it sound like a joke. Another double-edged comment, saying one thing and meaning another. She wished she could keep swimming, retreat again into the cool, silent water. But her limbs were trembling with fatigue. She would have to wait a minute before she could even let go of the side of the pool.

"I came looking for Kate," he said again. "But here you are."

"I don't think she's coming back. She's probably at home by now. You could call her..."

"I could," he said, still with the smile in his voice. "Or you could. She's your ride home, isn't she?"

"She—she had to go. I was planning to call Eric."

"No need. I'll bring you home."

In spite of the hard exercise, Celia was very cold. She thought of the fireplace at the heart of the Blackbird, and Rory beside it where she'd left him. He would be poking at the embers with a long stick, the firelight dancing in his eyes. He would be so warm.

"Come on out," Julian said. "I can hear your teeth chattering."

Celia snapped her jaws shut. But the tremors traveled down

her body and sent a ripple across the surface of the pool—now violet, shifting to red, casting an eerie glow around the room.

She didn't want to get out of the water. Walk up the steps with Kate's cast-off bikini drooping around her breasts, the bones of her hips and shoulders jutting against her skin. Just walk up to Julian and get her towel. A simple thing, but she didn't want to do it. Could not make herself do it. She gripped the edge of the pool as the cold locked in around her.

"Come on out, Celia," Julian said. His voice had deepened and gone quiet. A hypnotic, movie-star voice.

"You're afraid," he said. "And I think you have to ask yourself why that might be. If you really don't want me, you shouldn't be worried right now. You should be hoping I'll look at your body and see everything you think is wrong with it. You should be praying for that. Because if I lose that attraction, it's all much easier for you. You go on with your life. I go on with Kate—or without her, far away, which is even better if what you really want is to get rid of me.

"But that's not how it is. You're nervous. You feel shy. You don't want to get out of the pool and walk over here. And we both know it's not because you think I'll get sprung at the sight of you—you don't have that kind of confidence. It's because you think I won't."

Her mouth slipped below the surface.

"Arrogant prick," she said into the water.

"I'm not in a hurry," he went on, in a voice so deep it was barely audible. "I can wait. In fact, I can wait for a lot of things. I can wait for you to get tired. For that boy to get tired of you. Young men do, you know. But I'm older than you, old enough to see that you're an unusual girl. An inadvertent femme fatale, the damnedest thing I've ever seen. And I'll tell you this—because I get the feeling you haven't figured it out—that you have never in your life met a man who didn't want to fuck you. Every girl's got some of that mojo, it's true, but not like this. Not like whatever black magic you have conjured up."

From the corner of her eye, she could see him shift in the chair so that he was sitting forward, elbows on his knees.

"I'm a competitive guy, but I know when it's time to give up. We're not there yet, you and me. Not even close."

Celia closed her eyes. The light show was making her giddy and nauseous.

"You've got a stubborn streak. That's okay. Eventually you'll have to get out of the water and walk over here and get your towel. And when you do, you'll be thinking about what I said. Noticing how it feels to let me look at you. Maybe you'll realize it's what you want."

Just get the goddamned towel. Show him it doesn't matter. Get up, you coward. Jesus Christ almighty, just go and get your towel—put your clothes on. Fuck him. Fuck his almighty ego.

But the image of herself lingered in her mind. The sagging bikini, the jut of her hips.

It wasn't true. None of what he said was the least bit true. She liked to be covered. Where was the crime in that? She didn't like Rory or Eric to see her in a bathing suit, either. What did that prove?

"You're cold, honey. Come on out of there now. I can all but guarantee the sight of you will turn me on. Everything still fully functional in the old man, believe me."

The laughter was back in his voice. *The longer you stay in the pool, Celia, the more my opinion means to you.* It was a joke, some kind of game for the rich and famous. Slumming it, notching his bedpost, destroying her peace of mind to feed his self-esteem.

Celia damned her original decision to swim away and avoid him. It was cowardice again, always, and now he'd trapped her here. Whether she got out or stayed in the water, he would believe he had proved his point.

"And I thought I was competitive," he said. "You've got me—"

She dipped her head under the water and swam to the steps. She walked up and out, shuddering with cold, her skin drawn up tight and covered with goose bumps. But she didn't raise her hands to warm herself or even squeeze the water from her braid. She walked right up to the chair and stood in front of Julian, streaming water over his boots, her hands balled up at her sides.

"Atta girl," he said softly.

He held out the towel.

But Celia wouldn't take it. She stood looking down into his face, the patterns of light swaying across his features in shades of rose and violet.

Slowly he raised the towel, took her by the wrist and began to dry her. Shoulder to fingertips, one arm and then the other. Slowly, slowly, while she stood trembling at his feet. He dried her legs, her neck, her face and chest and hips and stomach. He turned her around and wrung the water from her hair. The towel was thick and soft, warm from being held against his body.

When he was finished, she turned to face him. He set the towel aside and reached for her. But Celia stepped back so that the tips of his fingers only brushed her hip.

She picked up her sweater and pulled it on, flipped her braid out from under.

"I thought I was competitive," he said again.

She pulled on her jeans.

"I'm sorry for you if that's true," she said. "The bronze must be quite a disappointment."

Julian stared at her for a moment, then burst out laughing.

"Goddamn, you're a bitch."
He got to his feet and held out her coat.
"Come on," he said. "I'll drive you home."

DECEMBER 24, 2008

RORY'S MOTHER HAD moved to Montrose when Rory was twenty. She had remarried, finally, to a Wyoming cowboy she'd met through an online dating service Celia had convinced her to try. Her new husband was decent sort, Rory thought. Slow and steady, with a smoker's croak and a perpetual limp slightly aided by an orthopedic shoe. Darlene had arranged a small ceremony in a chapel in downtown Montrose, followed by lunch at the Cracker Barrel with all their friends and a homemade lemon cake served on thick plates with scoops of ice cream sliding around the rims. Afterward she waved like a child through the dusty back window of Chuck Farrell's old Chevy pickup truck, trailing a dozen cans from the bumper that clanged against the blacktop as they drove away.

It gave Rory a pang to see her grinning that way, waving so hard. Celia had bought her a bouquet of white roses to carry, and boutonnieres for Chuck and Rory, and she'd found an antique silver-plated pitcher that she polished to a luster and wrapped in satiny paper with a big blue bow—paid for with her own money but signed, "With all our love, Rory and Celia."

They were a lot alike, his mom and Celia. When Celia

was small, she used to follow Darlene all around the house, gravely accepting any small task, happy to be near and, more than that, to be useful. Celia was never happier than when someone needed her help.

My little shadow, his mother used to call her. *A real little person.*

Rory, apparently, was not yet a person, more of a wrecking ball.

His mom used to dress Celia in ruffled outfits, to which Celia would add or subtract in sometimes bizarre combinations. A skirt over jeans, leg warmers on her arms, costume angel wings sometimes, even to school, or a headband with purple bunny ears on top. His mother's friends would shake their heads, but Darlene was charmed.

"Stripes and polka dots!" Grinning, her strong, rough fingers stroking Celia's cheek. "Now, I wouldn't have thought of such a thing. Don't you look pretty with all those colors, like a wrapped-up birthday present."

Together they would prowl the secondhand stores, filling Celia's room with clothes and costume jewelry. Darlene said it always started her day out right to see Celia coming down the stairs in the morning.

Between them was a quiet sympathy, the same willingness to be pleased by small things. The only time, in fact, that Rory could remember them fighting was years ago, when he and Celia were in their early teens. The day his mother had cut Celia's hair.

And that wasn't a fight, exactly.

Rory had come home from a soccer game and found them in the kitchen. Celia was perched on a rickety kitchen stool, her face and neck a savage red, thick with hives, eyes shocky and unblinking. Her hair lay in drifts of golden brown, which clung to Darlene's slippers as she circled the stool, scissors flashing, each swipe a dry screech like two rocks rubbing together.

He stood at the doorway, slack with surprise.

Celia's hair was her only claim to what truly could be called beauty: thick, silky, the spirals always floating around her head as though caught in a slight updraft. She used to call it her cape—she said it felt like that, patting against her back when she ran. It was what people talked about when they referred to Celia: *Oh, the girl with the hair? I know her.*

Now it was lying all around, in her lap and at her feet. The air was thick with the scent of Celia's strawberry shampoo.

Swapp!

The scissors closed again, and a last long strand slipped to the floor.

Darlene's lips were set in a grim line, her face as ashen as Celia's was red. Carefully she set down the scissors, wiped her hands and left the room without meeting Rory's eye. Her footsteps retreated down the hall. The bedroom door opened and shut.

Rory took a step toward Celia. She looked like a baby bird, all eyes and frail long neck.

"What happened?" he said.

She wouldn't look up. Her voice sounded trapped, as if she were holding her breath.

"She said it was too much. Too much, she kept saying. Too much."

Rory swallowed around the sudden tight ache in his throat. He took a cautious step forward, his hand outstretched as though to assess an injury.

She flinched away with a shrill cry.

"Don't!"

She leaped off the stool and ran from the room, slipping

on the hair as she rounded the corner. Her feet pounded up the stairs.

In the silence, he heard someone crying. It took him a moment to realize it wasn't Celia.

Slowly he shrugged off his backpack. He went to the closet and got a broom and a paper sack, swept up the hair and stuffed it in the bag. One long tendril was caught at the top of the bag. He lifted it out. It dangled from his hand like a spiderweb, twisting gently in the draft from the open front door. He found a piece of tape in the kitchen junk drawer, bound the cut end of the tendril and tucked it into his pocket.

He stood with the bag in his hands. The thought of throwing it into the garbage can hurt him somehow, as if the bag contained the body of a beloved pet. Finally he took it to the side of the house and held a match to a corner of the sack. Celia's hair turned black and frizzled, then faded to ash. It was very quick.

When it was done, Rory kicked some dirt over the ashes and went inside.

Darlene apologized again and again. She offered to take Celia down to Telluride or even Montrose for a real haircut to clean up the ragged ends and make a style of it. Celia refused. She was quiet afterward but not sullen. She insisted to Rory that it was fine.

"It's only hair," she said. "It'll grow back. I just don't feel like myself now, you know? My head feels..." She raised a hand to her bare neck. "Loose."

"You're still pretty," he lied.

The truth was, he missed her hair. And so did Eddie Dark, who was angrier than Rory had ever seen him.

"Goddamn it, Darlene," he said, so drunk he sounded almost toothless, his tongue rolling around his mouth. He had been drinking steadily for hours, since first coming home to see Celia's haircut. "Why'd you do that?"

Rory pressed his ear to his bedroom door but missed his mother's reply.

"She ain't your daughter," Eddie said.

"Of course she is." Darlene's voice faded and then returned. "Ed, I'm trying to help..."

There was a pause, then a glassy crash and the bone-jarring slam of the front door.

Afterward, an uneasy silence settled over the house. Celia rarely spoke, but took to following her stepmother around as she used to do when she was a younger girl, asking for chores. To Rory she seemed restless and vaguely apologetic, which baffled him. She helped with the meals and did the dishes every night after dinner without being asked. Then she'd go straight to her attic bedroom and stay there.

Sometimes Rory would follow her, and they'd lie on her bed listening to music. Celia would rest her shorn head on the pillow, one long leg crossed over the other, flicking her ankle.

He tried to find out what happened.

Celia only shrugged. "She said it was a good idea."

"I don't get it," he said. "Why was it a good idea? Lots of girls have long hair."

"That's what I said. But she kept saying, 'Trust me,' and that it was too much, and she had this funny look on her face, like..."

"Like what?"

"Like it was important."

"How could it be? That doesn't even make sense."

"I don't know." Celia's voice was sharp. "Anyway, what are you worried about it for? It's not your hair."

She got up then to change the music. But Rory had seen something in her face, something that looked like anger but felt a lot like fear.

All that was behind them now, Rory thought as he helped set his mother's table for Christmas Eve dinner. Celia had brought a white cotton tablecloth with a border of embroidered mistletoe. It was worn and aged to thinness, with a small stain in the middle, but so heavily starched that it stood out around the edges like a crinoline. Celia put a thick candle on the stained spot, took some ornaments off the tree and some pinecones out of her string bag, and in two minutes the old oak table looked like a picture from a magazine, making the cheap cotton curtains and nicked-up chairs seem somehow intentional.

His mother brought in the roast turkey with corn bread stuffing, mashed potatoes and rich golden gravy. She might have left it at that, but Celia craved a colorful plate and had added a bowl of glossy green beans, cranberry sauce and honey-glazed carrots. For dessert, an apple crostata. They ended up with so much food that Chuck had to bring in a side table from the living room to handle the overflow.

"This is enough to hold us until the spring thaw," Darlene said, hands on her hips.

"You've forgotten how much I can put away." And Rory's stomach growled, right on cue.

"He's not kidding," Celia said. "Last week I saw him eat six cheeseburgers in a row."

"And they weren't even that good," Rory said, pulling out a chair for his mother. "Willy Pete's."

"It's amazing that place is still open," Darlene said. "How is the old coot? And how's Jeanette?"

For some minutes they filled their plates, chatting about

their friends in Jawbone Ridge, and the young couple who had bought Yard Sale, Darlene's old shop on the High Street, where she used to sell secondhand ski gear and clothing.

"The shop looks good," Rory told her. "Christmas lights all year long, and in the summer they sell outdoor stuff. Camping gear and whatnot."

"How do they get customers in the door during the off-season?" Darlene wondered.

"They don't," he said. "eBay."

"Huh. I wish I'd thought of that."

But there was no envy in his mother's tone. She wished the young couple well and always stopped by to visit when she was in town.

Rory looked at her affectionately. After Eddie Dark left when Rory was thirteen, the three of them had to struggle harder than ever to make ends meet. Both he and Celia had started working early—under the table at first, years before they could legally collect a wage in the state of Colorado. They did odd jobs, mostly. Cleaning the big houses dotted around the mountain, babysitting, shoveling driveways. At fifteen, Celia took a steady job as a barista at the Java Hut, and Rory found a maintenance gig at a small hotel in Telluride. His mother had always hated to take their money. She wished Rory could have stayed in soccer, maybe learned to play an instrument. She badly wanted him to go to college. But he was a lousy student; he'd only made it through high school at all because of Celia's help. She had done all his reading and most of his homework—often at the expense of her own.

With exams, though, he was hopeless. Celia had tried to get him to cheat. She said he was clever with his hands; he could probably learn to palm some notes to boost his scores.

"It would make your mom happy," she said.

Rory was offended. "I'm not a cheater."

Celia gave him a crooked smile and handed him a book report to copy in his handwriting.

"That's not the same thing," he said, his neck growing hot.

"No," she said.

But there seemed to be a lot of opinion behind that syllable.

Now, across the table, Chuck was asking about the Blackbird. Where were they with the renovations?

"Well, the floors are done—" Celia said.

"Thank God," Rory put in.

"Rory..." his mother said.

"Sorry."

"The plumbing's good and the roof is solid, and I'm almost finished with the walls. Hopefully I'll have the kitchen done within the next month or so, and that'll be the last of them."

"And what are you doing about decorating it?" Darlene said. "Where will you get all the furniture?"

"A lot of it's done already," Rory said. "Celia has the magic touch, Mom. You wouldn't believe how good the place looks. Julian calls Celia the gypsy queen, decorating her palace."

"Gypsies don't build palaces," Celia said. "They keep moving—that's the point of being a gypsy."

"He means it as a compliment."

"Does he?"

"Sure. Why would he be there if he didn't think it was cool?"

"That's a good question."

"Wait," Darlene said. "Who's Julian?"

"Julian Moss," Rory said. "He's kind of a legend, actually. Back in the day he was a world champion downhill skier, took home a bronze in the Olympic Games. Anyway, he's building a house right now in Telluride and wanted to stay someplace nearby, so he ended up with us."

"But I thought you said the place wasn't ready."

"No, it's not, not at all. But Julian's cool with that. In fact, he's been pitching in with a lot of the work. Even—" Rory hesitated. Julian had been quietly siphoning money into the place. A lot of money, much more than Celia was aware of. Julian wanted to keep it on the down-low.

"Even what?" Celia said.

"Nothing. Pass the green beans, will you, Chuck?"

Rory took a heaping spoonful, trying not to notice the look in the older man's eye. He wondered how much Chuck knew or guessed about what went on inside the Blackbird Hotel.

After dinner, Chuck said to Darlene that it was time to go. The Christmas service would be starting soon.

"Last year we were late and had to stand in the back," Darlene said. "And by late I mean twenty minutes early."

"Go," Rory said.

"Why don't you come with us? It's the reason for the season, you know."

"Naw, you know we're only in it for the stocking stuffers," Rory said. "We'll do the dishes and watch *A Christmas Story*."

"I've raised a pair of heathens," Darlene said.

But she didn't argue. She and Chuck shrugged into their coats, gathered up two bags filled with gifts for their friends at church and they were off.

For a few minutes, Rory and Celia raced back and forth between the TV and the kitchen, calling out the lines they'd learned by heart during one epic childhood Christmas when they were both down with strep throat, entrenched on the couch while the show played on a loop in the living room.

When their favorite scene came on, Rory reached out and dragged her into his lap.

"Ho, ho, ho. What do you want for Christmas, little girl?" He drew his head back and leered at her. The curve of her ass was pressed between his thighs. His dick began to rear up against his jeans.

This girl, he thought. Goddamn.

She glanced at his crotch, both hands clasped under her chin in mock delight.

"Just what I wanted! Oh, Santa…" She pulled at his waistband, peering down his pants like she was opening a Christmas stocking.

"You'll shoot your eye out, kid," he said.

She crumpled against him, shaking with laughter. He kissed her open, breathless mouth, pulled her closer with one hand as with the other he unfastened his jeans and the buttons of her shirt.

This was what they needed. Things had been so heavy between them lately. They were working too hard, stressed out over money. But everything would be better soon. She still was his; she still knew they belonged together. She turned to straddle his lap as he pulled her clothes aside and bent to take her breast in his mouth, both hands sliding up her bare back to pull her closer, and his mind tripping in circles as he stroked her soft skin. This girl, this girl…

Abruptly she turned away.

A key clicked in the lock. The door sprang open, and his mother walked in.

"We were all the way to the 145 when I realized I'd forgotten Michelle's—"

She stopped in the doorway, her face blank with surprise.

Rory grabbed a blanket and pulled it over his lap.

"Jesus, Mom."

Celia was slower. She adjusted her shirt, lined up the buttons and began to fasten them. A deep red flush suffused her face, and her lips were pink where Rory had bitten them.

For several seconds, no one spoke. His mother stood where

she was, swaying a little as if hypnotized. The TV carried on in the background, an eerie parody of childhood, no longer comical but grotesque and damning. Rory reached for the remote, but his mother's voice stopped him.

"There's something you should know," she said. "I was wrong to keep it from you. I see that now."

Her voice was colder than Rory had ever heard it. She was looking straight at Celia.

A jolt of alarm passed through him. "Mom—"

"He left because of you."

Next to him, a huff from Celia, as if she'd been punched or had fallen flat on her back.

Rory felt his own breath snag in his throat. The words were out there now, part of the atmosphere. They formed a box around Celia and another around his mom, and he felt the walls close around him, too, as real as the floor under his feet. Across the room, the Christmas lights flashed red and green and the TV children screamed as they slid away from Santa's lap, but the sound was tinny and hollow as if it were coming from the bottom of a well.

His mother was sturdy now with her feet wide apart, one hand on the doorknob. She repeated the words carefully, with equal emphasis on each one. Her eyes were locked on Celia's face.

"Your father left because of you."

She bent stiffly to pick up a gift from the hall table. Then she left, shutting the door behind her.

The room had gone hollow, and a metallic ringing filled his ears. Celia got to her feet and Rory followed, pulled her cold hands into his as he rushed into speech.

"What the hell," he said. "Don't listen to that. I don't know what she's thinking to say a thing like that, Jesus Christ."

He struggled to keep his eyes still, suddenly hyperaware of

every muscle in his mouth and cheeks. She stood looking up at him, her eyebrows tightening with suspicion.

"What do you know about this? Tell me—what did she mean?"

"Nothing." Too fast, and his eyes were too steady, but he couldn't think where to look.

"Tell me."

"I don't know. It's nothing, swear to God."

Celia gave him a withering glare as she yanked her hands free. She turned and went down the hall to the guest room.

Rory followed her to the door. "What are you doing?"

She pulled her battered suitcase from the closet and dropped it on the bed, sprang the clasps to open it.

"She doesn't want me here," she said. "She won't want me here now."

"She was just surprised. I think we can give her that—come on."

Celia turned to him, blazing with disbelief.

"Surprised," she said. "Surprised is, 'Oh my God, you little slut, get your fucking hands off my golden boy.'"

"Jesus, Cee—"

"Surprised is, 'Dear Lord, heavenly father, a semi-incestuous love affair under my own roof. And on Christmas, too!'"

"All right—"

"This was anything but a surprise. She's been waiting for this. Waiting to say that, you saw her. And you—" Celia's voice broke, but she paused and held it together. "You won't even tell me what the hell she's talking about."

He reached for her. Celia shoved him away with one hand flat to his chest.

"Leave me alone, Rory. You've got nothing to say."

A sudden righteous rage surged up his body, carrying his voice with it.

"Hey, you've been waiting, too," he said. "How long were you going to let it go on like this? I've been loving you since we were kids. It's sick how much I love you—"

Celia hissed dismissively. She grabbed her clothes from the dresser drawer and flung them into the suitcase.

"This is love to you? Keeping secrets—"

"Secrets! Secrets are all you know. Don't preach to me." Anger snapped his chin back, inflated him with an acid buoyancy. "You live for that shit. Keep me with this knot in my gut for years, Celia, for a decade already, worrying over you and me and Eric, and your fucking secrets. Don't tell me."

"Well, that's all over now, isn't it?"

She swung her case off the bed and headed out the door. Rory followed her down the hallway, grabbing for her arm. A furious pressure roiled through his neck and ears.

"Maybe it is," he said. "Maybe you wanted this to happen, so we'd be done with all this sneaking around."

"Oh, yes. Yes, that's it exactly." She dropped her suitcase and turned to him. "Tell you what, let's just take this party right into your mother's bedroom. Surprise! Surprise!"

"Hey, let's. Let's be done with it, then." His voice boomed in his ears. "You really want to know why he left?"

The color ebbed from her face, leaving dints of white around her mouth and splotches of violent crimson on her neck and the tops of her cheeks.

"Yes."

"Bullshit. You don't want to hear it. You just want someone to blame."

Her mouth snapped shut as a hard tremor shook her body.

"Well, here I am. You can blame me and you wouldn't be wrong. Or you can blame my mother, or your father, or you can blame yourself if it makes you feel better." He jerked his chin, dropping his eyes to her clenched fists. "Go on, then.

Hit me if you want to. Hit me, but don't pretend you really want to know."

She started to turn away, but Rory caught her by the shoulder. Her eyes shifted left and right like a hunted animal.

"Go on," he said. "He's dead. He's fucking dead, and I'm not sorry."

She pushed him away with both hands. He moved to block her, and a second later felt the ringing crack of her hand against his cheek, stronger than he thought she could be. He ground his teeth to bite back his reaction even as his muscles tensed for a fight.

"Go on—get it out of your system. There's more where that came from, right? What are you waiting for?"

But as she raised her hand to slap him again, he ducked, grabbed her arms and pushed her through the bedroom doorway.

"What did she mean?" she cried.

"Fuck, Celia, what does it matter? To us? Now? He's dead. He left us and he died. What more do you need to know?"

"Why are you being like this? My dad was good to you."

Rory hissed with disgust. "Christ, you're oblivious. What do you remember about him, anyway? Because I think your memories must be different than mine."

"He treated you like a son."

"A son! He wouldn't teach me a goddamned thing. Remember the camping trips? Me running around after him, wanting so bad just to help, and all he could say was how he had no time to go around cleaning up after me. He wouldn't even let me take a whack at a tent stake or rig up the fishing gear. Fuck, I couldn't even gather the right kind of wood for the fire. Everything I did was wrong. It was that way at home. It was that way everywhere. He treated me like a nuisance."

"He was trying to teach you."

"Bullshit. To him I was..."

A word hovered on the tip of his tongue. It was a word he could never take back, and they'd had enough of those for one night. Rory swallowed it back.

"He was a pain in the ass. He was never my dad."

"Well, he was mine. Mine!"

She turned away, both hands over her face, crying mutely with the tears trickling down the sides of her thumbs.

Rory's anger dissolved. She was asking exactly what he'd be asking in her place. The only surprising part of her reaction was that it hadn't come sooner.

He pulled her into his arms. Her body seemed to run like sand through his arms as they sank to the floor. Her cheek against his was hot and sticky with tears.

"Oh, God," she said. "I really don't want to know."

TWO DAYS EARLIER

JULIAN SHUT THE DOOR and trotted down the front porch steps. The rumble of men's voices faded to silence as he crunched along the snowy trail, leaving Zig Campanelli's cabin behind him like a square of amber in the blue Alaskan dusk.

He took a deep breath, exhaled a plume of steam into the cupped silence of the night sky. The atmosphere at the cabin seemed strained this year. Always before it had been himself and other men his age: Campanelli, of course, and Vann James and Charlie Sims. All of them restless, nomadic, alighting occasionally in some younger woman's nest, but falling or flying out of it before anything might happen to seriously undermine their autonomy. The yearly ski trip gave them all something stable to latch the time on to, the way family men had holidays and kids' birthdays and weekends. As a group they'd always found the humor in that, congratulating each other on the latest lucky escape.

But this year was different. Their machismo had become a little strained, their voices self-consciously loud and laced with the rhythms and slang of a younger generation. It was embarrassing to hear them talk that way around Eric Dillon, a man who actually was young. His presence made Julian feel exposed, fraudulent—and resentful, in spite of the fact that it was Julian who'd invited him, who'd overcome every objection, who had paid Eric's way and brought him here.

"You should come with me," Julian had said. "There's room in the cabin. You and Rory keep talking about how you want to ski the Chugach."

"Rory won't be able to make it," Eric said. "He can't take that much time off work."

"I know. But I'm not asking him—I'm asking you."

A memory of Eric's hungry, hopeful face slid through Julian's mind. That disbelieving pride showing for just an instant when Eric realized he was being invited and not Rory.

Still, convincing him had taken some doing.

"I don't know, man. Celia's got a list of stuff we need to do long as my arm. Kind of shitty of me to bail on them for a month."

"Some advice, kid?" Julian said. "The money man comes and goes. You bought the place. You bought yourself some freedom. If Celia complains, you just remind her of that fact. I guarantee she'll quiet down."

"Celia won't complain."

"You think it will piss Rory off?"

"No," Eric said slowly. "No. They'll want me to go."

It had been in his mind, even then. Rory and Celia alone in the hotel. But Julian had worked on him, a word-by-word excision of Eric from the Blackbird that took the better part of a week. Eric was smart, but he was young and insecure and intensely competitive. Eventually he caved, as Julian suspected he would, to the idea of getting one up on Rory.

Julian stopped now, rocking back on his heels as he looked around. Before him was a small lake with a jagged edge of ice like broken teeth, the shore whiskered with grass poking up through the snow. He felt himself alone in the silence, small and still as prey. There were bears in the area. Big cats, maybe wolves. But Julian's hand in his pocket was curved around a gun, and he was a damned good shot. It was the last thing his older brother, Tony, had taught him, in the snowy woods outside their family's winter home in Connecticut.

"Hold your breath and squeeze," Tony had said. "Don't close your eyes, you pussy, you really want to do this with your eyes closed?"

He snatched the gun away and squeezed off a couple of shots, both of which went far wide of the mark.

"Do as I say, not as I do."

He laughed, a loud, happy barking sound, shrugging his big shoulders. Tony was always laughing in those days. He was a clown, a buffoon, but looking back Julian understood what he hadn't at the time: that it was Tony's youth and good looks that made him so popular. His behavior would have been considered boorish from an older man; only Tony had never reached the point of maturity. They all could remember him now as he had been before the accident. An overgrown puppy with more balls than brains, rollicking through the halls at school and at the supper table and down the slopes as if it had never once occurred to him that he might fall.

Amazing, really, the way people lit up when Tony was around. He had the whole long table in stitches at that last Christmas dinner, everyone screaming with laughter as though they'd never heard anything funnier than Tony's description of his Austrian ski coach—whose accent didn't sound remotely like the way Tony was bleating it out. But the table itself seemed to shiver with laughter, and no one minded at all when, using his knife and fork to demonstrate the position of his skis during one spectacular wreck, Tony left a flotsam of food particles around his plate and even managed to upend a full glass of red wine.

"Oh, Anthony," their mother cried. But she was laughing as she mopped up the spill, accepting his elaborate apologies and the dozen quick kisses he pressed to the back of her hand.

"*Mamacita!* That wreck was so big it's still going on!"

She just shook her head, her face full of love and tolerance and more than a little exasperation, all wrapped up in a pinkish glow of motherly pride. "What am I going to do with you?"

"Plastic on everything, Mom. I've been saying it for years..."

Later, gathered around the piano with their aunt pressed into service at the keys, he led them all into song, deliberately mangling the lyrics to the delight of their four young cousins. "Nine ladies drinking, eight midriffs showing, seven hussies stealing, six teens a-laying, five gooold teeeeth..."

Julian looked around in disbelief at the faces around the piano, all turned toward Tony. No one the least bit annoyed or wanting to clamp their ears shut as Julian did.

Tony didn't even care that he couldn't hear the pitch. He sang all the time, in spite or even because of how badly he could butcher a tune. He knew all the songs from *Hair* and would belt them out, his head thrown back, bellowing like he thought he was Treat Williams. He sang in the shower, the kitchen, the car, the street. He especially liked to sing outdoors, nostrils flaring, wildly off-key, full of what their mother called "Anthony's joie de vivre."

Tony knew the singing annoyed his younger brother. He would sometimes catch Julian in a headlock and scream songs in his ear, rubbing the top of Julian's head with his knuckles at the same time.

Their father loved it. He was a big man himself, but sickly, with four older brothers who'd tumbled around him like puppies but with whom he never could join in. He told Julian to accept Tony's roughhousing as a sign of affection, and he'd give Tony a good-natured pop to the back of the head when he went too far.

Tony was their father's favorite, but Julian always knew he was loved. Maybe not as much, but enough.

Really, it should have been enough.

"Don't think about it, Jules," his brother used to say. "I can see you're thinking about it."

Which always triggered an irritated response from Julian.

"I'm not."

"Man, you should see your face. You look like an old woman."

"I'm trying not to—"

"Yeah. You're trying not to miss." Tony laughed. "You're such a pussy, Jules. What am I always telling you?"

And Tony would repeat his favorite mantra: "Don't think about it."

Kind of a bad joke at this point. Tony hadn't formed a thought in twenty years. Hadn't done more than shit and drool, as a matter of fact. He spent his days eating oatmeal from a spoon, staring at *Jeopardy!* with blank black eyes while their mother called out the answers between bites, scraping the slobbered oatmeal off his chin and pushing it tenderly back through his lips until Tony's thick tongue finally worked it backward to his gullet and he swallowed it down.

Julian felt sorry for his mom, who, before Tony's accident, had kept flowers on every table and powdery sachets tucked between the folded sheets in the closet, dishes of fancy molded soaps in the bathrooms. Those had long been replaced by medicinal cleansers and stacks of adult diapers in a blue cloth hamper. There were no more dinner parties. No one to impress. Her world had shrunk to the size of a flat-screen TV. Tony's condition had trapped her in a freakish maternal parody: white-haired mother with a giant diapered baby, whose hands curled under his chin like an infant's fists, cradled against his chest.

Julian called her often and sent flowers at every holiday. But he rarely went home to visit, and never at mealtimes.

With his toes at the frozen shore, he took the gun out of his pocket. The weight of the thing never failed to surprise him. He remembered the way it had felt in his hand when Tony walked up to reset the tin cans they had piled on a stump at the edge of the woods. He had been entranced that day by the line of bare skin at the back of Tony's neck, between hairline and collar like a chink in armor. Looking at it, the gun had suddenly seemed too heavy to lift and too unstable. Julian didn't trust himself to raise it. He had stood in place, the gun dangling at the end of his arm as the scene around him wavered behind the fog of his own breath.

The cans haphazardly stacked, Tony had turned to face him. As their eyes met, he stumbled quickly away, only a step, but with an expression of wary surprise that Julian had never seen before. As if, for a moment, he sensed the proximity of danger and even where the danger was coming from.

Afterward they laughed it off.

"I'm not turning my back on you," Tony had said. "Not with that look in your eye. What were you thinking about, Jules?"

What was he thinking about.

On the hill above him, a shadow moved across the window. Julian raised the gun until the square of light was obscured by the barrel.

What was he thinking about.

He hardly knew.

FIVE DAYS EARLIER

CHARLIE PUSHED BACK from the table and closed his laptop.

"Looks good for tomorrow, kids," he said.

"Hot damn," Zig said. "You got the bird set up?"

"Yup. It'll be here at seven."

Julian grinned across the chessboard at Eric.

"Ready to meet the Lady, dude?"

Eric looked up, blinking. His eyes had gone a glassy pink and he was cradling his head in one hand. He'd been staring at the chessboard for a while but couldn't seem to decide on a move.

A smart kid. Brilliant, actually. He'd beaten Julian several times over the past few days, but tonight Julian was nursing a second beer, while Eric was annihilated on Vann Jimmy's San Francisco Kush.

Needs must, Julian figured. He didn't like to lose.

"The Lady's a bitch," Charlie said. He held up one hand nearly vertical, his fingers pointed at the floor. "Eight hundred feet, straight down. She'll rip your balls off, you approach her the wrong way."

Vann Jimmy wrapped his arms around his body. "Hold me. I'm s-s-scared."

Eric leaned forward and finally shifted his chess piece. Julian checked it immediately with his queen.

"Fuck me," Eric muttered.

Julian took a pull of his beer. "The Lady is a bitch, straight on. But you can approach from the side. Much more doable."

"Much more pussy," said Vann James.

"It's not pussy for a man to know his limits," Julian said. "We're not trying to get dead here."

"Might as well be dead, you let fear choose the way down a hill." Vann James flicked the lighter and held it to the swirled glass pipe. The flame-light danced along the scar on his cheek.

"'A fool flatters himself, a wise man flatters the fool,'" Julian said.

"Who's that?"

"Bulwer-Lytton."

Vann James snorted out a cloud of smoke.

"Oh, Jesus. You are the only man I know who would quote that guy unironically."

Eric stretched out a hand and lifted his knight.

Clever kid, thought Julian, annoyed.

A pity they weren't competing on the slopes. A loosened binding or buckle, a little something in his drink that would show up later on a piss test. It was harder to engineer a swerve like that in chess.

Charlie had picked up his phone and was tapping at the screen.

"Oh, Jesus Christ," said Vann James. "Are you texting that chick again?"

"Nope," Charlie said. "Not me."

Zig returned from the kitchen with a fresh beer. He twisted off the bottle top and tossed it toward the garbage can.

"You got to let her miss you, man," he said. "You got to let her get dry."

"Really," Charlie said without looking up. "This works so well for you?"

Zig laughed, saluting him with the beer bottle. "Yeah, I'm full of shit. I tried to get my chick to send me a crotch shot, and she was like, 'Oh my gawd, I'm not that kind of girl.'"

"Yeah, but you wish she was," said Vann James.

Zig wobbled his head.

"Sometimes. But, I mean, you also don't want your chick's business all over the internet."

"No, I get you. You want a classy slut."

"Hell, it's not even that so much." Zig dropped into a chair and stretched out his legs. "It was that when I was younger, sure. But you get older, you want to work a little. You want a woman who's got some pride, who knows better than to get involved with the likes of you. Because when you get that woman, who gives it up in spite of herself? Mmm..."

Julian moved a pawn and slouched back in his chair.

Celia's face drifted through his mind. She wasn't the type to say so, but it was clear from the lack of give on her end of the conversation that she disliked him. It hadn't been that way early on, when he first met her. She'd been friendly then, could even be called bubbly when she had a drink or two in her. But now when she looked at him it was with an air of dogged patience, as if she were a kindergarten teacher dealing with a tiresome child.

She didn't look that way at Eric. When Eric came into the room, that lanky girl with the odd clothes and crooked teeth was transformed. Her slanted face became suddenly fragile and mischievous. Her voice curved with flirtation. Her skin changed color, even, like a chameleon, a delicate pinkening that made the freckles seem to dance across her nose.

And Julian, watching, would feel a hard, sucking pull at his heart, as though it were tightening, shrinking inward to an inelastic knot that ached and struggled against his ribs.

Earlier in the day while the others were out skeet shooting, Julian had gone into the bunk room he and Eric were sharing. His own things were hung neatly from the clothes rail, but Eric's bag looked as if a small bomb had gone off inside. Clothes were strewn all around—uncharacteristic for Eric, who was almost as tidy as Julian himself. His shaving kit was lying open on the floor.

Julian stood beside it, looking down.

This is an asshole move. Leave it alone.

But he recognized this as a token protest, from a powerless, womanly source in the recesses of his mind.

He dropped to his knees and started to rummage through Eric's bag. Good-quality clothes, he noted mechanically. Jeans, sweaters, socks, ski skins. But at the side of the bag he found an inner pocket, and in the pocket a paper envelope. He pulled out the envelope and opened it.

Inside were three photographs of Celia. In the first she was gazing out the window of what was maybe her childhood bedroom, those wide gray eyes on the horizon, one bare leg stretched toward the camera and her hair lit from behind like a flame. This must have been years ago, because her hair was only just past her shoulders, and the lines of her cheekbone and jaw held a childlike roundness. In the second picture, probably taken within minutes of the first, she was laughing, her head thrown back, slender throat arched like a swan's neck and one shoulder turned as if to ward off Eric's humor.

He had seen that gesture a dozen times but always from a distance.

He flipped to the last photograph, a black-and-white: Celia, her chin lifted, staring straight into the camera from under a tangle of hair. Her arms were drawn back to expose her breasts, so small and delicate they barely cast a shadow. And she was wearing makeup, a lot of it, a dark shadow smudged around her eyes as if she'd gotten into her mother's makeup drawer and put it on with her fingers. Her lips were swollen and blurred with lipstick, open a little and with her tongue against her teeth. She looked arrogant, defiant. A little dazed.

Freshly fucked. That was what she looked like.

He sat on the edge of Eric's bunk with the picture in his hand. A teeming pressure sank painfully into his groin.

What had Eric done to get her like that?

Was she fooled by the bad-boy tattoos, the pierced ears, the unpredictable aggression? Eric was a good-looking kid—was it anything more than that? Surely she could see this boy was a coward. He didn't deserve her admiration any more than Julian deserved her coldness. But the proof remained, in black-and-white.

For Eric she'd painted her face.

Across the chessboard, Eric shifted his pawn. Julian smothered his resentment and dragged his mind back to the conversation.

"You know how other women say a girl's being cheap when she does shit like that," Zig was saying, "with the cameras in the bedroom and whatnot. It's a good word. I mean, obviously it's sexy and I'm as much in favor of porn as the next guy, but a chick like that does degrade in value."

"So why'd you ask for the crotch shot, then?" Charlie said.

"'Cause I'm a guy."

"It's all on her."

"Well, yeah. Sucks for her, I guess."

"The hell it does," said Vann James. "I'd love to be able to look at a chick and go, 'Yeah, I'll do her,' or 'Mmm, no, can't be bothered,' and have it all be up to me. Unfathomable. That's power right there."

"They've got more than they know what to do with."

Charlie had pocketed his phone and was perched on the arm of the sofa. He picked up the Tupperware box and started to break up some weed.

"But can you imagine," he said, "how awful it would be to be a chick? Men are disgusting—look at us. Zig with his pube beard—"

"Hey," said Zig, stroking his chin.

"Vann Jimmy, burping and farting all night—"

"Jules made chili!"

"And never will again," Julian said.

Charlie shook his head. "Disgusting. Men are fucking gnarly."

"You've got a point," said Zig. "We're clearly getting the better end of the deal."

"I don't know about that," Julian said. "Women don't get their hearts broken."

"Not true, to hear a woman tell it."

"Yeah, but that's bullshit," Julian said. "Do you really think a woman is going to get herself as worked up about you as you are about her? How many times have you broken up with a woman and felt like you were dying? Literally dying. You can't eat, you can't sleep, can't think of anything but her. You'd do anything to get that woman back. You'd howl outside her window like a dog if you thought it would change her mind."

Julian reached over and dropped another couple of logs onto the fire. Eric's eyes followed, glazed with weed, lit with orange firelight. Unreadable.

"And any other woman you could lay your hands on means less than nothing," Julian said, "because it's that woman, that one particular chick, and you can't even say what it is, but it's that one woman you need more than you need your next breath. You don't think a woman feels that way, do you?"

"No," Zig said. "A few years back I got lit up that way about a chick I met in rehab. She was pretty fucked up but she had this way of looking at me. Like I was a god, man, like she was hanging on every word. And when she stopped looking at me like that—"

"Hell," Eric said under his breath.

Julian stared into the hearth as the first tongues of flame curled from the underside of the logs. He remembered something else he'd found in Eric's suitcase: an orange prescription bottle, now buried in the snow twenty yards behind the cabin.

"'This look of thine will hurl my soul from heaven,'" he said softly. "You start to feel that woman belongs to you, and you get that fire..."

The shadows danced across the chessboard. Julian picked up the black king and set it down. "Checkmate."

The next morning, Eric couldn't find his meds. He was on his knees beside his duffel bag, the contents of his shaving kit turned out on the floor.

"Have you seen my prescription?" he said. "Little orange bottle, I thought it was right here..."

"Goddamn right I have," Julian said. "You left it on the bathroom counter, and it's a good thing, too. You can't take that shit out here, skiing these runs. It will slow your reactions."

"Dude, I've been taking it for years and my reactions are fine. I need it."

"Says who? Celia?" Julian shook his head. "Look, man, I know she means well, but some women just want to keep a guy placid. That's not you, not now. This mountain is the only thing you need."

From the distance came the throb of the helicopter blades. The men outside sent up a whooping cheer: "It's on!"

"Not a good time for this conversation," Eric said. "Where's the bottle?"

Julian clapped Eric on the back, hard enough to nudge him toward the door. With his hand on Eric's shoulder, he kept them moving through it.

"I'm doing you a favor, kid. Get your board."

The helicopter set them down at the top of the Isthmus. Julian's boots sank into the powder as Eric hopped down next to him, both of them ducking under the thunderous beat of the chopper blades, trudging through the snow to make way for the others. They collected their gear from the basket, and Julian waved the pilot away.

The mountains tumbled out beside and below them, white-capped spines and unforgiving stone cliffs with the helicopter retreating along them like a fly on the bedroom wall. All around the sky stretched to thinness, laced with clouds so close that Julian could feel them on his cheeks.

He glanced at the young man next to him.

Eric was well able to ski this mountain, right down the face. But physical ability and mental readiness were two separate things.

"Here it is, man," Julian said. "You ready to do this?"

Eric lifted his chin and looked around. His head bobbed in short jerks like a bird, eyes moving too quickly to alight. He drew a deep breath and blew it out, puffing his cheeks. Next to them, Zig and Vann James had their heads together, gesturing as they picked out their lines, while Charlie framed up a picture on his phone.

Julian sidestepped over to point out the landmarks.

"You got some pretty gnarly shit on the other side of the spine. You drift too far left and you're in a world of hurt. No way to recover, either, because if you miss it left you'll be diving off a cliff. But you want to stay out of the chute, too. It's tight right there. You want to really watch it."

Eric nodded, sharp little nods all in a row.

Julian gave him a sidelong glance, noting the quick puffs of steam clouding the air around Eric's face.

"Tell you what, though," he said. "If you swing down the right-hand spine, you'll have a much prettier ride. This one here's the kamikaze, but it's just a bullshit showpiece if you want to know the truth. More trouble than it's worth. No shame in it if what you want is a sweet double black through the powder."

He grinned at Eric.

"No point getting dead, you know?"

Eric craned his neck, comparing the options.

"They both come out in the same place," Julian said.

Charlie had set his board. He gave them a small salute and slipped over the edge. The slope was so steep that for several seconds they lost sight of him. Then he reappeared, tucked and soaring, before disappearing behind a snowy ledge.

Zig went next, then Vann James, his jacket shrinking to a bright red dot, darting over the snow. In the distance, they saw him barreling over the rocky point, tipping sideways as his arms swam through the air for balance.

"Shit," Julian said. "Hope he doesn't blow out that knee again. On the other hand, at least he missed the cliff."

He pushed off, calling back to Eric, turning his back to hide his grin. Eric would be taking the right-hand run—he was sure of it. The kid was all shook up.

"See you at the bottom."

* * *

Eric stood at the top of the mountain, the veil of clouds settling over him. The pearly air was dizzyingly silent.

It was never this quiet at home. Though the slopes of Telluride were famously uncrowded and contained pockets of momentary noiselessness, there hung over the mountains at least the possibility of sound. Another skier might come by, or a bird might sing, or there might be the far-off squeak of the lift. Here was a silence beyond that. Above it.

A wave of homesickness washed over him. Not for Colorado, exactly, or even for Celia, but for Rory. If Rory were here, he'd be brimming, delighted, full of enough confidence not just for himself but for Eric, as well.

It had always been that way, since they were little kids. Rory was the instigator of dangerous games, the one to send them charging down a tree run, jumping from the roof, barreling on their bikes around the hairpin turn at the far end of town. There had been innumerable batterings of their small bodies against the earth, though none stood out in Eric's mind like the tumble he took on the edge of the Ridge.

They must have been about ten at the time. They'd both gotten bikes for Christmas, and by spring were so desperate to ride them that it was almost all they did until the end of summer. But on that day the road was still muddy, and Eric had forgotten that the brakes were now on the handlebars instead of the pedals, and he'd skidded through the scrub and stinging gravel before coming to rest with his legs hanging over the ledge, the weight of momentum having carried him halfway over.

He screamed then, and the shame of screaming superseded even the terror of knowing he was going to fall. Then Rory was beside him, flat on his belly, his hands like a vise around Eric's wrist and their faces nose to nose above the scrabbly mud. Rory's vivid blue eyes locked on his. But Eric remained paralyzed with fear, one hand in Rory's and the other on a rock, which was slowly uprooting itself from the ground.

"You're not going to fall," Rory said. "Grab my arm."

The confidence in his voice snapped Eric's frozen joints apart, and he scrambled up, using Rory's outstretched body like a series of tree roots, until they were both on solid ground. They rolled over and lay for a minute, panting and trembling under the indifferent sky.

Then Rory sat up and said, "How's your bike?"

Like he hadn't just saved Eric's life, totally ignoring that scream.

The kindness in Rory went all the way through.

If he were in Alaska with Eric right now, he'd pretend not to see that Eric was scared out of his mind to take on the Isthmus. He'd be sunny, matter-of-fact.

You can do this. Just keep yourself pointed in the right direction and you're golden. Follow me down.

And he'd be off, tugging Eric after him.

Don't stop to think about it.

That was the problem. Eric was thinking. Overthinking. He wondered what had happened to Vann James, whether he'd blown out that knee—or worse. What if he'd gone the wrong way, gotten too far off course? And how much was too far? How did a person go balls-out down a forty-five-degree run with no more advice than "Not too much to the left"?

His heart was leaping up his throat. He leaned forward, peered over the edge.

Fuck.

SEPTEMBER 2008

A BASKET FULL of Celia's clothes sat on the floor of the laundry room, ready to be washed. She hung out her laundry every Thursday, a colorful bunting made of blouses, scarves, long skirts, cutoff jeans and tiny pairs of white cotton underwear that she hung in clusters from a single clothespin.

The clothesline seemed indecent, somehow, to Julian. Sleeves waving, hollow skirts floating upward, teasing glimpses inside a shirt as two halves parted at the buttonholes. He hated the way the empty garments hung there, spread wide across the line. It was like seeing her undressed in public.

"Must be hard to get your clothes dry in the winter," he had said the week before, trying to keep the mocking tones out of his voice.

She clipped one shoulder of her blouse with a clothespin, then the other. In the delicate cloud-light, her skin absorbed the colors of the pinned-up clothes: green, blue, pink, a shifting tint as she moved along the line.

"I use the dryer in the winter."

She never would follow him into a joke, even when he teed it up ready to go. It was a form of rudeness, in a way. A level of aloofness and brevity that made him feel like a fool every time.

It had amused him at first. Like sparring, flirtation. But lately he had the feeling that she wasn't playing. She wanted something from him, some particular response. Damned if he knew what it was.

She had stopped, pointing to the grass.

"Look," she said. "Oh, look."

A sparrow had collided with the kitchen window and lay there on the ground with its twig-like legs curled in the air, its eyes shut tight. One brown wing fanned out beside its body, the feathers pristine and utterly still.

Celia backed away a step, her face twisted with revulsion and fear, as if they'd encountered a wreck on the freeway instead of a small harmless creature, barely dead at all.

Julian stared at her curiously.

"Pick it up," he said.

"No, I can't."

"Why not? Are you afraid of birds?"

She shook her head and took another skittish step back.

"It's dead," she said.

"So it can't hurt you."

"I can't touch anything dead."

He clacked his tongue. "We'll all be dead someday."

"I know." She shuddered. "Doesn't that freak you out?"

"I don't think about it," he said truthfully.

"I do. I think about it all the time."

Julian picked up the bird, cradled its cold little body in his palm. Celia shrank back as if she thought he was going to throw it at her.

"What a strange girl you are, Celia. I didn't know you felt that way."

She stared at the sparrow as if she hadn't heard.

"I had a parakeet once," she said, "when I was about five. It was fine, totally fine, chirping and fluttering around its cage.

But when I woke up in the morning, it was dead. Hard, stiff, like it had turned to wood. It wasn't…real, anymore. It was just a thing, a hollowed-out thing. Its eyes were open, but there was nothing…"

She looked up at him, hushed and urgent.

"Don't you think it's awful that we have to die?"

He grunted a laugh and tossed the bird over the rocky ledge.

"There are things worse than dying," he said.

"Like what?"

"Like using up your life's experiences too fast. And then the years just go on and on, with nothing to look forward to."

He brushed his hands together, but still could feel the ghostly weight of the bird in his palm.

"It's a young person's world, Celia. After forty you begin to disappear. Like that bird of yours—you're not real anymore."

She frowned. "But you *are* real. You're here in the world, with the sun on your face and the ground under your feet. You're alive. You could be dead right now, with all the things you've done."

"Easily," he agreed.

"Then why—"

"Don't you get it? I wish I had been killed sometimes, in a blaze of glory and preferably within sight of the cameras. Now it's too late. I've outlived my relevance." He shook his head at the blankness of her expression. "You're too young to understand. I forget, sometimes, how young you are."

"But why should you need to be relevant? Why not just live?"

He caught his breath at the simplicity of that.

"Maybe I phrased it badly. Maybe I'm frustrated because all my wishes were granted before I really knew what to wish for."

He heard the awful, spooky weakness creep into his voice.

Immediately she withdrew and turned to hang the last of her laundry.

"Maybe you've gotten into the habit of wishing for the wrong things."

"Yeah? I thought I'd finally figured it out." He stepped closer. "I'd take you anywhere, you know, anywhere you want to go. I'd give you anything."

She picked up the laundry basket and settled it on her hip. A rummaging breeze stirred the clothesline.

"I have everything I want," she said.

"Do you?"

She started past him to the kitchen. He caught her by the elbow. Her feathery hair looped around his fingers.

"You don't want me, Celia? I think you do."

Her face in profile was distant.

"It seems like I already have you."

She left him standing there, shutting the door gently behind her.

A cruel girl. A strange, cruel girl.

He looked down now at the jumble of clothes beside the washing machine. Under a sky-blue shirt he saw the strap of Celia's underwear.

Reduced to this, he thought.

But he bent down, tugged the underwear out of the basket and shoved them into his pocket. As he straightened, he saw Kate pass by in the kitchen. His heart did a guilty stutter-step. But she didn't glance his way or slow down.

Surely she hadn't seen him.

Upstairs he closed the bathroom door and turned the lock. He pulled Celia's underwear from his pocket.

The cotton was soft in his hand—a tiny triangle in front, a slightly larger one in back, and in between the fabric had creased into a slight V shape. He ran his fingers back and forth over the point of the fold. The fabric held just a trace of her, some wheaty residual warmth. The scent quickened his blood, a visceral snap that got him instantly, painfully hard. He unzipped his jeans and let them fall to his knees, pumped out a palmful of lotion.

His mind's eye turned to a girl he had known at a tennis camp in upstate New York when they were both fourteen. At the end of a summer's worth of increasingly desperate machinations, he found himself finally on a bed of hot sand, the girl lying over him in a spindly, sun-warmed embrace, the scraps of their summer clothes creating pockets of inaccessibility between them. His fingers slipped along the dewy channel of her spine, all the way to her nape and sneakily down, every time a little farther. Her hair fell around them, collecting their breath and the wet suction sounds of their mouths, and as his fingers slid finally past the cottony folds of her bathing suit and right around her ass, she squirmed in his arms, sighing, the sultry air thick with anxiety. A sound came up her throat:

Naghhhhh…

A no, meaning yes, meaning she wouldn't, but oh, if she could…

Then, as now, the sound engendered in him not longing but a gnashing rage. He had upended the girl, left her flat and startled on the beach, and stalked away. In another bathroom, which he remembered now for the infuriating height of the sinks, he had rid himself of her in a few quick strokes, spit her right down the drain.

If only he could be so easily rid of Celia Dark. She had beguiled him somehow, imprinted herself inside his eyes, laced her scent through his mind like a madness.

And she wasn't even beautiful. With those crooked teeth and the bizarre clothes—she couldn't even be bothered to wear makeup. She wasn't even trying, a fact that made him angrier than almost anything else about her. Her rejection would be so much easier to accept if she were beautiful, or rich, or famous, or otherwise unattainable. She was none of those things. Why let himself act the fool for this girl when she was so monumentally unimpressed with him? He had Kate, who was pretty and fun, who wore skimpy clothes and would accept whatever he wanted in the bedroom. He could have any number of women and all of them would be more beautiful and accessible and fuckable than Celia Dark.

But his mind circled relentlessly around her. Those wide-open eyes and crooked mouth, that slim body swaying mysteriously under her clothes, the tawny mass of her hair. She'd been fucked hard, of course she had, but still there was something untouched about this girl. She was the dark virgin princess in a nightmare castle on the hill: wicked, aloof, catastrophically vulnerable. He didn't know whether he wanted to rescue her or rape her.

His teeth snapped together as he came in the bathroom sink.

"What do you think about this place?" Kate said.

She rolled over and lit a cigarette, leaned back on the pillow and sent a smoke ring floating toward the ceiling.

Julian lay back on the rumpled sheets, hollow and sluggish after the last retreating waves of orgasm. He closed his eyes and laid his arm over his forehead. Unsatisfied, even now. Like he was suffering some painful, insistent itch that was always just beyond his reach.

It was unfair, he knew. Kate was passionate, she was pretty and, the point was, she was here. Love the one you're with, he told himself.

With some effort, he pulled himself into the conversation. "Unique," he said.

"Yeah. I wasn't sure what Celia was trying to do at first, but now it's starting to feel like a gypsy caravan, with all the cushions and candles and everything low to the floor. It makes the place feel—"

"Warm."

"Exactly."

"Not a bad thing after a day of skiing."

"No, but I wonder whether we like it so much because of Celia, because of all of them. Do you think it will work as a B&B, with strangers coming and going?"

"Why wouldn't it?"

She reached over and tapped the ash off her cigarette. "It's just that it's all so personal. I feel like I'm sleeping in her bedroom."

He saw what she meant. Every object in the room had been found and brought here by Celia herself. The moss-green wallpaper had been peeled from the wall in strips, then sanded and waxed so that the remaining patches of paper and the wall behind it took on a lustrous glow by the light of the antique chandelier and the candles around the room. The Oriental rug, polished dresser, the drapes made from heavy scarves that hung from pegs over the window—all blissfully dim and comforting after a day on the icy-bright ski slopes. All intensely personal.

He thought of Celia's underwear, now crumpled in the corner of his drawer.

"Again," he said. "Not a bad thing."

Kate nodded. Her voice dropped to a low musing tone.

"Everybody loves Celia."

He rolled over, propped his head in his hand.

"What was she like as a kid?"

Kate paused a moment before answering.

"Not that good as a playmate, to be honest. She'd do anything you wanted and she was always really sweet about it, but she would never really throw herself into a game. I always got the feeling that she liked being kind of outside, watching everybody else but staying out of it. The girls at school hated her. They were vicious. But the boys..." She inhaled and blew a chain of smoke rings at the ceiling. "When we were in middle school, this older girl named Marcie called her out and they got into a fight. Girl fight, you know? But Celia was too bewildered to do much more than cover up and wait for it to be over. I don't think she even knew what it was about. Afterward she had a black eye—seriously, a shiner, like someone had thrown a glob of purple paint at her face. And it was the weirdest thing, the way all the boys came around her then. Boys who had never talked to her before. They would follow her and circle around, really quiet, like they'd found the Virgin Mary or something, like they were in a church."

Julian tried to imagine Celia as a child, drifting through the corridors, distant and alone with a cloud of silent boys trailing after.

"The girls left her alone after that," Kate said. "Until the end of high school, anyway. Rory was, as you might imagine, insanely popular and no one wanted to piss him off by talking about his kid sister. But after he and Eric left, the rumors started up that the three of them had been sleeping together. I'm not sure how much of that she took on board—I was wrapped up with this boy I was seeing, so Celia and I weren't hanging out much at the time. I've always felt bad about that. I didn't even notice when she dropped out. One day she was just gone and didn't come back."

"She left because of the rumors?" Julian found this hard to believe. Celia's eccentricity made her seem impervious to public opinion.

"I don't know," Kate said. "Maybe not. I didn't know her that well, not well enough to ask. I was more Rory's friend."

"A childhood romance?"

"Yeah, definitely. I adored him, in a puppy-dog kind of way. He's a year older than most of my friends, so automatically he was higher up on the kiddie social ladder."

"And Eric?"

"Not much to look at when we were kids, if you can believe it. If I'd known how he was going to turn out, I'd have put my dibs on early."

"Ah, but then you'd have missed out on this fine opportunity."

He expected her to laugh and agree that it would have been a loss. But she was following another train of thought.

"The three of them didn't really get close until her dad died."

"When was that?"

"Seventh grade, I think. He was already gone by then—"

"Gone?"

"Yeah, he'd moved out a few months earlier." She stubbed out her cigarette. "Moved out is maybe too strong a descriptor. Really he just left one morning, packed a suitcase and booked it out the door. He didn't even say goodbye."

"Had a fight with his wife?"

"I doubt it. He was a happy-go-lucky kind of guy. I can't think of anyone who didn't like him. But one day he just walked away."

"Another woman," Julian said. "Obviously."

"You would think. But where he'd have hidden her in this town is anyone's guess. Anyway, he always seemed like more of a family man to me. Really devoted, you know? He was always taking them fishing, camping. He used to make these elaborate family meals—Cajun food. You could smell it all the way down the street. He'd feed anyone who happened by." Kate shook her head. "A sweet man. And funny, with that accent. It made everything sound like a joke."

"So what do Celia and Rory say? Surely they know something about it."

"I don't think Celia has a clue. And if Rory knows, he's not telling."

"Hmm. And then her father died?"

"He was working in Boca Raton as an exterminator in the crawl space underneath some old lady's house and hit a live wire. The lady who lived there couldn't get him out, and by the time the ambulance got there, he was dead."

"Ouch."

"Mmm-hmm. Anyway, after that, Celia and Rory went everywhere together. I think he felt responsible for pulling her through it. He never let her out of his sight."

"Yeah. You know, I've always found that a little odd."

"Odd how?"

"That it's still going on. That Eric puts up with it. Seems like he'd want his chick to himself once in a while."

"Oh, no. No. Rory and Eric are like brothers. They love each other more than either of them will ever love Celia."

Kate stretched lazily, and the sheet slipped down past her bare breasts. She went on in that same musing tone.

"Though it is strange, in a way. Rory's been one-upping Eric his whole life. And Eric's a pretty insecure guy. You'd think at some point he'd have gotten tired of always being upstaged."

Julian looked at her. Something in his mind shifted, the first glimmer of light over a river of cracked ice. An image of his brother, Tony, snapped to his mind: Tony's face when it still had been animated, when Julian had been the one at the bottom of the slope, hearing the applause and hoots of approval and none of it for him. The gnawing jealousy, the wish to clamp his hands over his ears to drown it out.

Eric's a pretty insecure guy...

He rolled forward and kissed Kate, drew the back of one finger down the center of her body and under the sheets. She sighed happily.

So easy to read. Sweet little Katie.

"Keep talking," he said. "I like the sound of your voice."

DECEMBER 31, 2007

WHEN JULIAN INTRODUCED himself to Celia Dark, he pretended not to recognize her. Yet he'd seen her three times before since arriving in Telluride for the holidays. He noticed her first from the window of his hotel room, as she jogged alone down the snowy sidewalk, past the colorful speckled Christmas lights and the long golden windows. Her hair, oddly light, floated out behind her like a bride's veil. A strange, thin girl, long legs encased in tight black running pants, fists clenched and her breath rising in thin plumes of steam around her face. He'd been nervous, watching her. He expected her to slip and fall. Everyone else was walking in measured steps along the sidewalk, their hands out a little to the side, just in case. This girl didn't seem to notice the ice. She never skidded and she never slowed down. As she bobbed around the corner and out of sight, Julian felt the tension uncoil from his body, as if he'd been watching a gymnast or ski jumper having successfully stuck the landing.

A few days later he saw her again. He was riding up on a lift as she passed beneath him—bundled and obscured by layers of clothing, her face blotted by heavy sunglasses. But that hair of hers was hard to miss. And there was something, too, in her movement, some elasticity in her hips, an unworried connection to the ground that reminded him of his brother, Tony. She skied like she was swimming, with long, languid strokes pushing through the powder.

Julian was not the kind of man to turn around and ogle a woman. But he remembered her, was half-consciously looking for her when, the following night, they ended up together on the corner of a sidewalk, waiting to cross the street. The sun had slipped behind the horizon, leaving the sky purple and close, animated with snowflakes that drifted through the squares of window light and the teardrop lamps along the sidewalk. She wasn't dressed for sport this time, but was wrapped in a thick woolen shawl, her feet swallowed up by a pair of fleece-lined UGGs. Her hair hung in a shining braid over her shoulder, with a white feather tucked into the end. As Julian hesitated, trying to decide what, if anything, to say, a thick-wheeled SUV roared up the sloppy road, picking up speed as it passed them, swerving at the last second to splatter them both with filthy snow.

Julian yelled after it, furious, smacking the snow off his coat and jeans.

"Did he get you?" he said to the girl.

"Oh," she said, as if it had just occurred to her to check. "Maybe."

She swiped vaguely at her shawl. There was mud in her hair.

"What a dick," Julian said.

"Yes," she said, and that was it, and she was gone.

Julian stared after her, surprised. Not because he'd been rebuffed—which was not entirely without precedent, even for him—but because he hadn't been noticed at all. She'd barely glanced at him, was looking into his face and straight through as if he were a window, some transparent barrier to the scenery.

As he stood there, a feeling swept over him of déjà vu.

He had been here before. He knew this girl. She was going to round the corner and go up the steps to the wine market, through the glass door on the right, and as she passed through she would be looking right at him. The image was strong as a memory. Her shawl would catch on the door handle and she'd laugh with someone inside as she freed herself.

He stood there waiting, absolutely certain the scene would play out the way he'd imagined. For a moment, his life unfurled before and after this point in time as if he'd lived it already, had punched through some invisible membrane that separated past and future so that the present seemed to stretch infinitely onward like the reflections in a pair of facing mirrors. And, yes, there she went, up the front steps, her hand on the door. She was looking at him. Laughing, tugging at her shawl.

The déjà vu faded. Julian pulled his coat around him and continued on to the pub. Odd, the way the universe toyed with your head. Like everything was preordained, and you were just riding through life on a track you had already laid in the snow. Now and then you could look up and see the pattern of the landscape, the terrain at the edges of your vision, and know that you'd traveled this way before.

By eleven o'clock on New Year's Eve, the 760 Bar was wall-to-wall, a bobbing mass of sunburned faces, spilling out to the lobby of the Adelaide Lodge. The music throbbed in Julian's ears as he shouldered his way to the bar with Zig running interference just ahead.

His eyes slid around the room, cataloging the glances that registered recognition. Those were the hard-core ski crowd, who might not remember him for the bronze but would have seen his movie, or had him pointed out by those in the know: *That's Julian Moss. Badass motherfucker. One of those guys who skis all over the world. He made a film about it—you can see the clips on YouTube*... And man or woman, seeing him, would approve. His Irish grandmother would have said that Julian cut a fine figure in his black turtleneck and peacoat, slim black jeans and boots. A fine figure of a man who took some pride in his appearance.

Zig handed him a beer and chinked their bottles together. "Good times," he said and disappeared into the crowd.

Julian glanced around the room. Most of the other men were dressed down, in ratty jeans and sweaters, their hair smashed flat around their skulls, sometimes with the dents of a helmet still pressed in. He found his reflection in the mirror behind the bar and his confidence rose. He looked prosperous, assured, a little older than these twentysomethings maybe, but in an up-the-food-chain sort of way. The peacoat was a good choice.

He sipped his beer. A big blond kid walked by, circling the edge of the bar crowd as he made his way across the room. His face was vaguely familiar, but Julian couldn't think where they might have met. Might have been at another party or some skiing event. Clearly the guy was an athlete, maybe even a professional. He had that look about him: deeply settled in his skin, deft and familiar with his body like he'd already put it through some trials and was satisfied with the results.

As the kid took a seat at one of the semicircular booths, Julian got another look at his face and remembered. They'd shared a lift earlier that day. The guy worked for the forestry service or something and was part of the ski patrol. They'd made small talk until almost the top of the run, when the kid said shyly, "You're Julian Moss?"

"Guilty."

"Man, I've seen your films. Amazing, seriously, I can't even imagine all the places you've been..."

They talked about skiing until they reached the ramp, where they parted amiably, the kid with his radio in hand, skiing out to meet a snowmobile that was buzzing up the slope, trailing a stretcher.

Altogether a likable young guy, and as good a place to start as any.

Julian made his way toward their table. As he'd hoped, Ski Patrol saw him and beckoned him in. Their booth was tight full and littered with empty beer bottles. There was a dark-haired guy with tattoos on his hands, his back turned, talking to someone behind the booth, and a girl sitting next to him who looked up as he approached.

His heart sank and leaped absurdly. She was smiling right at him.

"So you're the wizard," she said over the din.

"The what?"

"Ski god, playboy, Olympic medalist..." She spoke carefully, ticking the description off on her fingers.

Ski Patrol took over the conversation. "I told her I rode up with you this morning. I might have gotten a little fangirlie about it."

"A little." The girl rolled her eyes.

"Playboy is a new one," Julian said.

"Retro," she said.

She scooted around, pressing up to the tatted kid on her left, to make space for Julian. But there was still not enough room, and he didn't try to sit down.

"I'm Rory McFarland," the blond said. "This is my sister, Celia, and that's Eric Dillon, and over there is Kate and whoever's hitting on her at the moment."

"Julian Moss," he said to the girl.

He carried the conversation easily with Rory, asking about the casualty Rory had gone out to retrieve when they met earlier. But inwardly his heart was light. He kept repeating her name, like a song that had stuck in his head: *Celia, Celia, Ceeelia…*

After a few minutes, Rory laid some bills on the table and motioned for Julian to take his seat.

"Listen, I'm going to leave you for a minute. I ordered some drinks. Keep her glass full, will you? She's on a roll but broke as hell."

Julian slid into the booth. The girl turned halfway in her seat, curling one leg under the other so she could look him in the eye. Her gaze traveled over his face with the unironic absorption of a young child. The crowd around them seemed suddenly too loud, deliberately clumsy, as though the whole room were filled with teenage boys vying for her attention.

He sipped his beer. He had pretty good horse sense when it came to women. They liked to be noticed, didn't mind being watched as long as you didn't come on too strong with it.

"You don't remember me," he said.

"No," she said, with a wary lifted inflection like a question.

He told her in careful detail about the three times he had seen her: what she was wearing during her run, the way her hair looked, billowing out behind her, the way she'd skied beneath him on the lift, the long swimmy strokes of her skis. The sudden burst of anger he'd felt at seeing her splattered with mud. He kept his voice low and self-amused and diffident, watched as her mouth slackened and her eyes went cloudy, drifting over his face.

"I keep having this déjà vu," he said. "Have you ever felt that, like you've been through it all before?"

She nodded.

"I keep thinking I know you already," he said, which was true, though he only realized the truth of it after the words were out.

"You don't," she said.

"Maybe not."

"And I don't know you..."

"You can, if you want to. Ask me a question."

She blinked up at him. He couldn't find a trace of makeup on her eyes or lips, which gave her face an almost shocking air of nudity in the flaring light. Her skin was smooth and translucent as a child's, scattered with tiny round freckles across her nose, which was pierced on one side and adorned with a fine gold hoop. The pace of her conversation was achingly slow. Long pauses followed by an unsatisfying trickle of words, but wielding the sort of pressure a young child will exert—eyes wide, full of trust and with the clear expectation that the other party will find the vocabulary to carry the conversation forward.

A waitress arrived with two Tanqueray and tonics. Julian left Rory's money on the table and paid for them himself, took Celia's empty glass and set it on the tray.

He turned back to her as the waitress walked away.

"Ask me a question," he said.

Celia leaned on the back of the booth, one hand cupped around the side of her neck. She took a long swallow of her drink.

"If you were going to build something," she said, "what would it be?"

He smiled. He'd once been interviewed by his eight-year-old cousin for her school newspaper; this felt like that.

"Let's see," he said, playing along. "Is money an object, or no?"

She considered this, her soft little eyebrows drawn to a crease over her nose. Her next words surprised him, a sudden flood of syllables rolling off her tongue as though she was parroting back a line she'd heard elsewhere.

"That's a good question. A hypothetical should have parameters, or people start building towers on top of Kilimanjaro for no apparent reason—"

"It could happen," the tatted guy said over his shoulder, then turned back to his conversation without missing a beat.

Celia swirled her drink. "Let's say you have enough for a big project. But not enough for a tower into space."

"Okay," Julian said. "And can I build it anywhere?"

"Anywhere." She gestured with her glass and a drop of gin sloshed over the rim to the table.

He shuffled through the possibilities. What would charm a girl like this? What was he expected to say? She was watching him, unblinking, as if his answer was the most important thing she'd hear all day.

He stalled for time.

"Well, I wouldn't build the Taj Mahal. It's been done."

"Yes."

"And a dead woman wouldn't appreciate the effort."

"True."

"I wouldn't build any sort of monument—"

"Not even to yourself?"

A teasing smile crept across her lips. For a moment he wished he'd come straight off the slopes and into this party, hat-head and all. He had never felt more overdressed.

He plunged ahead as if he hadn't heard.

"I wouldn't build a spaceship," he said. "Or a museum, or a time machine, or a robot sex doll."

Unexpectedly she laughed, a gratifying sunburst lighting up her face. A scratchy answering heat suffused his body. He pulled off his coat and laid it on the seat beside him, pushed his sleeves up over his forearms, wiped his upper lip with the back of his hand.

She'd be fantastic in bed, this girl, not easy to get but strange and wild and worth the effort once he had her. She'd be into some kinky shit. She might want to be pushed around—he could feel the challenge and the heat of her. He'd been with women like this, who were usually much older and tired of boys and were dying to be with a man who knew what they needed.

He took a pull of his drink and continued with a teetering confidence.

"I wouldn't—would *not*—dress her up in kneesocks and a pleated plaid skirt, or tie her hair in pigtails, or program her with phrases like, 'Oh, Daddy, I've been a very bad girl,' or 'Give it to me, big boy!' or 'You can put it *anywhere*.'"

He thought he might have gone too far, but Celia dissolved into a silent and breathless hilarity, one hand across her eyes, her cheeks glowing pink in the pulsing light. Her slender shoulders hopped up and down as her breath fanned up at him, sweetly liquored and warm.

The heaviness in his dick was undeniable, and the night seemed alive with possibility.

"Well. I'm glad we got that straight." She wiped her eyes with her knuckles, pressed both palms to her cheeks. "So what would you build?"

Back to the beginning, but now he had an idea.

"I'd want something practical," he said. "Something that would provide for my future. A big casino in Vegas, maybe. My own personal money machine."

There was a pause. He sensed that his choice had landed heavily.

"Oh!" she said. "That's clever."

She may as well have said, "That's idiotic." She kept nodding as though she'd forgotten to stop.

He had the feeling that he'd failed a test he didn't know he was taking. A strange constriction lodged in his throat. "What would you build?"

She drained the last of her drink, straightened her shoulders and pushed a stray tendril of hair off her cheek.

"Nothing," she said. "There's enough in the world already."

Her tone was offhand, disinterested, but underneath he felt a subtle reproach that annoyed him. A trick question, and he'd walked right into it.

The music had changed. A driving, sensual groove throbbed in the air.

"I need to get up and dance or I won't make it to midnight," she said.

Julian brightened. He opened his mouth to say, "Come on, then," but before he could get the words out, she'd turned from him to link her arm through Eric's. She said something in his ear that turned the kid's head on a swivel until they were nose to nose. Then she opened her mouth and kissed him, her slender hand slipping up to curve around his neck.

Julian looked on from the corner of his eye. A prickly sensation filled his chest, as though his organs had been removed and replaced by an icy liquid.

Celia turned to him, smiling, distracted, rubbing her thumb across her lips. "Hey, can we scoot past you?"

Julian got up and they shifted to the end of the booth. Rory had come back to the table, but Celia linked her arm through his, leaning her cheek against his shoulder as she tugged him along.

As they started toward the dance floor, she seemed to remember Julian.

"A money machine," she said. "Really smart of you..."

Her words were swallowed up in a swell of music, and she was gone, weaving through the crowd with both young men in tow.

They formed a tight triangle and began to dance. Celia raised her arms, swaying her hips as she turned, glancing at Eric over her shoulder as her hair spun out around her. Through the crowd Julian tried to figure out what she was wearing. It must have been a long skirt and some kind of sweater, but the way the clothes hung down her slim body made it seem as though she were draped in a collection of pale scarves and long strands of beads. She seemed excessively covered up compared with the other women on the dance floor, with an unsettling disregard for her own beauty.

Or…maybe not beauty. On closer analysis, was this girl even pretty? The question teased at Julian as he watched her. What did she look like, really? Straight on, her face had a doll-like fragility, the wide eyes and lips symmetrical and perfectly balanced. But her gapped and crooked front teeth, combined with the high Slavic line of her cheekbones, conspired at times to render her so flawed she could almost be called ugly. The effect was perplexing, mesmerizing, like turning a kaleidoscope. You got a different pattern every time.

He turned away, aggravated.

At the other side of the booth, Kate's admirer had wandered off. Julian sat next to her and hooked his thumb toward Celia.

"She couldn't decide what to wear?"

"Bohemian," Kate said. "It only works if you're twenty years old and shaped like a coatrack. Put that outfit on a middle-aged fat lady and you'd expect to find her selling turquoise out of a pawnshop in Sedona."

"Meow," he said, and she laughed.

"I know, I know…"

This girl was a different type altogether: crudely put together, tending toward stocky, with thick shoulders and short strong fingers. But a smart girl who knew how to make herself look good. Even at this hour, her lipstick and eyebrows were perfectly drawn, dark hair shining, and she smelled delicious. He noted with amusement the trace of glitter over the tops of her breasts. A young one.

He ordered drinks.

"You live up here?" he said.

"Since I was a kid. We all went to school together." She nodded around the empty table.

"So what do you do?"

"Not a damn thing," she said. "My parents own this hotel."

It should have been an obnoxious, braggy remark, but Kate wrinkled her nose and laughed a little as she said it, as though she knew what it sounded like and she was in on the joke.

"Lucky you," Julian said. "And what about your friends, what are they into?"

"They're the competition, renovating one of the historic hotels on the Ridge. It's the crooked little place at the far end of town. Have you seen it?"

"I don't think so."

"Then you haven't. You'd remember if you had."

The light faded to black and a strobe came on, throwing the dancers into stop-action relief. Celia's arms trailed up toward the ceiling as Eric ran his hands down her body, around her ass, disappearing beneath her shirt and out again under cover of the flickering light. It was hard to be certain, but Julian thought Eric was watching Celia's brother the whole time, as if he had something to prove, or was showing off in some way by running his hands over the guy's kid sister. If so, the challenge went uncontested.

"You're the Olympian Rory was talking about," Kate said.

"Probably."

"You don't look like a skier."

"No? What do skiers look like?"

She waggled her head. "You know...a little banged up."

"Oh, I'm plenty banged up, believe me."

"Tell me."

"Knee, back, shoulder, plenty of broken bones. The usual."

"You look tidy, though. Sharp."

"Is that a good thing or a bad thing?"

"Depends on what you like."

Their drinks arrived. She tossed back the shot, not as careful of her lipstick as he would have expected, and crossed her eyes at him as she slammed down the glass. Julian was charmed.

"What do you like?" he said. "You like these boys with the chapped lips and helmet hair?"

"Some of them."

"Bullshit," he said. "Those are the boys who are trying to look the part. They love the helmet head, they love the peeling nose, makes them feel like they've accomplished something. But you put them on a mountain and they're flailing—they've got no groove at all. They're just trying to identify. Probably grew up playing video games and next week they'll be back home in Montecito, working the checkout counter at Target."

An appreciative smile curved one side of her lips. She tipped up her bottle of beer, swallowed, set it down again. "Whatever you say. I'm going to the little girl's room."

But this time Julian knew he was not being dismissed. She got up from the table and began to pick her way through the crowd. She knew he was watching; there was a self-conscious sway to her hips. A cute girl, expensive and easy. No strange angles, no mystery to work out. Tight jeans and a low-cut sweater, that red doll's mouth and confident dose of perfume. His kind of girl.

Just before she rounded the corner, she looked back and caught his eye. She raised an eyebrow and disappeared through the door to the ladies' room.

Julian drained his glass, picked up her unfinished beer and

followed her, waiting outside the ladies' room and a little to the side.

When she came out, her eyes went straight for the table he had just vacated. It was filled now with strangers, no sign of Celia or the others. Kate stood on tiptoe, searching the crowd. Her shoulders slumped in disappointment at seeing everybody gone.

Julian moved up beside her and hooked his hand inside her elbow.

"How do you feel about older men?" he said.

Her expression held a trace of embarrassment: she knew she'd been caught looking. But she recovered gamely, accepting the drink for a second time.

"I take it on a case-by-case basis," she said.

She never asked where he was staying—which was, as it happened, right here on the third floor of her parents' hotel. He could have taken her to his room. For that matter, she could presumably have taken him to any vacant bed in the place. A closet, even, or a supply room. Instead she'd led him down the stairwell to the freezing basement parking lot and, after a few perfunctory kisses, had dug a condom from her purse and handed it over. Easy as that.

And that was good, Julian told himself. She would have been one of those popular girls he remembered from high school, grinning at the kids in the hall, self-possessed and shadowless. She knew what she wanted.

He pulled her to the outside of the lowest flight of stairs, where the metal handrail formed a corner with the cement wall of the garage, and there he turned her around. He slid one hand up her sweater, unzipped her jeans, his fingers curling upward as hers gripped the metal tubing.

"Hurry," she said in a bossy voice that sent a grunt of laughter up his throat.

"You hurry," he said. "You come for me and then I'll fuck you."

With his free hand he pushed down her jeans. An easy, easy girl. Ass-up in a filthy garage, bejeweled fingers wrapped around the bottom of the steel railing.

Treat a lady like a whore, his brother used to say.

From the hotel above came a muffled cheer. It must be midnight. He gave her a celebratory slap on the ass as he fucked her. Then he let himself go, the orgasm unraveling from the base of his groin. He lifted her by the hips and banged against her, a dozen times or more, until with a bone-jarring shudder he was coming, hard enough to smack her head against the handrail. He pressed a hand over her forehead in apology, to rub away the sting, and slipped the other over her stomach and around her breast. She squealed at the cold and started, adorably, to laugh.

"Like being fucked by the abominable snowman," she said.

He went to the bathroom afterward, shut himself into a stall so he could flush the condom. The music thumped from a speaker inside the men's room, rattling the latch on the door.

The sex had left him faintly dissatisfied. He had asked Kate to stay with him for the night. He liked her, and he liked her friends. But a strange lassitude had sunk in, having nothing to do with sexual gratification and everything to do with the fact that he was here again in Telluride on New Year's Eve. Alone—or nearly alone. Another year stretched ahead of him, featureless, every option so available that not one of them had the power to beckon him.

He might stay in town for a while. There was no place else to be, no one waiting for him, no home to return to. He could maybe find a house to rent in the area. Or, even better, a B&B where he could get a hot meal every morning and someone to clean up after him. Anyway, it was nice to come back to an inhabited home at the end of a cold day on the slopes. Made the time there seem to go faster.

Threads of conversation floated in from the men at the sinks and urinal:

"...Revelation was wicked fast today...tore up my board on the bumps at five...champagne tastes like donkey piss, man, give me a beer every time...they're gone, I think...some crusty-looking old hound with his tongue out for Celia..."

Julian left the stall and went to the sink. He met the eye of the younger man who had been speaking. The kid's face, reflected in the mirror, reddened beneath his tan, and he stifled a laugh as he headed for the door.

"Aw, shit," he whispered to his friend. "Oops."

Julian turned off the taps and gripped the edge of the sink. The creases of his face were marked with shadow from the overhead lights, two lines running down from his mouth like the jaws of a marionette. For an instant he felt a congested sort of panic, clotting in the pit of his stomach.

He turned away quickly. His hand strayed up to smooth the wrinkles flat with his fingers.

JULY 2007

ERIC STEPPED OUT of the real estate office and into the clear summer light, an unstoppable grin spreading across his face. How his father would have hated the way Eric had spent his inheritance.

That broken-down hotel? What the hell are you thinking? No goddamn common sense, boy, that's what's the matter with you.

"I can't hear you," Eric sang as he crossed the parking lot.

The world was full of people just like his old man, who thought that because an idea was unusual it was impossibly fucked up. As if the way he had lived was better. He'd spent his money on himself when he spent it at all. Always tense, always wound up. Finally popped an aneurysm in his head from the pressure of being pissed off all the time.

Eric could have told him: the point of money was to make people happy. To give them things, if you could.

There wasn't much left now, but that didn't matter. They had the Blackbird and just enough left over to fix it up.

He climbed into his truck and called Rory. In the background, he could hear the noise from Rory's team, working to clear the debris from a trail near Wild Boy Lake: the ear-shattering drone of a chain saw, a male voice nearby calling over the din, "Dude, you got that upside down..."

"Hey," Rory shouted.

Eric held the phone away from his ear.

"Done deal," he said. "I've got the keys in my hand."

"Sweet. How's it feel to be the owner of the most craptastic hotel in Colorado?"

"Like it's time to celebrate."

He could hear the smile in Rory's voice. "What's the plan?"

Even in the summer, it was hard to get a reservation at Tango on short notice, but Rory had done some side work on the restaurant owner's home the summer before. There would always be a table for them.

They sat on the terrace beneath a flowering crab apple tree. Its blossoms drifted to the table, into their champagne, a pink confetti over a parade of small plates: rolled-up slips of eggplant filled with buttery ricotta; an oval dish of exotic mushrooms drenched in butter and wine; spiced chickpeas and warm hachapuri; honey-drizzled Brie, topped with roasted pears and candied hazelnuts; spheres of fresh goat cheese in olive oil; herbed chutneys and seared red grapes served with loaves of crusty bread; quails' eggs like tiny suns, running onto the plate. They ordered and kept ordering, filling the candlelit table with bite-size morsels they fed each other with their hands.

The luxury of the expensive meal released them. As they ate, they watched each other, unconcerned with how it might look to anyone seated nearby: the slow consumption, sticky squares of bread pudding dripping dulce de leche between their fingers, tipping their heads back with their lashes lowered in a trance of desire. Their table seemed enveloped in a haze of golden light, as if for the night the three of them were utterly alone and each existed for no other purpose than to bask in the pleasure of seeing each other—all, equally—in love.

At the feet of the Blackbird Hotel, Celia swayed a little, squinting up through the darkness. Eric offered his arm and she took it, a light weight but with her fingers gripping hard, like a bird alighting.

"You took the boards off the door," she said. "I'm glad. I hated seeing the Blackbird with its mouth stapled shut."

Rory produced a flashlight, and together they crossed the weed-choked gravel lot, their footsteps crunching on the pebbles, thumping in unison up the front porch steps.

Eric handed Celia the key. It should have been a gothic-style brass key, to go with the place, but instead it was small and round and ordinary, still marked with a handwritten paper tag on a string from the Realtor's office: 213 Ridge Road.

"You should do it," Celia said. "It belongs to you."

Eric looked down at her with a frisson of unease. She did understand about the Blackbird, didn't she? He'd always thought of the three of them as almost psychically connected, but sometimes, as now, a tiny crack of misunderstanding would appear, and he'd feel the earth beneath him thin as a sheet of ice: one wrong move and they'd all be in the water, with no one left on land to save them.

"It belongs to us," he said. "Open the door, Cee."

Rory propped the flashlight under his arm and slapped a drumroll on his thighs as Celia slipped the key in the lock and pushed open the door.

The stone fireplace stood agape at the end of the room, and the sheet-covered furniture loomed around them like tombstones in the murky dark. But for a second, Eric thought he could see the place the way Celia always had: crooked, unloved, but begging for company.

She would know how to bring it to life. She had a touch. When they were teenagers, he'd once left her for half an hour in his room while he went to get a textbook he'd left at a friend's house, and when he came back, the place was transformed. She'd moved none of the furniture but had rearranged everything else around it. His books were stacked by the bed to form a small table, his posters hung a little lower on the walls, in a more interesting arrangement, like a story, interrelated, that he could look at from the bed. She'd taken every small object and found its purpose and relocated it accordingly. Subtle changes, but for weeks afterward he'd felt a swoop of pleasure every time he walked through the door. The room made him happy in a way it hadn't before.

He never told her how his father came home that night and knew, without asking, that she had been there. His dad thought she'd gotten rid of things—things that Sam Dillon had bought "with his own good money, good as anybody else's." It was pointless to explain otherwise, and Eric had broken the rules anyway by having a girl in the house when his father wasn't home. The lacrosse stick had come out that night to punctuate the lesson, but none of that had diminished the pleasure Eric felt at going into the room after Celia had fixed it up.

He wondered now whether the magic worked on people. If he lived in her space, would it seep into him somehow? Would it make him the kind of person other people loved, the way she was?

"Wait here," Rory said.

He crossed the room and went upstairs, the bobbing flashlight marking his progress until he reached the upstairs hallway and disappeared. They heard his footsteps thudding overhead.

In the darkness, Eric pulled Celia into his arms. Her kiss was sweet and tangy as a summer peach.

"Promise me something," he said.

She looked up at him. He still could see the remnants of little girl in her freckled nose, the huge limpid eyes, lashes gone silver in the moonlight.

"Promise me I won't ever have to live without you," he said.

"I can't promise that. You might want to someday."

"Bullshit."

"People change," she said. "My dad changed. I never thought he'd leave, that he'd stop loving us. And then he did, and one day he was just gone, and even now it doesn't make sense to me. Everyone is stuck inside a doorless room. No one gets into anyone else's head. Nobody can ever really get out of their own."

"That's not true. You and me and Rory, we're all in the same room."

"Really? Do I know everything about you?"

"You know enough," he said. "You know as much about me as I do."

"And how much is that?"

He smiled. "Touché."

"You could be like him, you know. Someday you might decide to go, and then what will I do? Hunt you down? Drag you back at gunpoint, going, 'Hey, you promised...'"

"Be serious."

"I'm trying to be. But you're making me nervous. You're supposed to want to be here."

"I do."

"Then just stay. Why make promises?"

To her it was simple. How could he explain the feeling that had been gnawing at him, that they were all going into this with a different idea of what it meant. He had to be sure they understood each other. He had to lock it in.

He spread his arms wide. "There's nothing worth anything, after this. You and me and Rory. This is the big love, baby.

This is the love of our lives. What would I do afterward? What would there even be? Permanent anticlimax."

Her gaze drifted around the room and returned to his. Celia took her promises seriously, and he'd never known her to break one.

"I can't do it," he said. "Promise I won't have to."

Shaking her head, she bent and pressed a kiss into his palm, curled his fingers over the top, and she reached up to kiss him again on the lips. Quick and firm, as if to seal the envelope of a wartime love letter.

"All right," she said. "I promise."

Rory's footsteps sounded in the hallway. He came back to them behind a flaring light, turning the beam up to his face to turn the shadows upside down.

"Come with me, my pretties," he said in a crone's voice as he turned to light the way. And to Eric, in his regular voice, "Good job, man."

They followed Rory across the room and up the stairs. Deep inside the hotel, the silence murmured like the inside of a shell, echoing back on itself. The light jumped around the walls.

At the end of the hall, Rory fell back a step to let Celia open the door.

"Oh!" Her hand flew up to cover her mouth.

Eric had done up the room with dozens of paper lanterns and hung them from the ceiling like beads. Each one was lit inside with a candle, so that the peeling walls and bare floorboards gleamed with an amber light. In the center of the floor was a makeshift bed of quilts and cushions, a borrowed futon pad from Rory's place and the feather pillows from Celia's. The room looked like the inside of a gypsy's caravan, tattered and mysterious.

Eric pulled her into the room. He ducked to see her face, grinning at the shine in her eyes.

"Twenty bucks," he said to Rory, holding out his hand.

"What's all this?" she said.

"A celebration."

She shook her head, wiped her cheeks. Eric turned on the radio, and Celia walked around the room, spinning gently to the music, touching the walls and windows.

They kicked off their shoes and sprawled out on the cushions. Eric had remembered the bottles of champagne, a corkscrew and a cooler of ice, but hadn't thought to bring a single glass. Celia laughed and sat down next to him, told him to open the champagne and hand it over. So they passed the bottle between them, the bubbles tickling down their throats, laughter racing back up. Everyone started talking at once.

"Is it really ours?"

"Hell yes, it is."

"We've got a million things to do."

"That roof..."

"Plumbing."

"Walls, oh my God, miles of walls."

"And floors."

"That staircase..."

"It doesn't matter—it'll be fun."

Fun. Their inside joke. They dissolved in laughter.

"Fun! For about one nanosecond, and then we'll be wishing we'd spent that money on a trip to Hawaii."

"Fuck Hawaii, I can't be still on a beach that long."

"And you can't surf—"

"The hell I can't. Just like snowboarding, only the mountains are moving."

"Well, it's too late now."

"I'll buy you a beach ball, and you can pretend the snow is sand..."

"Is it really ours?"

"It really is, baby. It really, really is."

Eric reached into his pocket. "I almost forgot. Joss gave me this."

He pulled out a glass pipe and a bag of weed.

Rory's eyes lit up; he was reaching already for the bag. But Celia frowned.

"Just for tonight," Eric said. "I want to celebrate with you. It'll be fine."

Rory packed the bowl and handed it to Celia.

Eric drank champagne and watched the smoke drift around their heads. His heart ached as though pierced straight through.

"Cupid's arrow," he said, one hand on his chest.

Smoke poured into their lungs and out, lifting like fog to the lanterns overhead. The lights receded for a moment, then returned, with sharper edges and newly defined detail in the paper. Celia settled back on the cushions with Eric's shoulder for a pillow. She tipped her gaze over Rory's head, toward the velvety sky.

From her childhood bedroom, if you sat against the wall and pressed your cheek to the window, you could see the outline of the Blackbird Hotel, its filthy eaves draped with cobwebs that made it seem like a drawing from a child's book about Halloween. On summer afternoons, when she was supposed to be studying, she used to sneak out her window to visit the Blackbird, thread her legs through the limbs of the aspen at the foot of the house. The tree branches felt cool and frail in her hands, like the arms of a small but helpful friend. All around were the whispers of leaves in the wind, a tickle of leaf-tips against her bare legs as she shimmied down the trunk and pulled herself around the side of the house to solid ground.

She remembered the way the town of Jawbone Ridge slipped past as her feet patted the road; the post office, barely wider than its faded blue door; the scarred facade of Patsy's Café, leaking the scent of pancakes into the crisp mountain air; the Ruby Saloon, a Tinkertoy explosion of wood and brick, holding itself gamely upright against the downward tug of the mountain. Beyond the vacant miners' shacks and the pincushion of two-by-fours that kept them more or less in place, the road switched back and curved sharply uphill, but one summer day Celia kept walking straight, up the steep forbidden driveway that widened into a weed-choked parking area near the edge of the ridge. She crossed this and stopped at the front steps of the Blackbird Hotel, the farthest she'd ever been until then.

"I'm he-ere," she sang.

But the Blackbird was gruff, unwelcoming, as if it knew it was a hazard to children and was trying to protect her by holding itself aloof.

"You're not fooling anybody," she told it.

She walked around the corner to where the boards had been pried loose from one of the windows. Teenagers, she thought briefly. A chunk of tree stump was lying under the window. She dragged it a little closer and climbed up to peer through the gap. Blinded by the sunlight, she could make out only the outline of the windows across the room and the shape of the banister against the light. She climbed through the window, scraping her belly, and landed with a hollow thud on the wooden floor.

She rose to her feet, wiping her hands on the seat of her pants. Rods of sunshine fell through the boarded-up windows, leaving streaks of dust-sparkled light on the floor and walls. Ghostly humps of sheeted furniture rose from the shadows, and as her eyes adjusted she could make out the shape of the hearth across the room, gaping as if startled in the middle of a yawn.

Celia turned in a slow circle. The shuffle of her feet was

a heartbeat, a sign of life in a lifeless place. It excited her, to think she'd brought that noise to the Blackbird, had generated movement and life and sound inside this shell of a place.

Then she stopped, her heart leaping into her throat.

A beastly face leered at her from the shadows, its lips drawn back from a set of jagged teeth. Its desiccated eye stared at her through the swirling dust motes.

A cougar. A stuffed cougar, its head mounted on the wall. Its fur looked dry as autumn grass, and the dust was thick over its glass eye. She licked her thumb and reached out, meaning to rub the eye clean. But she couldn't bring herself to touch it.

Poor thing. Beheaded and nailed to a wall. And underneath, a spray-painted arrow and the words, "Got paws?" The ultimate indignity.

She crossed the room and mounted the curving staircase, stepping cautiously with her hand trailing along the dusty banister. The upstairs windows had been left uncovered, and the hallway glowed with afternoon sun streaming through the bedroom windows and the wide-open doors.

She walked to the end of the hall and through the last door.

The room had two wide windows looking over the ravine to the valley below. Groves of aspen lined the hillside in wide swaths of green and gold, shimmering in the afternoon sun. This was the opposite view from her bedroom, more expansive and magical than anything she had ever seen. She could see their house, slightly back from the edge of the ridge, and her room at the top with its triangular wall of windows. As she watched, a shape moved inside her room. Her heart lifted. It was her father! Home! Now he would explain where he'd been and why he hadn't been able to say goodbye. (He was a secret agent, he'd been kidnapped, he had amnesia, he'd taken a fall!) Tonight they'd make supper together, shrimp and grits. All her plans to sulk and keep away and demand an apology dissolved in an instant, because her father was home and he was looking for her already.

But as she watched, she saw his arms and legs slip through the window, shimmying down the tree as she had done, and realized it was only Rory. Her father was dead and he'd already come home, in a box, which was buried deep underground and miles away.

Even now, almost a decade later, she sometimes forgot. Literally forgot that her father was dead. She'd catch herself on the verge of asking after him and feel her face go hot and cold with the shame of forgetting, as if his death had left no impression on her mind.

She lay back against the cushions, mesmerized by the dancing light. A rush of longing swept through her, settling like a large hand against her breastbone. She saw the rooms transform in her mind's eye: the walls smoothed, the banister polished, splintered wooden floors like satin underfoot. Every room lit with candles and fairy lights, and the big friendly kitchen painted a particular shade of blue, its massive range chugging heat into the room. The windows would be scrubbed clean, each one offering a slice of this view: the snowy mountain valley in the wintertime, brightening to green for the summer, and the doors open wide to the pine-scented air.

No one would leave a house like this.

Rory and Eric were still batting words around, but their energy had grown nervous in spite of the weed.

"...windows."

"We'll have to get the range working..."

"And sweep the chimneys."

"The structure is sound," Celia said. "All it needs is love."

Eric sang the line back to her. "All it needs is love, love, love is all it needs..."

"Don't we all," Rory said. He reached out to trail the back

of his fingers down the inside of Celia's arm, back and forth across her palm. His blue eyes had gone dark, his pupils wide, the light in his gold hair like a halo around his head.

Eric lifted his shoulder to bring her mouth to his, his lean warm tongue tracing the edge of her teeth.

Little sister, they called her. They wanted it to be that way, incestuous and twisted. They loved the things she'd let her brothers do—all those childish tight-lipped kisses and sticky fumblings, the dark closet where they'd crouched behind her stepmother's clothes, where she'd clutched at the hangers as they'd rubbed against her with cheeks as smooth and round as her own, where she'd first felt their eyes on her body and nearly fainted at the sudden onrush of feminine power.

Dizzying, terrifying. This need of theirs to feel her body, the distant blankness in their eyes as if the sight of her bewitched them.

Let us see, they used to whisper. *Celia, just let us look.*

And she had; she did. They played games and sought out corners where, out of summertime ennui or defiance or simply out of the boredom that came from living in a small mountain village, they would exchange a series of terrified, breathless caresses, each of them following a pattern of advance and retreat like the whole thing was subject to a rule book that no one could locate.

Only somewhere along the way, they had grown up. The stubble at the edge of Eric's lips burned like sandpaper now, and Rory's hands were strong and clever, long past the point of fumbling as he unfastened the buttons of her blouse, his fingers slipping in and out of the buttonholes with a businesslike efficiency. The fabric dropped away and a breath of cool air swept across her skin.

Let me see, come on now, baby, there you go.

Rory stroked her bare chest with the flat of his hand, settling his palm over her thudding heart while Eric's mouth played decoy, busily opening hers as he turned his body sideways to settle her head on the pillow. So smooth, they were, the two of them, barely a word spoken and they had her half-naked and afire with longing, her neck straining upward and both hands lying limp upon the blankets.

They were reaching for her skirt, gathering slow bunches of fabric in their hands.

Let us see, come on, Celia, just a peek...

Just a peek, just a touch.

Where was the harm in that?

She wondered sometimes, under the amplified swell of their attention, how the transformation had occurred. Her peripheral vision filled with the shapes of them, wrapped in a nebulous light, graceful and quiet and distant, as if their everyday selves had stepped out of the room and left three wraithlike replacements locked in a carnal dance. Someone's fingers in her hair, someone whispering her name. It didn't seem to matter who was giving or receiving, who spoke or didn't speak, or on what side of the line they were treading. They were simply gone, all of them, to the far reaches of their minds even as the physical boundaries between them dissolved.

How had they come to this? Was it a choice she had made or one that had been made for her? Tendrils of memory drifted through her mind and faded. After all, what did it matter now? The past was gone and the future was a shining ribbon unwinding at their feet. It would start for them here.

Inside the Blackbird Hotel.

Untwining, they dropped back to the cushions almost as they had started. Rory and Eric pulled on their jeans, but Celia lay naked on the tangle of her clothes. Eric lit a cigarette and Rory reached for the pipe, and they all three gazed at her body as if it were a TV screen during the commercial break.

"You'll have some papers to sign," Eric said eventually.

Rory exhaled a lungful of smoke.

"I don't know, man. It still feels wrong to share the ownership. I mean, it's your money."

Eric waggled his eyebrows, one hand on Celia's thigh. "You think I don't know how to share?"

"Listen," Celia said. "Rory and I will still be here. Nothing will change, whatever the paperwork looks like. But the property should be yours."

Eric's smile faded. He dragged on his cigarette and turned to tap the ash into the empty bottle of champagne.

"The Blackbird is as close to marriage as the three of us are ever going to get. If we're in this, really in this, we need to do it right. We need to own the place together, all three of us equally."

His face worked anxiously. Maybe they really didn't understand.

Then Celia sat up and kissed him full on the mouth.

"Where do we sign?"

JANUARY 2003

CELIA WAS DREAMING.

She lay in a state of boiling half consciousness, ripples of dreams in a wonderland mixed with reality, impossible to separate.

Their kitchen at home. She was standing at the counter on the little yellow footstool her father had made for her. She could feel its smooth paint under her feet as she watched the knife flash in her father's hand. A whole onion exploded over the cutting board, bursting into tiny cubes that glistened like broken glass. Steam rose from a pan on the stove. Her father's voice drifted through Celia's mind: *Careful, chère, don' get too close.* And she saw that it wasn't a knife in his hand at all, but a fishing rod. Rory was there, too, and now they were in a small boat on Copperhead Lake, all of them fishing. The sky around them was a sheet of pewter, the water dark as oil. Celia's rod began to bend—a fish! She cranked the reel. Nothing. It was only a weed. Her line had gotten tangled, and no matter how she pulled and jerked, the hook would not come loose. *Cut it*, Rory said. *You have to cut the line.* Celia's father took the rod from her hand and worked it. His hand flashed in the sunlight, whipping the rod back and forth. Rory's voice had grown insistent, and Celia began to feel afraid, as if there were something dangerous just beneath the surface of the water. *Cut the line, cut the line.* Her father's hand was moving strangely, faster and faster, his lips curled back in a terrifying sneer.

In the dream she was suddenly awake, lying on the living room couch in the eerie glow of the TV across the room. Her father was standing over her with his hand moving fast between them.

Rory's voice screamed from inside the TV.

Cut the line! Cut the line! Cut the line!

She woke from the dream in a clammy sweat, in a darkness so complete she wasn't sure at first that her eyes had really opened. She swung around, disoriented, reaching for her bedside lamp even as reality came rushing back, along with the realization that she was not at home.

She found the light at last. She lay in its sour glow, curled around her arm, as her heartbeat gradually slowed.

Room 114. The Blue Pine Motel, just off the I-70 in Grand Junction.

"You might cramp a little," the doctor had said. She was tiny and deft, with thin white hair like dandelion floss and a gentle Southern drawl. "That's normal. And you'll bleed a bit more than you usually do."

She had patted Celia on the shoulder and called her honey. She was very kind.

They all were. The women at the clinic hadn't pushed when Celia said she didn't know who the father was, but that he wouldn't want this baby; there would be no one to help her care for it. Everyone understood and seemed to agree that Celia was acting wisely. They called it a procedure and told her what would and wouldn't hurt, and they set her up with the pill. Under the sympathetic gazes of the doctor and staff, it was easy to pretend the procedure was nothing more involved than a Pap smear.

"Lie back," the doctor said. "Try to relax."

Celia tried. Awash, snugly sedated, she let her legs open, let her eyes slide out of focus, trying not to think about what was being sucked into the little vacuum canister beside the table. Someone had decorated the ceiling in an underwater scene, with taped-on mermaids and dolphins, whales, tropical fish and bejeweled sea horses unfurling their tails. She could saddle one, she thought, like those on a merry-go-round she'd ridden as a little girl, with her father beside her. She still could feel the wind on her face, the cool painted neck of the bobbing sea horse under her hands.

"Hang on, darlin'." The lights on her father's face had flickered pink and yellow, flashing on his teeth and his soft black hair.

But Celia liked to fly. She spread her arms and let the sea horse swoop her up and down through the autumn air.

"Look at me, Daddy, look!"

Always Celia was trying to get her father to look at her. She loved the lazy swing of his attention, like a warm sun behind a veil of skidding clouds.

He was smaller than most other men, but more handsome and much more ready to smile. He had a deep drawling voice and spoke a secret language only Celia could understand. Darlene called it swamp slang and tried to discourage him, saying that they weren't in the bayou but Jawbone Ridge, Colorado, and he should try to speak so that other people could understand him.

"Ah, now," he said. "You can take the man out the bayou..."

But Celia was glad for the bayou. She loved her father's drawl, his thin cotton shirts with the mother-of-pearl snaps on the pockets, the acidic scent of his skin and the oily gleam of his cheek after he'd shaved. She could read things in his face that taught her about the faces of other men: if they were puzzling things out slowly or leaping to conclusions, showing signs of impatience, or were pleased and didn't want to show it.

He wasn't impatient at the carnival. They had all the time in the world. When the ride was over, he unbuckled the strap around her waist and helped her off the sea horse, and they strolled together through the crowd, his calloused hand enfolding hers.

At the entrance to one of the big striped tents, a sign read THE FLYING TRAPEZE, in old-timey red-and-black letters. Her father bought two tickets and some cotton candy and they went inside.

Celia had read about the circus. In books it sounded like a magical place, full of wonder, bright and colorful as Disneyland. This circus wasn't like that. The tent was disappointingly dingy, set right on top of the cracked blacktop with the remnants of the parking spaces showing through. The music sounded tinny and exhausted. Everything was crammed in; even the men at the top of the trapeze seemed too big for the space.

But it was date night. Time for just the two of them, and it didn't much matter where they spent it. Celia nailed a smile on her face and clapped extra hard as a small dark girl danced into the spotlight. She was older than Celia, maybe fourteen, with a narrow, supple body and a leotard of spangled purple. Her lips and eyes were painted, and on each cheek was a rosy circle sparkling with glitter. She climbed the ladder and took her place on the tiny platform near the top of the pole. She waved and posed, took the trapeze in her hands and started to swing. Back and forth, passing between the two men in a series of gymnastic flips and somersaults, her body curling up and snapping open, sequins flashing in the spotlight.

Celia glanced at her father. His eyes slid from side to side, tracking the girl on the trapeze. He was smiling to himself as if he was thinking of something else, as if he'd noticed something Celia hadn't. His fingers encircling hers had grown tense. He wasn't squeezing, exactly, but Celia's eyes began to burn and a fat lump formed in her throat.

He gave her a quick tight hug.

"You wanna fly like that, pop chock? Wan' be up high, swingin' on that trapeze?"

Celia nodded. She didn't want to swing on the trapeze, but he seemed to think she would and she didn't want to disappoint him.

"Want Daddy to catch you?"

"Yes."

He tweaked her nose, his teeth winking in the light.

The show ended to a ripple of applause. Celia wanted to get out of the tent, go back outside where the Tilt-A-Whirl and cotton candy were waiting. But her father led Celia toward the thready crowd of parents and children waiting to get the circus girl's autograph.

"You are sure a brave girl," her father said when it was their turn in line.

She looked up at him unsmiling, the pen and circus flyer in her hand. Up close, her spangled leotard was not so pretty; the shoulder had a line of uneven stitches at the seam and some of the sequins were missing. Celia noted this with grim satisfaction, eyeing one of the last loose threads that seemed to be holding them together.

"You been swingin' on that trapeze for a while?" Daddy said.

"Since I was four." Her voice was thin, with a slight lisp. *Like a baby*, Celia thought scornfully.

"Four years old!" Her father beamed down at her. "Cho! Just a lil bitty thing. You gon' be in town tomorrow, darlin'?"

"All week," she said.

"Good, good. I'll maybe come back this way—"

He stopped midsentence. The big circus man had materialized at the girl's side. His dark eyes glittered from beneath heavy brows. He said something to the girl in a guttural language Celia couldn't understand. The girl handed the flyer to Celia and darted away.

Her father was still smiling. But it wasn't a real smile anymore.

"Talented girl," he said. "She your daughter?"

The circus man said nothing. Just looked at her father steadily, then slowly, deliberately, he fixed his eyes on Celia.

Heat crept up her neck and prickled in her cheeks. Those shiny black eyes were communicating something dark and foreign, a subtle menace laced with some indefinable thrill that dropped her stomach like the crest of a roller coaster. Badly she wanted to look away. But she found she couldn't. She could only stand rooted to the ground, her mouth half-open, unable to breathe.

"Goddamn," her father said. "Just saying she a good, nice girl, that's all..."

He took Celia by the hand and pulled her along, muttering and shaking his head. She could feel the circus man behind her, all the way to the truck, all the way home.

In the motel bathroom she cleaned herself and wiped the drops of blood off the floor. So much blood, and somewhere in all of that was the seed she had managed to uproot.

She sat on the cold tile, her back to the wall. The mottled plastic veneer was coming loose around the bathroom counter, and a bulb was out in the vanity lights overhead. Everything in the room had probably started out blue, but the blueness had become exhausted and had long since faded to gray.

It seemed a more fitting place for a murder than the well-lit clinic downtown. Vaguely seamy. Possibly the scene of other crimes like this one, over the years.

She imagined Rory's face if he knew where she was tonight. He would hate this; he would never understand.

Why'd you do it, Cee? You know I would have helped.

But I don't know who the father is.

I am, he would say. *Eric is. Either way, you wouldn't be alone, Celia.*

But Celia knew it wasn't as simple as that. They all would be watching the baby. Would he have blond hair or black, blue eyes or brown? Who would he walk to with his first lurching little scarecrow steps? Who would he call Daddy? Would he grow up wondering, hearing the whispers, diminished in some way by the uncertainty? Would Celia have to choose between Rory and Eric, and have to make the choice based on the paternity of this child?

A baby would have been a rejection—her body's rejection—of one man in favor of the other. She imagined a microscopic slide, one helpless, moonlike egg under attack by a hundred determined sperm. One getting in, the others left to die.

Her body was trying to make her choose.

And she knew firsthand how it felt to be the odd one out of the triangle. Rory and Eric were together now in Vegas: Rory was working in Karl McFarland's construction company, Eric had started classes at UNLV. It had all been arranged; they couldn't let their parents down by quitting before they'd started. They swore they'd be back next spring when she graduated, that they all could be together, but Celia felt the sting of rejection all the same. She sometimes couldn't take their calls. Their laughter made her cringe, flushed with a jealous chill at all the inside jokes she no longer shared.

She found herself keeping secrets of her own. As a comfort or some sort of childish revenge. She didn't tell them she hadn't stayed to finish high school, or what people were saying about them now that they were gone. She pretended not to hear.

She'd never tell them what a task they'd left her with.

Rory's thumb hovered over the glowing white face of his phone. Celia had gotten a cell months ago, so technically the number should come up CELIA—CELL, but he liked the way it looked this way—the old way—when she called. HOME.

It was too late to call her now, it would have to wait until morning. He got out of bed and went to the kitchen. The refrigerator was nearly empty except for a couple of Cokes and some leftover pizza. He thought wistfully of the fridge back home, which was always crammed with food. Celia had long since taken over the cooking from Darlene. She kept the leftovers neatly stacked in Tupperware bowls with little pieces of tape on top, noting the date and contents. She said it made her feel like Nigella Lawson to find a use for every scrap.

Eric had laughed at that, juggling a couple of cantaloupes in front of his chest while they pushed a basket around Clark's Market.

"More than a mouthful's a waste," he said archly, just as a hunchbacked old man darted by on his scooter.

"Just open wider," called the old guy, rounding the corner.

They fell about the produce section, laughing so hard they couldn't make a sound.

But you had to cook to produce leftovers like that, and neither he nor Eric could do more than scrambled eggs and toast. Most nights they ordered out for pizza or Chinese, or stuffed themselves at a casino buffet. It was never enough; he was hungry all the time.

He grabbed a Coke and shut the fridge with his foot. A jar of pickles slid from one end of the door to the other, landing with a loud thump. "Shh," he said to the fridge, glancing down the hall to Eric's door.

The lamp was still on; he could see a crack of light along the floor. When they had first moved in, Rory thought Eric must spend a lot of hours reading late at night—he went through two or three books a week, flew through them as fast as Celia did. Later he realized that the light was never turned off. Eric slept with it on.

Rory couldn't blame him. Living alone with a father who drank as hard as Sam Dillon would make anyone feel the need to be prepared. All through their childhood, Eric had borne the brunt of his father's temper, collecting bruises inside and out. He had his own ways of coping.

It used to drive Celia crazy, seeing how resigned Eric was to the situation.

"Why don't we call child services?" she'd say. "Or tell a teacher? We could talk to Mr. Brewer..."

"And then what?" Rory said. "They take Eric out of the house and where would he go?"

"Maybe they could find his mom."

"Why? Would you want to live with yours? I sure as hell would not want my dad to be tracked down and saddled with me. They're MIA, Celia, all of them. They don't give a shit."

"A foster home, maybe? Or just—"

"Are you living in the real world? I swear, sometimes I wonder whether you know anything about life at all."

"Sometimes I wonder whether you even care what happens to him!"

"Of course I do. Jesus, Cee." He took a deep breath. "Eric's dad hurts him. He doesn't injure him."

"It's the same thing."

"No, it's not. Eric will get through this, and eventually he'll get to the end of his rope and lay the old sonofabitch out on the pavement, and that'll be the end of it."

"And in the meantime we're supposed to watch him get hurt and hope he doesn't get injured?"

"We're going to let him handle it. Back off, Cee."

She had turned away, pink-faced and frustrated. And she was right, of course. The line between hurt and injured was not always easy to see. There were injuries that didn't show up on the skin or on X-rays or medical reports. Eric was carrying a lot of those.

Rory popped open a Coke and carried it back to the couch, turned on the TV that was showing a commercial for $3.99 steak and eggs at some divey-looking casino downtown.

A strange city, Vegas. At first he had been agog—and appreciative—of the women on the billboards, tits and ass for the morning commute, and everything open, as it were, all day and night. But the novelty quickly faded. Now the city depressed him. So many hard surfaces: the cement and blacktop, the cracked desert floor, tightly packed rows of stucco houses in every imaginable shade of beige. The sound of a nail gun or table saw could travel unbroken for miles across the flat, arid sky.

He missed the mountains, the crooked little houses propped along the ridge, the damp hush of a snowy day. The seasons here were all the same; whether hot or cold, the sun hovered over the desert like a great blind eye.

He tried to hide his homesickness from Celia. By tacit agreement, he and Eric kept their calls to her short and upbeat. They told her about the apartment, the city, Eric's classes and Rory's job in construction.

They told her about the plan.

"By the time you finish school," Rory said, "I'll have almost a year on the job. I can get a job with the forestry service, and Eric can maybe take some time off school—wait tables or something. We'll find a place for the three of us, wherever you want."

Celia listened quietly, hundreds of miles away.

"Cee, what's wrong?" Eric said.

The phone on the table between them was silent, but they could feel she hadn't hung up.

"I'm eighteen," she said.

"Yeah..."

"I could be with you now."

"But you need to finish school."

Another pause.

"Yes..." Her voice was vague, drifting back to silence.

They hung up after that call with a sense of unease.

"She thinks we don't want her here," Rory said.

"I know." Eric's lopsided grin flashed out. "She's jealous, thinks we're out here banging each other."

"Bitch, please."

They laughed nervously.

Rory wished that Eric—the only one of them with the power to put things into words—would explain to Celia that it wasn't really about school.

He tried to imagine Celia in Vegas, under the glare of the sunshine and the flashing lights, on the littered, flat, dusty city streets, or here in the barren apartment, sitting on the brown plaid sofa. His imaginings took on the quality of a surrealist photograph: a mermaid in a taxi, or a flying tree with its roots exposed.

They didn't want her to come here. They wanted her at home, in Jawbone Ridge, waiting for them. It upset them to think of her in the coarse desert light, surrounded by plasticky mock-ups of things that did exist elsewhere—castles and pyramids and cities and canals. Things that were wondrous in their natural setting, here were only facades, outlined in strips of neon. The fact that she was at home meant the whole thing between the three of them still existed, was still possible. They could buy the Blackbird someday. They could live in it together, make it their home and livelihood. If Celia left Jawbone Ridge, even to be with them, the dream might disintegrate altogether.

It was fragile, this thing they shared. It could easily come apart.

Rory turned off the TV and went to the window. Outside the wind was howling like it never did back home. A single dry leaf skidded by, illuminated briefly by the street lamp before disappearing into the empty desert lot across the street.

It reminded him of the night his mother had sat them down side by side at the kitchen table and herself across from them to say that Eddie Dark had died and wouldn't be coming home.

Celia had sat for a minute in her orphan's haircut, dry-eyed in the paling light, as Rory asked what happened. Feeling nothing—nothing at all for the man who had raised him as his own.

"He touched a live wire," his mother said. "Under a house he was working on. He got a shock—"

"No," Celia said. "No, no, no, no—"

She leaped up and flew out the front door, down to the street calling "no no no" until she ran around the bend and out of sight.

Like a leaf driven by the wind.

Rory had found her later with Eric. He tried to bring her

home, but she clung to Eric's arm as if he were the only thing keeping her feet on the earth. When Rory reached for her, she turned her face to Eric's chest, her eyes squeezed tight, both hands clamped over her ears like Rory was a danger to her sanity—or the cause of all her trouble.

Uncanny. The instincts of that girl.

NOVEMBER 2002

"WOULD YOU LIKE to talk about what happened last week?"

"Not really."

Eric sat with his knees wide apart, slouching into the nubby green sofa. He wanted to bite his nails but was too well aware of the quick brown eyes of the man across the coffee table, who tilted his head alertly, as if Eric had agreed.

A small electric heater ticked on.

Eric plucked at his fingernails, pressing each one between two fingers of the opposite hand.

"Has it really been a week?" he said.

"Yes. A week today," said Dr. Paul. "Does that surprise you?"

Eric shrugged, but inwardly he was disconcerted. A week. How had an entire week passed? Where did it go?

"The last time we talked, you seemed a little unclear about what happened the day you came in."

Eric lifted his head. The doctor, a round-breasted bird of a man, was gazing at him as if he'd spied a juicy worm just breaking the soil.

Dr. Paul. It occurred to Eric that he didn't know whether

Paul was the guy's last name, or whether he'd just stuck a title on the front of his first name the way pediatricians sometimes did.

"Do you want to tell me what you remember from that day?"

"Why don't you tell me?" Eric said. "You're the one with all the papers in your lap."

"Do the papers bother you?"

"It all fucking bothers me."

"What does?"

"This." Eric spread his arms. "All of it. Locked up in here like a goddamn lunatic."

"You're not locked up. You can check out anytime you want."

"But you can never leave," Eric sang.

Dr. Paul gave him a mournful smile.

"I'm here to help you."

"I don't want your help."

"I think you do."

"Yeah? What makes you say that?"

The little man gathered his papers and set them on the table beside his armchair, handling them gingerly as if they were living, fragile things.

"Because one of the first things you said to me a week ago was 'Please help me.' Do you remember?"

Eric ripped at a hangnail, drawing blood.

"What made you say that, do you think?"

"I was confused."

Dr. Paul nodded.

"It's just…"

Eric stopped. The space heater clicked off, leaving the room in a silent fug. He pressed his hand to his forehead. He hated these thick pauses, the manipulation, that expectant look on the shrink's face like he was waiting for Eric to have a revelation. Patient, heal thyself.

"Go on," the doctor said. "Please. Finish the thought. You said you were confused. What did you mean exactly?"

"I don't know. One minute we were..."

"It's okay, Eric. Go on."

"One minute everything was more or less okay, and the next I was wigging out. I sort of forgot who I was. Not completely, but—"

"Who did you think you were? Do you remember?"

Eric swallowed.

"It's crazy."

"It's not crazy. I promise. You thought you were someone else?"

Eric leaned his head back on the couch. He still could see Celia's face, her long sleek body and sleepy mouth. Her voice, as if in a dream: *Rory, Rory...* Her breasts in their mouths, each of them fastened to her body, their fingers tangled between her legs.

"Rory," he said. "I thought...for a minute I forgot..."

"Who is Rory?"

"My best friend. More like a brother, really."

"And what's he like?"

"Rory? Oh, he's—" Eric searched his mind. "He's like Jesus, man."

The shrink raised his eyebrows, thin as feathers, floating above the gold wire rims of his glasses.

"Like Jesus? How so?"

"Well, not to look at. What I mean is that he's righteous. You know that line from the Bible? 'Great vengeance and furious rebukes'?" Eric lifted his sleeve and turned to show the tattoo on his arm: EZEKIEL 25:17. "That's Rory. You mess with one of his people and he'll rain fire on your head."

Dr. Paul nodded slowly, his head tilted to one side.

"I see."

"Righteous."

"And he's the one who brought you in?"

"Right, yeah. I think I scared him."

Rory's face flashed through Eric's mind: eyebrows drawn, shaking his head. Spooked.

Stop. Stop. Stop saying that, man. You're starting to freak me out.

"I did. I scared him."

"He doesn't sound like a man who scares easily."

"No. In fact, this might have been a first."

"Do you remember what happened to scare him?"

"Wouldn't you be scared if your best friend suddenly decided he was you?"

Dr. Paul bobbed his head, smiling a little. A light flickered from the phone on his desk: a call had come in.

"Aren't you going to get that?" Eric said.

"No. Tell me wh—"

"We were with Celia."

"Is that your girlfriend?"

"My girlfriend, his girlfriend. You can see how it might get confusing."

"You have the same girlfriend?"

"Well, technically Celia is Rory's stepsister, but it amounts to the same thing. I mean, we're both fucking her. At the same time, occasionally."

The words sounded ugly, put that way. He wished he could take them back and say something real. *We both love her. We love each other. This is not an emotionally incestuous threesome between us; this is a big romance.*

But he didn't say that. He wanted to sting this little birdman, who probably thought he'd uncovered some critical malfunction in Eric's sex life. He waited maliciously for his words to strike home.

The heater clicked three times, slowly.

"So anyway," Eric said. "We were with Celia."

"With her—"

"We were fucking her, yes." He bit his fingernail, caught himself in the act, shoved his hand under his thigh. "We were home from Vegas for a few days. To see our families, supposedly, but really to see her. We always come home together."

"Why is that?"

Eric shrugged. "More fun that way. Rory likes to watch. Celia likes to be watched."

Dr. Paul waited, letting the silence ask the question.

"Me, I like it all. I'm the conduit."

"The conduit."

"Yeah. They're a little shy, passive. I'm not shy at all. I'll say anything. I make it happen."

From a distance he heard his own voice, felt the warm curve of Celia's ear at his lips: *Open up, baby. There you go…*

"Rory wants to do the right thing. He feels like Celia's real brother—it fucks him up." Eric bounced his heels on the floor. He saw the shrink's eyes glance down but thought, Fuck it. At least he wasn't biting his nails. "He's not her brother, obviously, but they grew up together, used to share a bathtub when they were little, all that. And they still introduce each other that way. 'This is my brother.' 'This is my sister.' But they're not, so in theory it shouldn't be that creepy."

"Do you think it's creepy?"

"Me? God, no. I'm just explaining how they see it, why they need me."

The heater kicked back on.

"Can you turn that thing off?"

Dr. Paul got up and clicked off the heater. He went back to his chair, pulled the pages into his lap.

Eric smirked, pointing with his chin.

"I don't blame you. We three are smoking hot."

The doctor looked at him impassively. Not even pink.

"Why don't you tell me a little more about the night you came in," he said.

Eric sighed, puffing out his cheeks. He wedged his hand more tightly under his thigh. "Why don't you tell me? What did Rory say?"

"He said he was worried about you. He asked a lot of questions about the hospital. He seemed very concerned that you would be treated well."

"There you go. His brother's keeper."

"I'd still like to know what you remember."

Eric ran his hand through his hair, over his jaw. He must have shaved yesterday, maybe even this morning, though he couldn't remember doing so. Odd the way that kept happening. He laid his arm over the back of the couch, propped his head on two fingers.

"We were with Celia."

"Do you remember where you were?"

"In this old hotel, a place we've been visiting since we were kids. It's abandoned, really run-down, but Celia loves it." He raised his head to look across the coffee table at the doctor. "We didn't go there to have sex, by the way. We were just looking around. But we're combustible—any spark will do it."

He could see her, spinning through a wedge of sunlight, Rory holding up her hand like they were dancing. Her hair was so light, not even like hair but like feathers, floating through the light and the sparkling dust motes.

"So you were in the hotel. What was that like?"

"Dark, kind of murky. Spooky, you know. Quiet. You could hear your own heartbeat, if you stopped to listen."

Footfalls, the brush of Celia's shoe on the floor as she spun. He remembered hearing the whisper of her hair, like meadow grass in the wind.

"When we were kids, we used to try to get Celia to take off her clothes. Just to give us a peek. I can't even tell you what a fucking thrill that was. I used to plan for days, thinking what I'd say to her, whether I'd get up the nerve to say it. She hardly ever went along, but when she did…oh, Jesus, I'd go home and spank it like I was dying. Something about that girl, I don't even know… Anyway, someone, Rory or me, we were playing again, talking really soft. 'Lift your shirt, Cee, pull down your underwear…' Just to see if she'd do it. Only now she does. Really docile, too, and she just looks at you…"

He shifted a little in his seat.

"So, you know, two guys are never going to be short of ideas. But something about the place got to me. I started to feel…"

"Feel what, Eric?"

"We were getting her dirty. She had cobwebs in her hair, scrapes on her knees and the palms of her hands. I started to feel disconnected. My brain was churning, you know?"

Dr. Paul nodded.

"I wanted to fuck her. I think I was fucking her, or maybe not. Maybe that was Rory. But I felt way outside of it, like I was watching us on TV. I remember feeling sad."

"What were you sad about?"

Eric blinked.

"I don't know. She looked so small, between us like that. I felt like we weren't giving her what she needed. A family. A brother. She doesn't have that anymore. We took her family away. It upset me, thinking of that. I remember fucking her…maybe it was Rory…but I thought, what she needs is a brother, I'll be her brother…"

He closed his eyes and felt the heat and silence expand around him. His throat ached. When he spoke again, the words sounded garbled and heavy.

"We took her family away."

JUNE 2002

THEY WOULD JOKE afterward that no one should be allowed to see a Quentin Tarantino film while under the influence of anything but air.

It had to be the Tarantino, they decided. After all, they each had been to the Nugget Theatre a hundred times, on dates and in straggling groups. There was little else to do in Telluride and still less in Jawbone Ridge. In the winter they could ski up and over the mountain to take in a matinee, but summertime meant a long ride around to the 145, up through the mouth of the canyon. It seemed like a hassle most of the time, and anyway they had outgrown it. Most of their friends watched movies now in dimly lighted living rooms and bedrooms, out of the public eye.

But teenage nostalgia had crept up on them over the long, sweet summer after Rory and Eric graduated. They spent all their time in the places they knew best: the park at Telluride, with their skateboards and bikes, or lazing around the pool where Eric's friend Joss Mathers worked as a lifeguard; hiking up the Wasatch Trail, so familiar now that even the deer they encountered failed to startle; lunches at Patsy's, where they had worked their way through every condiment and combination of condiments to find the perfect dip for fries, a pastime that sparked an ongoing debate between the three of them over the proper ratio of ketchup to mayonnaise. In truth, by the last day of summer they were getting bored. So when Eric said, "Let's see the Tarantino. I've got some good shit to put us right," Celia had right away found her sandals, loaded her string bag with bite-size Hershey bars and hopped into Rory's old Ford pickup, sliding to the middle of the bench seat with the gearshift against her knee and a masterful position at the radio. As it turned out, she only needed the volume control. The station was playing an old-old Elton John, which she and Eric sang to each other, nose to nose, coming in strong where they knew the lyrics.

"Just like you, Cee," Rory said.

"Mohair would be itchy," she said. "But I'd take the electric boots."

He rolled down the window. The warm breeze poured over their faces. Celia's hair flew about and tangled around Rory's arm, so she braided it over her shoulder, found a piece of twine in her bag and tied a bow around the end. The sunlight streamed through the window, lighting the hairs on Rory's forearm so that his skin seemed bristled with fine gold wire. Eric's fingers, adjusting the volume, were pale and nimble, the inside of his forearm tattooed with a long black feather.

Celia had gone with him the day he got that tattoo, perching beside the bench as the ink puddled around the droning needles. Then a rub of the cloth and the puddle was gone, leaving a new bit of pattern behind. The artist had drawn the design from the crow's feather Celia was wearing at the end of her braid.

"I didn't know you liked feathers, too," she said to Eric. She'd been collecting them forever, and usually had one or more tucked into her macramé belt or dangling from a string around her wrist. In her room, she gathered bouquets of them into vases, strung them like beads around the window.

Eric tugged at her braid and said he liked them by association.

He had six tattoos, all in black-and-white. The biggest was also his first: a demented jack-in-the-box with a girl-doll springing out of its head. It covered the upper-right quarter of his back, draped over the rigid architecture of his shoulder blade and spine. He had his fingers done next, in bold letters meant to be read across, from one fist to the other: DARK LOVE. Later he got the Chinese symbol for "brother" on his calf and the reference to EZEKIEL 25:17 in black all caps, horizontally across his forearm like a stamp. On the other forearm was the feather, and at his wrist the letter *C* with four more letters in a squared-off pattern next to it: *e-l-i-a*.

One last piece he would get years later. A raven, flying across his heart. Noted and photographed by the young coroner's assistant as the site of the entrance wound. "Got him right through the eye. Freaky!"

Eric wasn't eager to go straight back to school that fall. He'd lobbied hard for a year off, but his dad said no, that Eric would get his ass into college now, before he got lazy and stuck in Jawbone Ridge. And though he hated to admit it, Eric thought he was probably right. There was nothing in this tiny village for him. Nothing but Celia, who didn't want him—at least, not the way he wanted her. She would let him get so far but no further, was up for anything he wanted to do except the one thing he wanted most.

Now, with the afternoon shadows advancing across the canyon, Rory pulled off the road and parked at the edge of town, three blocks from the theater, where a trailhead was marked with a wooden sign and two rough-hewn fence posts pointing the way up and out of Telluride. He rolled the windows halfway and killed the engine.

Eric dug a pipe out of his pocket and rummaged through the glove box.

"Whatcha got there?" Rory said.

"Some sexy, sexy dope, man," Eric said, twitching his eyebrows like a pantomime villain. "Not like that skunk weed Joss throws around. This is the chronic. I've been saving it."

"One last Rocky Mountain high?"

"You know it."

"Stop bragging and light me up," Celia said.

"Bossy chick," Eric said.

But he held the flame to the pipe and the pipe to her lips. The box canyon crowded around them in towering bands of green and gold, filling the windshield with color.

"I'm gonna miss this," Rory said.

"You don't have to go," Celia said.

"Hell yes, he does," Eric said. "You trying to pirate my roommate, Cee?"

"Neither of you," she said. "You, plural."

"Yeah, but what then? We sit around toking and skiing and tramping around the same trails we've been down a hundred forty-seven times—"

"Awful," Rory said. "That would be awful."

"Me, fighting with my dad. You stocking oranges in the produce aisle. That's what we've been doing all summer."

"I could get promoted to the checkout stand." Rory grinned.

"There are other options," Celia said.

"What options?" Eric waved the pipe, leaving a vapor trail through the cab. "What's here for us that's new? What would be the point?"

"Why does it matter where you are," Celia said, "or what you're doing? Shouldn't it be about who...who you..."

Eric turned to look at her, tipping his chin to blow smoke at the ceiling. "What matters is that we get on with things. The problem is that you hate change. Shh, yes, you do. You're gonna be one of these old mountain biddies serving coffee to the city boys, trying to convince them to buy the souvenir mug and another slice of pie."

This was uncomfortably close to what Celia's job at the Java Hut actually entailed. Though the challenge in his eyes was unmistakable, Celia didn't rise to meet it. Maybe he was right. Maybe she was living in the past, too timid to step into the future the way he and Rory were doing. But when she tried to imagine something more ambitious for herself, the vision wouldn't come, or seemed puny if it did. What she wanted was exactly what he said: more of the same.

Eric's challenge evaporated in the balmy air. They laid their heads back against the bench seat and closed their eyes, letting the heavy buzz fill their limbs.

"Oh," Celia said, to no one in particular.

"Which one of us is me?" Rory said.

"You're the big one," Eric said. "I'm the smart one."

Eric took a deep pull as he turned to Celia. He put his lips over hers and exhaled slowly into her mouth. The smoke was smoother and sweeter than it had been straight out of the pipe, like burned anise, and his lips were firm and damp.

He drew away, smiling. "And you're the girl."

"That's not very exciting," she said.

"The hell you say. I'm excited just looking at you."

He emptied the pipe and shoved it in the glove box. The movie would be starting in a few minutes. Rory patted himself down, Celia said "oh" again and they rolled out of the car and drifted down the street to buy their tickets.

Celia put the three stubs in her string bag. She would use them for years afterward, a neat little perforated chain, as a bookmark in her diary.

Celia half closed her eyes. The screen was awash with a series of disconnected images set to a soundtrack of twangy rock ballads, whining guitar overlaid with thin lyrics from bands she didn't know. She'd given up trying to follow the plot and had turned her thoughts to the boys, one on either side of her, smelling sweetly of weed and Hershey's chocolate.

No, not boys. Men. Much bigger than she was now. Years ago she could hold her hand flat to Rory's and their fingers would match up perfectly. Now when she pressed his hand open and laid hers over the top, there was a good half inch of space all around where she couldn't cover him.

Rory turned to look. At their hands together, at her face. His eyes gleamed in the darkness, dark blue from the movie screen, then flickering yellow. He laced his fingers through hers and didn't let go.

Tomorrow Rory and Eric would be leaving: Eric for UNLV, Rory to work in their uncle's construction business in Vegas. They planned to share an apartment in the city. They would be gone and she'd be here alone, unsure even about how to miss them.

Gone. The word clanged in her mind like a struck bell.

As if he could read her thoughts, Eric reached over and laid his hand on her knee. Just a pat at first, as if for comfort. He leaned over to whisper in her ear.

"Your skin is so soft. I can barely feel you."

His breath tickled her cheek. He ran his fingertips back and forth along the hem of her skirt.

The room grew black and distant for a moment, then came swimming back. Celia sat frozen, staring at the images on the screen, the solitary heads of the people in the theater around them. She felt Rory's attention turn from the movie. They were waiting, both of them, for her to make Eric stop, to catch his wrist and push it away, to redirect his attention to the screen. The fabric brushed her thigh as he plucked at the edge of her skirt, easing it higher.

Always before—during the tedious encounters with other boys, in the parking lot behind the school, and once in her own room, where she lay flat and stiff under Darrell Connors with her knees clenched tight together, listening to Rory's footsteps pause at the bottom of the steps—Celia had maintained a conscientious virtue. Not for herself, exactly, but because she sensed it was necessary. She felt herself the guardian of a precarious order that might change in frightening and unpredictable ways if she wavered.

"A boy will do whatever he can," Darlene had said. "You've got to be the gatekeeper, Celia. Same as it ever was."

Her tone was cheerful but left no room for argument. And the truth of it was borne out in time. Boys came hardwired with the need to touch.

Darlene had said nothing about the way it might feel to *be* touched. As if that part didn't matter.

Under the narcotic buzz of the weed, Celia felt an undercurrent of panic, a wire of erotic tension coiled around her heart. Eric's fingers burned her skin, but they made her body so shivery-cold that she had to clench her teeth to keep them from rattling. She gripped the armrests as he pushed his hand under her skirt. The side of his fingers brushed the fabric between her legs.

Celia glanced around the theater. A scattering of single men occupied the seats around them, and she knew there was someone in the back row where she couldn't see him. Eric's caress was hesitant, as if he had chosen this moment because he assumed she would stop him—because he wanted her to, maybe.

Same as it ever was.

Only it wasn't the same. The clock had run out, and tomorrow she'd be alone. For nights now she'd lain awake, her chest aching, imagining the absence that was coming. The heat of them, their big sheltering presence, the exotic, exciting maleness of them would be gone. All gone. She often dreamed that she was chasing them on foot, sobbing mutely, her arms swimming up and down as they drove away in the back of a yellow school bus. *Look at me*, she wanted to scream. But the sound was smothered by the underwater dampness of the dream, and they never turned around.

Eric turned his hand to stroke her with his fingertips. She heard a sharp hiss of surprise as she let him nudge her thighs apart.

Look at me, she thought fiercely. *Do I have your attention now?*

They had grown deliberate, all of them. She felt their eyes on her face, her bare legs. And between her legs, where a dense pulse struggled under Eric's fingers.

"You want him to stop?" Rory said.

His eyes were fever-bright and his cheek glowed red from the screen. The theater was filled with the sound of the character's breathing, a pause in the action. Her answer slid into the silence through her clenched teeth.

"No."

Eric slipped his hand inside her underwear. Stealthy at first, an exploratory maneuver, as a young boy will do across a school-yard boundary. Then a second time, and a third, slippery and emboldened.

Rory frowned in disbelief, his eyes flicking over her face. He slipped his hand around the inside of her thigh and pushed her skirt up to her hips—like a challenge, like a dare he was sure she'd refuse, that would snap her out of whatever spell the darkness had cast. She stared back, holding his gaze as she had when they played together as children, nose to nose on the living room sofa: Who will blink first?

She let her thighs move farther apart.

Rory's eyelids fluttered and his hand grew tense and heavy around her knee. She shifted in her seat, her nails biting into the armrests. The small movement lifted her to Eric's hand and sent a ripple of impatient desire through her body.

"Don't." Rory's voice was hoarse.

Don't what, she wanted to say. Who was he talking to?

Don't let it happen, maybe. Don't let us get carried away. *Eric, don't touch my sister, my little sister. Who the hell do you think you are...*

Anger roiled in Celia's chest.

Don't?

Watch me.

Rory's gaze broke from hers. He stared into the shadowy place between her legs where Eric's fingers dipped and sank inside her.

A boy will do whatever he can.

Do it, then. Who's stopping you?

She hunched down farther in her seat. Eric lifted his hand and pushed his damp fingers into her mouth. She curled her tongue around them, tasted her own fluids, salty as tears. He was staring at her mouth. They both were staring, their lips parted in surprise. The expression in their eyes was intoxicating, the gesture so needy and erotic that she could no longer be still. When Eric's hand returned to her lap, she began to move with him. He curled his palm and she pushed back, grinding against the heel of his hand.

Beside her, heavy and slow as if in a dream, Rory dragged his gaze from Eric's hand, drew her face to his and kissed her.

A surge of emotion rose through her body, settling hot and thick inside her throat. Rory was her brother. Present in her earliest fragment of memory, chasing her lost balloon. *It's gone, Cee-Cee, far away gone…* His sturdy legs churning, arms reaching to catch the ribbon even as the balloon bobbed into the vast blueness, shrinking to a dot as though the whole sky were pulling away from them. *Far away gone, Cee, you can have mine.* And the gladness of her own response—that he would give up his balloon for her. For her! It was impossible to imagine loving a person more than she had loved Rory in that moment. He had been there always, her brother in every way that mattered, yet always with this kink of genetic distance between them where the craving had taken hold. And now, in the space between two breaths, he was kissing her like a jealous lover, lips parted, his tongue pushing hard into her mouth as Eric's fingers slid inside her.

Slut, she thought, gripping the armrests.

I don't care! I didn't start it.

A car chase had erupted on the screen. The theater thundered to life, flogging the air with drumbeats and the petulant squeal of tires. The movie would be over soon. She imagined them sitting this way when the lights came up—Eric turned sideways, his hand between her legs, Rory looming over her with his mouth open on hers, now with his hand pressing at her breast. And herself between them, her feet on the seat backs, letting her legs slip apart like she didn't know any better than to let herself get finger-fucked in a middle of a matinee.

"This is what you want." Eric's lips were next to her ear, his voice seeping through the rising tide of music. "Come on and take it, then."

The movie would be over soon. Tomorrow they'd be gone, gone, gone.

A crackling fullness gathered in her belly. A swelling impatience, some nameless dread.

Don't stop, oh please, please don't stop…

They could feel it coming for her. They'd been bringing it on, hoping it would overtake her, pushing and pulling for as long as she could remember. She still could see their faces when their cheeks were as smooth as hers. Sidelong glances, plucking at her clothes, teasing in girlish voices but with a masculine persistence that frightened and compelled her.

A boy wants to touch. But, oh, the feeling of being touched. The winding tightness. The overwhelming sensation of both of them looking, watching, waiting. A wave of furious pleasure surged upward through her body and set the tops of her thighs ablaze, turned the air to fire in her lungs. She clutched at Eric's wrist.

"Oh *yeah*," Eric said.

He caught her climax in the palm of his hand, two fingers buried inside her. She tried to pull away to catch her breath, but Rory wouldn't let go. His kiss had grown brutal, teeth clacking against hers, his tongue stiff and angry. He clutched at her breast. He sucked away her air, swallowed up her cries.

At her shoulder she could feel Eric softly laughing.

The speakers around them went quiet, a vacuum of silence as though something vital had been sucked from the room.

Rory blinked. He leaned away. In a daze he stared from Celia to Eric, three fingers rubbing his lips.

Eric smoothed down her skirt, flashing a Cheshire grin in the darkness.

"Let's go to your house," he said.

No one said a word on the ride back from the theater. No one turned on the radio. Celia sat on the seat between Rory and Eric, her knees pressed together, breathless and shaken with her heart banging against her ribs. Next to her, Eric hummed a tune she couldn't catch over the growl of the engine, and on the other side Rory's hand gripped the wheel so hard that the tendons stood like wire under his skin. She felt an odd pressure to make conversation, to thrust something sharp into the bubble of silence, but could find nothing at all to say.

They walked silently from the truck into the empty house. Up the front steps, through the living room strewn with everyday debris: Rory's cast-off sweater, a half-finished puzzle on the kitchen table with Darlene's coffee cup beside it, a book of Celia's lying spread-eagled over the arm of the blue denim couch. A bowl of apples. An old notepad next to the kitchen telephone, littered with phone numbers and scraps of paper that had torn off inside the spiral binding. The ordinariness of the house seemed incriminating, as if the objects had been arranged by their morning selves in evidence against them.

They walked up the first flight of stairs, switchback, up the second set. The walls were lined with pictures of Rory and Celia, straight-ahead school mug shots against backgrounds of mottled blue. Rory's big engaging grin, chin up, nose crinkled with laughter. Celia, wide-eyed and unfocused as if startled by the camera.

At the end of the second-floor hallway, she pulled down the ladder and climbed up, passed through the silk curtains and into the golden light.

Rory and Eric followed, blinking. Their hair and eyelashes gleamed. Even the stubble on Rory's jaw caught the light, a scattering of hard bright glitter on the crescent of his chin. Shadows lay in streaks under their cheekbones and the hollows of their throats, but their eyes glinted with the miniature, triangular skyscape of Celia's window.

A tangible buzz filled the room, like the electric field around a convergence of power lines.

You can still back out, Rory's face said. *You can still say no.*

Eric inched toward her, creaking the floorboards.

They were waiting. Expecting something from her.

Celia reached up and began to unravel her braid, separating the strands of hair and combing it through with her fingers. She searched the room for something to listen to, but could hear only the dry sweep of their communal breath, the whump of her heartbeat and the endless sighing river far below. She peeled off her T-shirt, stepped out of her sandals, tugged the skirt down her legs and let it fall in a pool of cottony blue at her feet.

Her reflection flashed in the tiny mirror on the wall, revealing fragments of the scene she was standing in, her body slipping across the surface of the glass.

Eric left when Darlene came home, and Celia went to take a shower. She turned on the water and let the steam erase her reflection.

What had happened changed nothing. Rory and Eric would leave tomorrow. They would be gone and might never come back, like Kate's cousin Garrett had done. He'd gone away to college and no one had seen him since, or heard anything more than the occasional online comment or phone call to his parents, asking for money. He just went away and never came back.

Like her father had done when Celia was twelve years old. One night they were watching a movie on the couch, the next morning he was gone. Impossible to imagine that anyone could go so utterly absent in such a short space of time. Gone, with no explanation, as quick and complete as if he had died right then instead of six months later under some stranger's house in Boca Raton. Afterward she felt as if she'd been watching a stage performance in which the actor had walked off in the middle of the second act.

It should be easier to see Rory and Eric go. No surprises, no drama. But Celia was plagued by a deep, sickening rage, directed mainly at herself; even knowing their leaving was imminent, she could find no words to begin the argument that might keep them in Jawbone Ridge.

Passing Rory's room, she felt already the emptiness of the days ahead. His walls were bare, everything boxed and cased. He was leaving her behind.

She was a fool to hope that he would stay. There was nothing holding him here and a world beyond the mountains to explore and inhabit. That was the natural impulse, everyone agreed, but if so, it was lacking in Celia.

She went upstairs and sat cross-legged on the bed. A sharp moon had risen, casting a thin white light over the Ridge. Her body felt mangled, hot, an uncomfortable afterburn like a seltzer between her legs. But when she closed her eyes, she could see the way Rory had looked at her and feel again the thick weight of Eric, pressed against her thighs. The memory sent a pulse through her body like a ripple in still water, a memory of the cresting wave that had overtaken her when Rory pulled her knee over his hip and sank inside.

She heard a heavy step on the ladder and a couple of raps against the floor—it was how Rory always came in, a polite request for entry. But it seemed out of place now, and she didn't respond. After a moment, he put his head through the curtains.

"Hey," he said.

She motioned him in with one hand.

He dropped down next to her on the bed. He was silent at first, kneading the pad of his left hand with the fingers of his right. She'd been watching him do that since they were little kids. A pang of loneliness tightened her throat.

"I shouldn't have let that happen," he said finally. "None of that should have happened. I'm supposed to be looking out for you."

"You're always telling me we aren't kids anymore."

"That doesn't mean you don't need looking after."

"Maybe. But it's a little late for chivalry."

He nodded, staring at his hands. Then he got up and bent to kiss her forehead.

"Anyway, you're leaving tomorrow." Her throat was scratchy, and the words sounded strangled and thick.

He stroked her cheek with the back of his curved fingers. "Not for long. We won't be able to stay away now. You played it pretty well, Cee."

She caught his hand and pushed it away.

"I didn't start this."

"No?"

She turned away, staring out the big open window to the scattering of lights in the town below and the shadowy Blackbird perched above. Her eyes burned, and the landscape rippled like a dark sea.

"It's the three of us now, Cee. It's done." He pushed through the curtains at the top of the steps. "And you still haven't thought this through."

"Thought what through?"

He paused to look back.

"How it will end."

NOVEMBER 2001

ERIC HAD THAT light in his eyes. They could see it through the icy windshield as he pulled his SUV to a stop beside their house, where Celia and Rory were waiting at the end of the driveway.

"He's in the zone," Rory said, and she could hear the lift in his voice even as her own stomach swooped and fluttered in response.

Rory opened the passenger side door.

"Look who's rocking a new set of wheels. I hardly recognized you, brother."

Eric hopped out and let down the rear door. He took Celia's snowboard bag and stowed it with the others behind the backseat. His dark hair curled around the bottom of his knit cap, tipped with airy snowflakes that drifted through the rosy glow of the taillights.

"I still can't believe the old man coughed it up," he said. "Thought I'd be getting a matched set of SAT study guides for my birthday."

Celia climbed into the backseat next to Kate. They had all been there yesterday when his father handed Eric the keys. They'd run out after him to see what was waiting in the driveway, had witnessed the shy disbelief in Eric's face when his father said he'd earned it and heard the abruptness of his father's grunted laugh, as though he was as surprised as any of them that he'd finally done the right thing.

Celia saw the whole scene again as a blissful afterimage: Eric, arrow-straight against the sun, his hand on the hood, puddles of light on the bright blue paint. It felt like a new start for Eric and his father, a shift in their relationship.

In the seat next to her, Kate yawned.

"It's so early," she said. "Do you know how hard it is to attach a set of falsies in the dark?"

"No," Celia said.

She handed Kate a thermos of coffee.

"You're a saint," Kate said. "Java juice?"

"What else?"

Celia had been working almost a full-time schedule at the Java Hut. She went straight in after school each day and stayed until closing; the scent of coffee clung to her through the frigid walk home, too pervasive to be scrubbed clean by even the sturdiest winter wind. At night, her body falling away from her into sleep, she would sometimes catch that chocolaty bitterness on the sheets and twitch awake.

It was the same for Rory, pulling early hours at Clark's, where he stocked produce. *I swear, Cee, I spend half my REMs sorting apples. Old ones up, new ones in back. Like counting sheep, only redder.* One morning she had come in to find him at the kitchen table, leaning forward with his head on his arms like a child, fast asleep. She sat at the table with him for a while, watching him breathe. Then she rinsed out his half-eaten bowl of cereal and made him a plate of fried eggs.

A day at Crested Butte was exactly what they needed. Celia could feel the energy pouring into her limbs. As they pulled onto the road, she turned to watch the town disappear around the bend. The old Blackbird Hotel huddled unlit on its perch at the end of the ridge, its profile rising dark against the purple sky.

Rory cranked the music. To wake everyone up, he said.

"Wake us up with something good, though," Eric said. "What is this?"

"The new Torey Graves. It is good, listen."

Eric listened for about two seconds. "Yeah, no."

"Come on, now."

"The problem with you is that you like everything."

"Not true."

"Really. Name one song you don't like."

Rory paused. "Give me a minute."

Eric hooted with laughter. "There you have it. I can tell you ten songs I hate in ten seconds."

"Bullshit. You can't even come up with ten songs, period, in ten seconds."

"You're on. Loser buys pizza."

Rory looked at his watch. He raised one finger and let it fall.

"Go."

"'Like a Bird.' 'Jet.' 'Pretty Good.' 'This Is Real' (which, for the record, one hundred percent sampled). 'Faded.' 'All for You.' 'Run.' 'Love Ain't Free.' 'I Will.' And anything by Chrissy Hinden."

"Damn," said Rory. "You had two seconds left."

"'Irresistible.' 'More Than Me.' 'Drowning—'"

"Okay, okay."

"You gotta know what you like, brother."

Rory just shook his head.

Eric could go on this way for weeks at a time. Speed talking, wired, the words zinging out of his mouth with a nervous sharpness that rendered his mind in a sort of auditory Technicolor. His energy flooded the space and lifted them along with it, better than the best weed on the planet.

"I got my SATs back yesterday," Kate said, with an air of serene indifference.

"Well?"

"High sixes."

Celia gave her a round of applause, muffled by her knit gloves.

"Did you hear that?" She shoved Eric's seat with her knees. "Katie murdered the SATs."

"Congrats, Kate."

"Right on," Rory said. "Not that it's a surprise, obviously. You still thinking UNLV?"

"Yeah. My dad says he'll set me up at one of our properties if I get a degree in hotel administration."

"Sin City. I'll be there, too. My mom's sealed it up for me to work in her brother's construction company. If Eric gets in, we can all hang out."

"Movie night. I won't even make you sleep on the couch."

Rory raised his eyebrows. He turned back to Eric, who was trying to change the music again. Their argument resumed, an amiable squabble that faded for Celia to white noise.

"Did you get your scores yet?" Kate said.

"Yes," Celia said. "And there were no sixes, let me tell you."

"Only because you won't try."

Celia wobbled her head. She supposed it was true. But college had always felt like a waste of time. Though she understood the point of university in Eric's case—he planned to study engineering—she wasn't sure why it mattered so much to Kate. Her family had been in the hotel business for generations; they could train her on the job.

"It might be Kate herself who wants the degree," Rory had said. "Something to hang on the wall."

"All that money and effort for wall art?" It wasn't the way things worked in their home.

"For ego," he said, as if it were self-evident.

In the seat next to her, Kate was brainstorming Celia's career path.

"You could study design," she said. "Fashion design, or maybe interiors. It wouldn't be like a real school."

"No?"

"Not really. I mean, you wouldn't have to study math or science or anything. You'd just—I don't know, draw and learn about color schemes and how to put together a room." Her face lit up. "You could design our hotels. My mom will be retiring soon. You could apprentice with her and work your way up. Maybe even take her place someday."

Celia leaned her head against the seat cushion. *Design* was a Katie word, a way of making something difficult out of what should be easy. When she got dressed, Kate was Putting Together an Outfit. She struggled into clothes and peeled them off and switched bras and shoes and accessories. Her bathroom contained an array of cosmetics, and she used it all: lipstick, mascara, eyeliner, even glitter sometimes, a wash of silver under her eyebrows. Dressing for Kate was a process, like building a beautiful, tight-fitting shell.

Celia picked out her clothes for the sensual pleasure of wearing them. In the summer, she loved the feeling of light cotton skirts that brushed her bare legs, blouses that slipped across her breasts, long strands of beads that thumped against her chest and slid inside her neckline and all the way down her stomach, surprising her sometimes when they rolled cool as water across her nipple. She never understood why some colors matched or didn't match, why you couldn't mix stripes and plaid, why a hiking boot didn't go with a peasant skirt or a scarf shouldn't be worn around the thigh, the ends swaying like meadow grass against her calf. She never understood the point of being uncomfortable, not for a minute.

None of that would make sense if she tried to explain it to Kate.

Instead she shrugged. "You know me. Can learn, cannot be taught."

"You won't get a job that way, though, Cee."

"I already have a job."

Kate clicked her tongue. "At the Hut. You won't want to be making cappuccinos when you're fifty."

"True. When I'm fifty, I'll turn my talents to alcohol and become a bartender."

"You're being stupid. You need a good job, something that's going to pay the bills."

Rory turned around in his seat.

"Celia's smarter than any of us. Not everyone needs the fat stacks, Kate."

He smiled to take the sting out of the words, but Kate seemed to feel them all the same. She subsided into the corner, the thermos of coffee tucked like a child's blanket against the side of her neck.

The base at Crested Butte was ninety-four inches deep, and they'd gotten a little more the previous night, a buoyant layer of powder that seemed to levitate them down the mountain, each languid turn whispering off the back of their boards. The snow was smooth and luminous as a sheet of silk, glittering in the sunshine, tinged blue with reflected sky.

No one wanted to stop for lunch. No one wanted to stop at all. They found a trail through the woods and skied it single file, Celia pulling up the rear because she liked to stop sometimes and listen. The mountains here had a brighter sound than the dense hush of Telluride; the voices of children rang in the distance, and the squeak of the ski lift jumped around the snow so that she kept looking up, expecting to see it directly overhead. From the lower trail, a snowmobile droned and then faded away.

At the bottom, they lined up for the last run of the day. Rory hung back to tighten his boot as Celia came up behind him. Kate waited ahead, next to Eric.

Rory waved them on.

"Go on up. We'll be right behind you."

Celia saw the flash of disappointment in Kate's face as she looked back from the lift. A moment later, Eric's quick grin and an exaggerated eye roll.

"You have an admirer," Celia said, kicking the loose snow off her board as she and Rory swung into the chairlift. "Better sharpen your knife—you'll be adding another notch to the bedpost."

Rory pulled off his glove and unzipped his pocket to pull out some lip balm. "Seems like you're developing quite an edge yourself."

"You're right. That was an awful thing to say."

"I like it. At least it's honest for a change."

Celia lifted her face to the sun as the lift bore them gently up the hill.

"You've been avoiding me," Rory said. "You don't want to be alone with me anymore."

"We're alone now."

"Don't act like you don't know what I'm talking about."

"I don't."

"Right, it's just me. Me in fantasyland." He jerked his glove back on. "You can be such a bitch, Cee."

Celia's face flushed, and she felt a rush of tingly vertigo. She wrapped her arm around the bar of the chairlift.

She often felt this way at night. Lying in bed, the velvety

darkness pressing at her ears, the mattress would seem insubstantial all at once, and though she'd remind herself that you couldn't fall when you were already down, she would sometimes grip the sheets so hard that her hands ached.

At 2:00 a.m. the night before, she had given up on sleep and padded to the kitchen to make a cup of chamomile tea. As the first small bubbles began to vibrate inside the kettle, she heard Rory's bedroom door open. A moment later, he appeared around the corner, blinking into the sharp light from the bulb over the stove.

They'd met this way in the tiny kitchen a hundred times. She'd seen him just like this: rumpled and bare-chested, a cluster of knobby muscles above the waistband of his boxers, herself in a cotton nightgown—it happened all the time.

But last night something was different. He stood looking at her, motionless and surprised as if he were holding his breath. Something about his stillness seized her attention, made her limbs heavy and her stomach queasily light. His gaze tilted slowly down her body, and his face filled with something like shock, as if he'd found her dead on the floor instead of propped against the stove making tea.

She turned away, fumbling with the wrapper of her tea bag.

Go away. Go back to bed, Rory. Go away.

He edged up behind her, reached over her shoulder to get a glass from the cupboard. A hundred times before, they'd been here. A thousand. This was nothing new; this was nothing at all.

But that night, his nearness made the hair rise on her arms, sent a chill across her skin. Her muscles had gone springy, unpredictable, like those of a small child. The wrapper crinkled in her hands.

He closed the cupboard door but didn't back away. She could feel his body—his whole body from his shoulders and all the way to the floor—push against the sliver of space between them. His hand next to hers gripped the edge of the counter, his fingers curled under and the knuckles standing white against his skin.

She didn't move. Couldn't breathe.

He pressed his face to the top of her head.

"Fuck, Celia."

The kettle began a petulant whistle. A cloud of steam poured from its spout. She reached quickly to pull it off the heat, and when she turned around, Rory was gone, the empty glass abandoned on the counter.

Now Celia wound her arm more tightly around the bar. The snowboard tugged at her feet, so heavy that she was afraid its weight might drag her right out of the chair.

"You're my brother," she said.

"I'm not your brother," he said quickly. "Not really."

"Maybe I want you to be."

"Really? Because if that's what you want, then stop…stop…" His voice trailed off.

The chair chattered over the last pole before the ramp at the top of the lift. Celia gritted her teeth and hung on.

"Is it Eric?" he said.

It didn't sound like a question.

At the top of the run, where Eric and Kate were waiting, Celia clamped down her binding and took off before Rory could say another word. She stayed right under the lift, the quickest way down, weaving a tight line through the bumps.

Eric passed on her left, darting in and out of the late afternoon shadows. He caught some air and hung for a moment, his arms outstretched like wings against the sky.

Rory watched Celia slide away, leaving a fan of softly carved snow in her wake, and all the words he couldn't say still trapped inside his throat.

It was Eric who talked best to Celia. He offered extravagant compliments, an unending flirtation, a constant low-level howl outside her window. His hands roamed freely over her back and arms and even her ass. He liked to touch her hair, which had grown out since Darlene cut it, and now fell in thick waves to the middle of her back with a point at the end like a flame. Eric wrapped her hair around his hand, kissed her easily on the cheeks and the inside of her wrist—and another time, full on the lips while she was standing at her open locker outside the high school gymnasium. He surrounded Celia, and she responded with gestures so supple and generous that Rory could never be sure whether they were meant to include him. He looked on with a wretched envy as Eric pressed Celia's palm to his lips, swept his mouth across her shoulder while she smoked his weed. Eric burned with a fiery energy that seemed to suck all the oxygen from the room, so that Rory could only find sips of air that never filled his lungs.

Sometimes he found Eric looking back at him with his faun-like grin, one dark eye winking closed. He was flirting with both of them. Probably he knew how Rory roiled inside, how he thought of Celia when he was with other girls, and paused beneath her attic bedroom in the desolate hours of the night when he'd already emptied his body and still could not stop the blistering pornographic course of his thoughts.

I'm not your brother, Rory had said, and it was true. It *was* true. They were not even distant cousins; they were not at all related. There was nothing to stop them.

He thought about the way she looked the night before, the pearly outline of her body inside the nightgown, the scent of her hair. A sudden tense awareness, and his own voice stretched like wire in his throat. His hands had ached with emptiness; he'd clenched them shut, leaving a row of purple half-moons in his palm.

I'm not your brother.
I'm not your father.
I'm nothing like him.

The mood of the house became strained after Darlene cut Celia's hair that day years ago. At dinner they would make desultory conversation for a few minutes: How's your day? Did you do your homework? I heard they caught the guy in Grand Junction who kidnapped that little girl. But the effort seemed too much for sustained chat. They'd finish the meal to the clatter of cutlery and the creaks of the roof settling under the weight of heavy snow.

Eddie Dark was quiet and sullen, his formerly sunny disposition darkened with an unrelenting resentment directed at Rory's mother. And something else, beyond resentment. An undercurrent Rory couldn't understand.

Like Celia, he tried to make himself useful, vaguely aware that they both were inserting themselves into the cracks of their parents' relationship, but unable to think of any more positive or direct intervention. He replaced some lightbulbs, oiled the door hinges, rehung the shower rod in the bathroom, washed the dishes.

All jobs were subject to critique.

"C'mon in here, boug," Eddie would say. "You got to tighten them screws. You gon' have this whole thing down on our heads."

And he'd watch, brimming with impatience, as Rory got out the tools and tried again.

In his work, Eddie was a perfectionist. The house was never done; there was always something to fix or change, something that was driving him crazy. The edges of two strips of wallpaper that didn't match up, or a shelf that was not quite level, a faulty window shade that bothered him endlessly until he got his tools out and fixed it. He was impatient, always snatching a hammer or drill from Rory's hands, and inclined to come along after them even in the kitchen, to rewash the dishes that were already stacked in the cupboard. The house was full, overfull during that time, with the swelling and shrinking of his stepfather's mood.

It was on one of these long thick nights that Rory came out of his room, headed for the bathroom down the hall. He glanced into the living room as he passed.

Celia had fallen asleep on the couch. She was curled on her side, a pillow bunched under her cheek. Her slack face was bathed in a soft blue glow from the TV, her lips slightly parted, one hand tucked between her knees and the other curled like a flower under her chin.

Rory stopped in his tracks.

Eddie Dark was standing over her, leaning with one hand on the wall behind the couch. The other hand was down the front of his pants, moving fast. He was staring down at Celia with a grimace, like her sleeping face hurt him somehow.

Rory felt suddenly warm, uncomfortably warm, a scalding heat at the nape of his neck, beads of sweat seething under the surface of his skin. He heard his voice travel up his throat and quiver into the space between them.

"What are you doing?"

It wasn't the right question. Rory knew exactly what Celia's father was doing. He just couldn't believe it.

Eddie's head swung around. The shock on his face was so complete that it wiped away every trace of expression. He froze as if locked in place.

"What are you doing?" Rory said again. His mouth felt sticky, each word peeling off his tongue.

Eddie jerked his hand out of his pants and lurched away

from the couch. He shoved past Rory to his bedroom and shut the door.

Celia hadn't stirred. Her shorn head never turned on the pillow.

Rory stood with his feet halfway on the carpet and half on the cold linoleum floor. The heat leached away and left him stone-faced and heavy with shame.

He understood then why his mother had cut Celia's hair.

It's too much, too much…

The temptation, she meant. She had been trying to protect Celia.

He fetched a pillow and blanket from his room and made a bed for himself beside the couch, at Celia's feet. He strained to track the shallow sound of her breath, praying she would not wake up to the roar of his heartbeat and wonder what he was doing there.

Don't wake up, he thought to her, over and over, his body desperately still. *Don't wake up, don't wake up, nobody move here.* He clutched his pillow, his eyes trapped open and glued to the screen. He was seized by a terrible emptiness, a violent hollowed-out sadness as if he'd been gouged.

The minutes ticked by.

An hour later the bedroom door opened. Eddie came out carrying two fat duffel bags. Rory watched as he shrugged into his coat.

They stared at each other through the blue darkness.

Then Celia's father picked up his bags and he was gone.

"Do you know how much a trillion dollars is?" Eric said.

The road home was dark again and rutted with snow, the pines a smeared shadow that rose and fell above the white embankment. Celia breathed a patch of fog onto the glass and drew a smiley face with a curlicue on top of its head like a baby.

Eric and Kate had been talking about politics, something about the national debt, arguing stridently for and against the new president. Celia had lost the thread of the conversation, but the trillion-dollar question intrigued her.

"Um, a trillion," Kate said. "A trillion is a trillion."

"It's a dollar every second for thirty thousand years."

"Dude," Rory said. "That can't be right."

Kate worked out the number on her phone's calculator. It was right.

"Mind. Blown," she said.

"And did you know," Eric said, "that if you took the average adult's circulatory system and laid it out in a line—"

"Eww," said Kate.

"—the whole thing would be nearly sixty thousand miles long. You could circle the Earth two and a half times following a trail of Rory's capillaries."

Celia rested her head against the cool glass, lulled by the hum of the engine and the tired buzz of her muscles. The tops of her thighs would be sore tomorrow, but tonight she felt better than good. Eric had managed to smuggle some beers from his dad's stash, which they transferred to Big Gulp cups and brought with them into the pizza joint, sipping the bitter liquid through fat red straws. Celia didn't like the taste at all, but she enjoyed the warm and watery blur it made of her surroundings.

"I've got one," she said.

"Factoid Mary," Eric said. "Go."

"The Great Wall of China."

"Heard of it." Eric smiled; she could see his eyes in the rearview mirror.

"Did you know that the men who served as guards there

during the Middle Ages were sometimes born on the wall? They lived their whole lives up there and were buried inside it when they died."

"No women?" Eric said.

"You don't get babies without them," Rory pointed out.

"The women went there to get married," Celia said. "Then they were trapped there, too, raising their children on the wall. Imagine the view, trees and water as far as the eye could see, only you can never reach it. You're on the wall forever."

A silence fell over them. Celia thought of the view, tree-tops like moss on the hills far below.

"Why would any woman agree to that deal?" Kate said.

"There was no agreeing," Eric said. "Women did what they were told back in the day."

"Dragged kicking and screaming to the wall, married off to some disgusting unwashed Chinaman. Not a good time to be a woman."

"Some of them probably liked it. Even an ugly woman would be guaranteed to get laid."

"Not every woman wants to get laid," Kate said.

Eric clicked his tongue.

"What?" Kate said.

"You're so fucking politically correct," Eric said. "Of course women want to get laid."

"Not like men do."

"Bullshit. Women want sex just as much as men."

"Which is why men get raped so often." Kate rolled her eyes and flipped open her phone.

"Women get raped because society encourages them to pretend they don't want to have sex."

"You're an arrogant, misogynistic pig, Eric Dillon. Did your father teach you that?"

Eric's eyes glinted in the rearview mirror. Celia had thought he was messing around—he loved nothing better than to jerk Kate's chain—but now she wasn't sure. Nothing was guaranteed to set Eric off like a comparison to his father.

"I've got another," he said. "Did you know that half of all American women will get raped at least once during their lifetimes?" he said.

"Not true," Rory said. "Not even close."

"Fifty percent," Eric said, ignoring him. His eyes flicked from Celia to Kate. "Who do you think is more likely? The chick who gives it up willingly or the one who walks around like an ice princess with a stick up her ass?"

"Rape is not about sex, you idiot," Kate said. "It's about control and violence."

"And sex."

"The sex is beside the point."

"Oh, my God. No, baby. It is the entire point."

"You don't know what you're talking about," Kate said. "And I'm done with this conversation."

A splintery smile from Eric. "What about you, Celia? You think I'm wrong?"

"Dude, move on," Rory said.

The truck shifted gears, trundling up a long hill.

"Come on, Cee," Eric said. "The Mona Lisa act is strong, I'll give you that, but you should be careful not to carry it too far. You send a guy away with blue balls every time he sees you, he's gonna get frustrated. You might find yourself alone with a guy like that and find he's gone from frustrated to pissed off—and then, who knows? I'm thinking it would behoove you to cultivate the art of the hand job. A virgin's best friend. In fact, I believe you've got a couple of willing tutors right here. What'd you say? We can start your rape prevention training right now."

His voice had narrowed and gained speed like a river through a crevice. Beside him, Rory's head rotated slightly left, but his gaze was locked on the road.

"Fucking lunatic," Kate said.

"Oooh, did I scare you?" Eric made a spooky face as he turned back to look at them. The light from the dashboard skimmed his face, shadows pooling under his eyes. The engine revved and they accelerated down the hill.

"Watch the road," Kate snapped.

Eric's laugh sounded strange, a guitar string wound too tight. Behind his laugh was a song Celia realized was playing for the third time in a row: *You arrive before daylight, hopeful and tired, bearing flowers, stay for hours, and you make us late for school, you make us late for school...*

"I never can figure out why you girls think you're in control." He waggled the steering wheel. "Who's driving, anyway? Who's driving the car, Celia?"

They were flying now. Through the windshield Celia could see a yellow road sign indicating a sharp curve ahead. Her fingers clenched around the armrest.

"Let's keep it between the lines, brother," Rory said.

Eric cranked up the music, one hand on the wheel as the truck swung around the curve.

"Come on, Cee," Eric said. "Tell me. Who's driving the motherfucking vee-hicle?"

Celia stared into the mirror. You are, she wanted to say. But the words would not come. Her leg tensed as though stomping on a nonexistent brake.

He jerked again at the wheel. The engine growled, throwing them back against the seats.

"Stop!" Kate yelled.

There was a sudden absence of vibration. The truck began to slide, fishtailing down the road. The landscape slipped sideways across the windshield—a clump of trees now in front of them, now beside. Rory's hand shot out to catch the wheel. But it was too late. The tires hit the icy shoulder of the highway and the truck whipped around. They careened down the embankment with a series of stony thumps that slammed Celia's head against the side window and her neck against the sharp edge of the seat belt. The truck dove to the bottom of the ditch and stuck there.

Everything was still. Only the music carried on, a blur of vibrating bass and a woman's slow voice chanting the chorus.

You arrive in the nighttime, drunk and inspired, bringing tears, stay for years, and you make me late for school, oh, you make me late for school…

Kate was the first to recover.

"Eric, I swear to God." She flung open her door and scrambled out.

Celia unsnapped her seat belt and tried her door. But it was wedged against something and wouldn't open. She climbed out the passenger side and hunched at the side of the car, hands on her knees. The blood rang like an electric current through her body.

"Everybody okay?" Rory said as he got out. He laid a hand on Celia's back.

"No," Kate said. "Not okay. Fucking Eric…"

Eric. He was still in the car.

Celia picked her way over the icy rocks and scrub, around the back of the truck to the driver's side door. Rory was right behind her.

Through the windshield, she could see Eric staring straight ahead, his face washed in the green light of the dashboard. His eyes were glazed, unfocused, his hands locked tight around the steering wheel.

Celia tugged at the door, her heart in her throat.

"Eric. Eric, are you all right?" She slapped at the window.

He blinked. He released his seat belt, unlocked the door and clambered out of the car, scrambling back a few steps to survey the damage.

The truck was headfirst at the bottom of the embankment, one front wheel perched six inches off the ground. There would be no driving it out.

"It's not that bad," Celia said.

"Not as bad as it looks," Rory said as he flipped open his phone. "Not at all. I'll call us a tow. I've got four bars."

Eric stretched out his fingers to touch Celia's forehead. They came away wet with blood.

"It's only a scratch," Celia said.

But Eric's body started to shake, long jarring spasms that locked his jaw and brought a sheen of tears to his eyes.

"S-sorry," he said through clenched teeth.

"Shh, don't worry about it," she said. "Eric, it was just an accident."

He shook his head, staggered away and began to vomit.

Three hours later, the tow truck pulled up to the house. Kate got into her car, which she'd left at Eric's that morning, and took off for home, still muttering and cursing under her breath, flipping him off in the rearview mirror. Celia stood with Eric on the driveway while Rory helped the driver unload the battered truck.

The driver, whose name, Manuel, was stitched on the pocket of his cotton shirt, had wanted to take Celia to the hospital. She refused, so he dug a plastic first aid kit from the tow truck's glove box, and Rory cleaned up the cut and put a bandage on it. They rode back to Jawbone Ridge with Manuel shaking his head and scolding them gently in Spanish.

"Si eras mis hijos," he kept saying, *If you were my kids*, and Celia imagined him at home, calm and confident with his wife and a passel of black-haired boys. Laying down the law. Manuel wouldn't have let them drive all the way from Crested Butte in the dark—he said it didn't make no sense.

"I seen a lot of wrecks," he said. "You got off easy."

After the truck was unloaded and Rory had paid him, he shook Rory's hand and gave him one final admonishment before turning the truck around and trundling away. He thought Rory had been driving.

A crack of light showed through the blinds at the front of the house. A few seconds later, Mr. Dillon surged through the big double doors, screaming at Eric from the door and all the way down the sidewalk.

"I knew you'd wreck this truck. I knew it, right from the start. Told your mother this was a mistake, but oh no, she said it would be good for you. Good for you! You couldn't even make it last one day. One fucking day! What in God's good name is wrong with you?"

Celia glanced at Eric. He'd lowered his head and wouldn't look up. But at his side, his fists were clenched, both arms stiff and quivering. He was breathing strangely, in short, quick little gasps as though preparing for a long underwater dive.

Mr. Dillon skidded onto the driveway and stopped a foot in front of Eric. He half rose on tiptoe, expanding sideways as well as up, his arms stuck out from his body like a boxer's. He should have looked comical in his sweats and cowboy boots, his gray hair standing straight up on his head. But there was nothing funny about the way he was coming at Eric.

"What the fuck is wrong with you?" he said. No questions about whether Eric was okay or what had happened. He was yelling as if they were already in the middle of a fight, picking up where they'd left off.

Eric didn't say a word.

Look at him, Celia wanted to say. *Don't just stand there—look up.*

"What in fucking hell happened to this truck?"

Eric, look up, look up.

His father raised his hand and smacked Eric hard across the face with his open hand. The crack rang out in the darkness like a branch snapping in two.

Eric didn't move. His head jerked around with the force of the blow, then came squarely back with his gaze resting as before on the icy concrete. His feet remained locked in place. He reminded Celia of a documentary she'd seen about the young marines in training camp, the soldiers standing for hours under a torrent of abuse, nonreactive. This must be a well-rehearsed behavior for Eric—for both of them. They fell into it so easily that it was as if Celia and Rory weren't there at all, that it was just the two of them and a long-established routine.

A wet sickness rose in her throat.

Please, Eric, oh, God, look up.

Eric's father was thumping the side of Eric's head with his knuckles as though banging on a door, punctuating each sentence.

"I want you. To tell me. What happened. To this truck."

She started forward. Rory's hand shot out and he held her in place, not looking down at her but straight at Eric's father, a weird, flamey light in his eyes.

"Eric," she said.

Eric's gaze slid along the snow toward her.

"You better listen when I'm talking to you," Mr. Dillon said.

A burst of heat sprang up in Celia's nose and eyes. The

scene began to swim and blur. She wanted to scream: *Look up, Eric, look up!* as if all their lives depended on it. Panic careened through her in quick shuddering waves.

"What the fuck did you do?" Mr. Dillon's hand spread out, the fingers stiff and locked together like a paddle. He raised his arm.

"No!" Celia cried.

As she tilted forward to stop him, she felt Rory rush past, setting her aside as he went. His left hand reached out, flat to Mr. Dillon's chest, right arm already up and swinging. His fist arced through the snowy air and landed with a sickening crunch on Mr. Dillon's mouth. The big man collapsed backward, his feet shooting up as his head thumped the frozen ground. Celia saw something fly up and land on the snow at Eric's feet, where it lay glittering and important like the image on the cover of a book.

A bloody tooth.

For a moment, the night was absolutely still. Then Mr. Dillon climbed slowly to his feet, his hand pressed to his mouth. Blood poured through his fingers. He appeared to have shrunk on the way back up, so that Rory and Eric towered over him against the background of the huge pale house. When he turned, Celia could see the shocking glint of tears in his eyes, his shoulders crumpled as though succumbing after a long struggle to an overwhelming exhaustion.

He didn't say another word, didn't look up from the bloody ground. His boots squeaked as he turned and shuffled up the walkway and went inside.

When the door closed, Eric turned to Rory. There was no gratitude in his pallid face, none of the savage righteousness that blazed in Rory's. His chest heaved and his voice was choked with anger.

"Why did you do that?" he said. "Why do you always do that?"

Rory stooped to pick up the tooth. He pressed it into Eric's hand.

"Because I love you, dumbass. Nobody fucks with that."

JULY 1998

"NO, BUT WHAT did he say after that?"

Celia cupped her chin in her hand. Kate had asked the same question a dozen different ways in the past hour, and she had given the same answer. Even the river at their feet seemed to sigh at another repetition of the story.

"That's all," she said.

"Oh, my God," Kate said. "He's definitely not asking Erica, then. But he didn't say who…"

"No, but you know how Rory is. Homecoming is two months away. He might not even go."

"But you'll tell me if he says anything?"

"Sure," Celia said, but she didn't mean it. There were only so many ways to get around the truth: Rory didn't like Kate, not that way. If he went to the dance at all, it would be with Jenny Parker or Claire Richardson. Likelier still, he'd forget about homecoming altogether and hang out in the living room playing Realm Defenders with Eric.

She leaned back against the rocks, holding up her hand to see the pattern Kate had painted on her fingernails. Red with black dots, like ladybugs. She had painted Kate's, too, a shimmery pale pink that was all Mrs. Vaughn would allow her daughter to wear.

One of the dots had gotten smeared. Celia took up the bottle of black polish and tried to repair it.

"You don't know how lucky you are," Kate said, her eyes drifting closed as she tipped her face toward the sun. "Living with Rory McFarland. I'll bet he walks around in his underwear, even."

"Sometimes," Celia admitted.

"I would never leave the house."

"He also leaves toothpaste in the sink and towels on the floor. Once I even found a jockstrap hanging over the shower curtain."

Kate laughed. "Okay, that *is* kind of gross."

"Totally."

"I'll have to tame him."

"Good luck with that. The boy is clueless."

"And what about you? How come you never talk about the boys you like?"

"There's nothing to say."

"Nothing to say because you don't like anyone, or because you don't want to tell me?"

Celia placed a dot of black polish on her nail and blew on it gently. "Telling is a jinx."

"No, it's not. You should put things out there. That's what makes them come true. If you don't say anything, you're sort of telling the universe, 'I don't care what happens.' You're supposed to make wishes. Everybody does."

"Hmm," Celia said.

After a second, Kate said, "Remember Leo? He broke up with you because you wouldn't say anything, right? He never knew what you were thinking."

"And your point is..."

"You should talk. That's what girls do."

Kate got to her feet, collected the bottles of nail polish and pushed them gingerly into her pocket with the tips of her fingers.

"Are you sure you don't want to go to Dorrie's with me?"

"Dorrie hates me."

"Because you let her. Just show up, be nice."

"Next time," Celia said.

"'Kay, well, maybe I'll stop by your place on my way home. Would Rory be there, do you think?"

"You're obsessed."

Kate grinned. "You say that like it's a bad thing."

After Kate left, Celia sat on the riverbank, her guitar on her knee and a book of children's poetry spread open on the grass in front of her. The text was woven into a delicate pen-and-ink drawing of a wrinkled giant bent over a simmering pot, steam rising in wavy lines around the verses. She strummed out the melody she had composed, a slow waltz tempo in a minor key, and sang the old poem in a low voice.

My age is three hundred and seventy-two,
And I think, with the deepest regret,
How I used to pick up and voraciously chew
The dear little boys whom I met.

I've eaten them raw, in their holiday suits;
I've eaten them curried with rice;
I've eaten them baked, in their jackets and boots,
And found them exceedingly nice.

But now that my jaws are too weak for such fare,
I think it exceedingly rude

To do such a thing, when I'm quite well aware
Little boys do not like to be chewed.

Her father used to read to her from this book; when he got to the line about little boys being chewed, he would change the words to "little girls," and he'd bury his face at the side of her neck, making loud snuffling, chewing sounds. Celia would squeal and laugh so hard that he sometimes had to read the poem a second time, so she could play her part the right way and lay her head on the pillow at the end.

He was gone now. One morning, gone, and all their life before wiped cleanly away as if it had never been.

"He would have come back," Darlene said. "Eventually."

Celia knew that wasn't true. It was something her stepmother said to be kind. The truth was something else; Celia could see it tugging at the faces of Rory and Darlene, in their shoulders that stiffened when anybody mentioned her father's name.

Always Celia looked away in a panic. You couldn't unsee something; she knew that now. She'd barely glanced at her father's lifeless face, yet she still could see the row of tiny stitches under his eyelashes, his puppet-hands lying wooden and inanimate, folded on his chest. For months she had spent her allowance on NyQuil and cough syrup, a dizzying circular quest to get herself back to the time before this time, the vast lazy whiteness of the not-knowing. Her drugged-up mind grew sluggish, even in the bustling school hallways, where the shrieks and chatter only served to punctuate her own interior silent befuddlement.

Rory had put a stop to that. She had watched in a sullen misery as he upended the bottle and poured the cherry-red liquid down the bathroom sink.

"No more," he said.

And that was all. But he opened his strong, thin boy's arms and she walked into them, and found herself crying. Finally crying after all those months, in big messy sobs and gulps and shudders that racked her body like an exorcism.

Afterward he handed her a wadded-up handful of tissues.

"Well," he said, and the inadequacy of that stung them both with a bout of semihysterical laughter. They sank to the floor, shushing each other, blotting the tears off their faces.

Three words, she thought now. Three words from Rory and she was out of the fog.

And so I contentedly live upon eels,
And try to do nothing amiss,
And I pass all the time I can spare from my meals
In innocent slumber like—like this.

At the end of the last verse, she turned her head, listening, and pressed her fingers flat to the strings.

Rory and Eric. She heard them on the path above.

Their voices had changed over the past year, as if the source had sunk from the top of their throats to a hollow cavity deep inside their chests. The sound had gathered resonance, she could feel it behind her own breastbone when they spoke. She imagined their voices as tracings, needles on paper making long deep waves of sound, and her own barely visible, a narrow blip lifting off the page.

They had followed her, far up the river from where they usually met, out of sight and earshot from Jawbone Ridge and anyone who might report the truancy, collect Celia and put her back on a bus to the Telluride Middle School, where she was supposed to be making up a math class in hopes of improving her grade. She didn't need the class for credit, but

Darlene said she could do better than a D+ in algebra and she should take it again over the summer.

Her stepmother was right, of course. Celia could do better.

But not today. Today she'd packed a bag and hid it behind the ski shed, then circled back to retrieve it after Darlene had gone inside. She slung the strap over her shoulder and started up the riverside trail, around the point of the ridge where the Blackbird cleaved to its perch, overlooking the town. There, at the base of a tall slab of granite, was a pool of still water: the Palm, named by some long-ago generation for the columns of cracked stone that resembled fingers, so that from the top of the ridge, the pool appeared to be cupped in a giant hand.

The Palm was a local place—no one's favorite swimming hole because it was so hard to get to, the water mountain-cold even in the middle of summer. The path had never been fully formed, so the past twenty yards was a fight through a patch of thorny scrub, then a long clamber up and over the clutch of boulders at the base of the Palm before coming to the tiny waterfall that filled the pool. There Celia had cleared a small patch of prickly grass and furnished it with a fat disc of pine trunk and an old tin pitcher she'd dragged from home. Sometimes she'd fill a backpack with linens and iced tea, candles and books and fruit, and she'd decorate the clearing as if it were a room, with beads draped over the aspen and her guitar propped against a tree.

She had started coming here the previous summer, just after her father left. At first, she was sure he'd come home and didn't want to be there when he did. Being at the house when he got back would have signaled a forgiveness she didn't feel. Let him come. She wouldn't be there. And if, walking up the road for home, she saw his truck in the driveway, she'd run to Eric's house instead. Her father would have to come find her, and when he did, when he stood at Eric's door asking had anyone seen her, Eric would stand very straight in his path and tell him no, and who did he think he was to leave without a word and then come strolling back into their lives like nothing had changed?

Get off my step, Eric would say. *Celia isn't here.*

But the truck never did come. Only a message, delivered by Darlene, saying Celia's father was dead. And later his body, dry and inert as a length of cut wood.

No closure, Eric said, as if diagnosing an illness, and Celia imagined a circle with two loose ends flapping, unable to connect.

Behind her, his buzzy new voice rang out as the two of them thundered around the boulder at the end of the path.

"Dude, you said the same thing last time you wore those shoes."

Rory threw down his canvas bag and dropped to the ground beside it. He kicked off his rubber flip-flops and crossed his leg to examine his toe.

"Why didn't you remind me?" he said.

"I'm not your mother."

Celia strummed a chord on her guitar.

Eric did a mock double take, one hand over his heart.

"Why, Celia, what on earth are you doing here?"

He put his hands on his hips, palms facing out, like Mr. Welding in fourth period. His voice rose to a trilling falsetto.

"This is highly irresponsible, young lady. Highly irresponsible. You know your mother paid good money for you to learn the quadratic equation. I will not have you show her such little respect."

"I don't have a mother," she said.

"His mother, then, impudent wench." He hooked a thumb at Rory, then resumed his normal voice, muffled for a second as he peeled off his T-shirt. "You're gonna be toast, you know."

"Yeah, t
to find you
"And lo
a toe in the
on my tan.
But Ror
first. They
howling.
"Jeeeees
Rory grab
dunking each
flinging the hai
their heads like the
and they spun in pla
ing them around, Eri
yellow-green bruises lik
bloom again in a few weeks or a month, round and purple as tulips, clustered around his shoulder blades and down his ribs.

He would grin sometimes at Celia's distress.

"Don't worry about me. I have a plan."

"What kind of plan?"

"I'm going to take him by surprise. He's forgotten I'm a growing boy. One day I'll be bigger than him, and then…"

And he'd smack his fist into his palm. Or a wall, or a door.

"I'm gonna knock out all his teeth and wear them on a chain around my neck," he said. "Swear to God, Cee."

She could smell the excitement on him, acrid and metallic like the scent of wet pennies.

"You don't think I'll do it?" he said. "You think I'm a pussy?"

"No."

"But you don't think it'll happen."

good person, Eric. You
ove."
asn't sure. She never could be

In bare feet she padded to the river's
he water like a baptism. Her yellow sun-
Her hair, now grown to shoulder length,
d under the water. Rory and Eric's splashing
a, almost silent. Surfacing, she could hear their
yful as ever, but distorted by the new sharp depth.
ey were grown men pretending to be boys.

he water was too cold for a long swim. They climbed out of
he pool and stretched out on the flat boulder at the base of the Palm, their heads propped on bunched-up towels and T-shirts, limbs woven together like a mat of intertwined roots.

Gradually the heat of the rock warmed them. Celia sank into a honeyed drowsiness, the drone of locusts in her ears.

"I'm going to marry you someday," she said.

The words lay, blurry and directionless, under the blanket of heat they were sharing. A sparrow began to chirp and a crow answered back, screeching from the top of the pines. She watched it dive out of the trees, its wings like an arrow against the sky.

Eric turned and laid his hand on her chest. His palm was cool and solid over her heart.

"But you'll always love me best," he said.

JANUARY 11, 2009

4:38 p.m.

ON JULIAN'S LAST DAY on a pair of skis, he was thinking of his brother, Tony. Two years older than Julian, stocky and barrel-chested, with thick limbs that never seemed to fully straighten and flat, oar-like feet, his brother had the build for skiing and took to it right away. His turns were artless and brutal, but it hardly mattered. Tony Moss simply pointed his ski tips downhill and crouched over them, grinning and screaming threats at the skiers in his path. He was heavy and cumbersome as a snowmobile. He expected everyone to get the fuck out of the way, and mostly they did.

Julian disapproved. His turns were elegant, graceful, even for a downhiller. The fastest way down would always be over the snow, not plowing through it. He skied with a clean snap off the edge, right back to the flat of the skis. It was about balance and common sense. You didn't have to shove the whole goddamn mountain out of the way.

He paused at the top of the run to check his watch. One of the diamonds was coming loose at three o'clock, but it had been that way for decades, since the day his father had given it to Tony.

Tony. Tony again. Kate had been asking questions lately about Tony's accident. How had it happened, and what became of him afterward?

"What became of him?" Julian said. "Nothing at all."

"But where is he now?"

"Right where he has been, at my mother's house. He gets physical therapy, some nursing care, but basically my mom takes care of him."

"Doesn't your dad help?"

"Can't help. He's dead."

"Oh." And after a moment, "How did he die?"

"Heart attack, the summer after. Or, as my mother would say, his heart broke."

"Your poor mom."

"It's her choice, though," he said. "Being with Tony. She could put him in a home, I've told her that a hundred times. It's not like he knows the difference."

Kate had looked at him sideways. "She would know the difference."

There was a sound of judgment in that statement. As if Julian were missing the point. As if it were his fault, somehow, that his mother had adopted this maddening, almost Catholic attitude of penance in refusing to leave her home. She *wanted* to be with Tony, she said. He needed her, she couldn't leave him. And no amount of persuasion could shift her. Eventually Julian stopped trying.

Let her stay there, if that was what she wanted. It had nothing to do with him. Nothing at all.

He pulled his glove and the cuff of his coat over the smooth golden disc and pressed his goggles more firmly against his cheeks. In good weather he would be seeing the distant outline of Jawbone Ridge, meandering at the edge of the ravine and half-hidden by a rise in the hill. But today he could see no farther than the smudged gray shapes of the pines that lined the run. The snow had been coming down all night and day and lay now in foamy sheets that disguised every edge and erased all the shadows. The white sky seemed part of the mountain, everything condensed to a foggy swirl that made it difficult to find the horizon and read the texture of the snow. A dangerous light for skiing.

But he'd dealt with much worse. He pushed off confidently from the lip of the run, pounding straight down the face, his upper body quiet while his knees folded and unfolded like shock absorbers, following the bumps. No wasted motion, that's what he'd been taught. Take only as big a bite of the edge as you need to maintain the line. It took courage to point the skis downhill, to really ride the snow. Courage and arrogance, to think you were never going to fall.

Tony had that. It helped if you were not the contemplative type.

Don't think about it, Jules. You pussy...

And he'd tear off down the hill, singing louder every time Julian asked him to stop.

Ten whores a-leaping, nine ladies drinking, eight midriffs showing, seven hoodlums stealing, six girls a-laying, five gooold teeeeth...

An obnoxious, nasally repetition, setting Julian's teeth on edge.

Tony was singing that last morning on the banks of Long Lake. It was the day after Christmas and the lake had frozen over, apparently solid and smooth, with a lattice of earlier skate tracks carved through the snow-dusted surface. In the distance, Julian could hear the shouts and laughter of their friends, their bodies like small birds darting across the whiteness.

Tony tucked in his laces and stepped onto the ice.

"Hurry up—I'll race you," he said.

Julian didn't answer. Everything was a race with Tony. Just eighteen, he had started training a few months before with Gustave Pollan, who said that Tony was one of the most gifted downhillers he had ever seen. Tony had the build for it, the temperament, and even the mantra.

Don't think about it.

Tony skated backward onto the ice, grinning.

"Come on," he called. "If you beat me, I promise not to sing for the rest of the day."

"Thank fuck," Julian muttered as he got to his feet.

"But if you don't..." Tony spread his arms wide, singing at the sky. "Five goooold rings—"

The air was split by a sudden loud crack. Tony disappeared into the lake as if a trapdoor had opened at his feet. For a moment there was silence. Then he came up spluttering.

"Shit! Julian!"

Julian gathered himself to spring forward and skate to his brother's side. But somehow he wasn't moving. Only his heartbeat accelerated, preparing his body for a command from Julian that never came.

He would always wonder what might have happened if Tony had been closer to the shore. If Julian hadn't been at his wits' end over the singing, if his father hadn't given Tony his own gold watch that Christmas—the watch he had promised Julian, that Julian had admired aloud again and again. If Julian hadn't so far to go before he reached the hole in the ice.

Because somewhere in the space between the shore and his brother, a tiny warmth was smothered, like an ember blinking out and finally turning to ash. The future arrowed out and away from him, with some version of himself on the other side, looking back. And it looked good. Life without Tony would be quieter (thank fuck, that godawful singing); it would be calmer without that jangling presence in the house. No more stone-knuckled charley horses, no more of Julian's girlfriends being more impressed with Tony than they were with him. He'd have his parents' money one day. All of it. He'd have his father's undiluted attention.

Tony was trying to pull himself from the water, but the ice kept breaking out from under him.

Julian stood transfixed, watching his brother struggle.

"Julian! Get a branch!"

But Julian didn't move. He felt his organs pulling inward, sucked to the center of him and then vacuumed away. His body was hollow. His mind watched impartially, from some faraway point, unconnected to the scene before him.

This wasn't his fault. He hadn't pushed Tony; he'd never raised a hand. The big dumb ox had strayed onto the thin ice all on his own. Showing off. Singing (that godawful racket!), maybe ignoring the warning snaps of the ice. It was his own damn fault. Julian could not be blamed.

The seconds ticked by. Tony's voice grew hoarse, constricted by the cold. His wet lips darkened to a violent blue. His eyes rolled upward in their sockets.

"Jules..."

Far in the distance he saw their friends approach. They must have seen the commotion, or heard Tony's cries for help.

Julian dropped to his knees and eased forward. He reached down.

And slipped the gold watch off his brother's wrist.

As the bumps smoothed out, he swept into a side run where the snow was light and soft. This trail had been cleared decades before by the community of Jawbone Ridge, in order to give skiers access to the town and bring in their share of tourists' dollars. Julian sometimes stopped on his way back to town in order to clear the snow from the small brown sign at the side of the run, run his gloved fingers through the troughs of the carved yellow letters and the arrow pointing right.

At the moment the sign was barely visible, but it would be pointless to clear the snow away. He flashed past, catching a flat bit of air, then driving his edge into the final turn. He lowered himself over his skis and took the last bit in a hurry, eager to be back indoors.

The run narrowed and wound through a small stand of evergreens. A tall dark shape appeared through the snow, its long windows glowing with a pale yellow light. Julian pulled up at the edge of the tree line and popped off his skis. He slung them over his shoulder and carried them to the side of the hotel and into the mudroom and left them with the others outside the kitchen door. Judging by the collection of footgear, everyone was here except for Kate, who was skiing in from a green run after they'd parted at the top of the lift.

"You go ahead," she'd told him. "I can't ski in this. I feel like I'm going to wrap myself around a tree."

"I'll go slow," he said. "You can follow me."

"Your slow and mine are two different things. Go on—I'm not skiing a diamond in this stuff."

He should have stayed with her, to make sure she got back safely. That would have been the gallant thing to do. But gallantry had never been his strong suit.

He kicked Eric's boots aside and sat his in the corner next to Celia's, then gave himself a brush down to get the snow off his shoulders and out of his hair. He unzipped his coat and hung it up to dry on a peg by the window. It gave him a peculiar warm feeling to see all their coats hung up that way. Everyone would be inside, waiting, and Celia would have something ready to eat, an open bottle of wine on the table. He wished he could burst in the door, calling, "Honey, I'm home!" like in an old-time sitcom or a black-and-white movie. The kitchen at the Blackbird felt that way.

He opened the door.

The bottom scraped on something, as though a piece of wood or glass was trapped underneath. He put his head around the door to investigate.

An unfamiliar smell assailed him—coppery, acidic. A scent he felt he should know, that raised the hairs on the back of his neck and sent a cold river of adrenaline down his spine.

The room was in a shambles. The floor was strewn with broken glass and crockery, and a chair had been overturned and was lying on its side against the cupboard doors. A can of paint must have tipped over, he could see a pool of it spreading across the floor.

He stared at it uneasily.

Blue paint, it was supposed to be. The cans had been lined up on the floor, dots of color on each lid to show what was inside. Turquoise blue. Celia had talked about it, said how pretty that paint would be in her kitchen. But the paint on the floor wasn't blue; it was red. Dark, dark red.

Now he remembered that smell. It was the scent of emergency rooms.

The scent of blood.

He took a cautious step into the room.

Rory was lying on his back in the paint. Oh, God, wait, no. Not paint. The paint was blood, a huge perfect pool of it like a cartoon drawing. Rory's eyes were half-open and vacant, with a dull film over the irises. His mouth was crusted around the edges, his teeth streaked pink, with lines of dark red drying between them like spilled wine.

Julian stood perfectly still. His own blood raced inward, so that his arms and legs felt empty and his torso overfull. He reached numbly for the countertop and stared down at Rory in disbelief.

He'd just seen him. Just this morning. Big, young, sandy-haired kid. This morning Rory had been chopping wood—and not even with a chain saw, but with an ax like Paul-fucking-Bunyan. A huge pile of logs lay beside him, ready to be hauled inside and stacked next to the fireplace. He'd stripped out of his jacket, and a cloud of steam rose around his head as he swung the ax and sank it cleanly into the heart of the wood. The log split apart with a thick crack.

He'd looked up smiling, wiping his forehead with the back of his glove.

"Taking the Plunge this morning?" he said.

"Thought I might." Julian set his skis against the wall as he pulled on his hat. "Why don't you meet us up there?"

"I might, if Celia lets me out of here. Got my eye on the bowl today, though."

"Jesus, son, it'll be running with avies today. Don't break your head."

Rory grinned, his teeth flashing white in the sunshine. "Okay, Grandpa."

Julian had hopped into his bindings and slid away without a word, Rory's confident young voice echoing in his head. *Okay, Grandpa.*

Arrogant prick.

Now here he was, blue-lipped and preternaturally still. Empty. His heavy chest and shoulders and legs seemed full of latent power, but it was the strength of a Thoroughbred in peak condition that breaks a leg before crossing the finish line. His brawn was worthless now. A big, beautiful waste.

For a fleeting moment, gazing down at Rory, Julian felt his own body throbbing with life. The pulse in his ear. The dizzying push-pull of his lungs. His very uprightness felt like winning.

But on its heels came a rush of fear, swarming up the back of his neck. An impulse to call for help, to be surrounded by other living souls.

The phone was in the common room. Julian crossed the kitchen, avoiding the shards of ceramic and glass, and rounded the corner to the side table at the foot of the stairs where the phone sat. As he picked up the receiver, he turned and got a second shock.

The side door was standing open. Through it he saw Eric lying in the snow outside. One arm was wedged underneath his body, the other flung out beside him and bent at a strange angle, palm up, his legs stretched perfectly straight like a felled tree.

The phone hummed a dial tone.

For the first time, Julian realized how quiet it was. His thoughts on finding Rory had not progressed to the point of wondering what happened. But they went there now. His mind collapsed to a small, dense point, spiraling inward, centered around a name.

Celia.

A sharp bang cracked the stillness.

He dropped the phone and plunged across to the stairs. His legs had gone numb, heavy, and the staircase loomed above him. He stumbled upward, dragging himself along with his arms, as if his body had divided in two: one part sodden with dread, the other disbelieving, clear-eyed, certain she was just as he left her.

She wasn't here; she couldn't be. She must have taken Rory's truck around the mountain to Telluride. Maybe into Montrose for a hardware run—they did that all the time. Not here, she wasn't here, it was too quiet, she was far from this nightmare

Julian had stumbled into, she was far away and safe, of course she was. Of course she was.

But at the back of his mind was Celia's voice—her ordinary, everyday, sleep-husky voice telling them over breakfast, "Today I'm going to spackle the kitchen and tape it off, maybe get started on those pillows for the blue room..."

She hadn't planned to leave the hotel.

Julian staggered up the curving steps to the long hallway and the row of doors, four on either side. He pounded at them with his fists as he passed.

"Celia! Celia!"

A horrifying vision swam through his mind: Celia on her back, her mouth full of blood. Eyes gone dull and sightless, fixed on some distant point as if searching for the source of a far-off sound.

His mind tripped along a series of fragmentary sentences.

Oh, God...not...not, not, not...it's fine, she's not even here...

The door at the end of the hall was locked. Julian rattled the handle, banged at the door with his open palm, began to pummel it with his shoulder. He backed up and charged at it. Once, twice. On the third try, the doorjamb cracked apart. He kicked it open and he was through.

He edged into the room.

A small shape lay huddled on the bed—laundry, he thought, weak with relief. She's left her laundry, that's all it is. But a thick tawny braid snaked across the pillow, tied at the end with a piece of twine and adorned with a sparrow's feather.

Julian's knees locked. He braced himself against the wall to stay upright. A wave of inundating heat passed through him, from the top of his head to his feet, like diving headfirst into a pool of hot water. His lungs ached for air, but his chest had constricted so tight he couldn't draw a breath. His tongue tripped at the roof of his mouth.

He crept stiffly up to the bed as though he might wake her.

His eyes slid over the bed and came to rest on her hand, drooped around the gun. Her thumb was curled around the trigger. Her lips were still moist, slightly parted; a tendril of hair lay unmoving across her mouth.

He stared at it, all the baby-fine hairs like a veil, the edge of one pearly tooth gleaming through.

A burst of hot water filled his mouth.

His eyes darted from her face. He noticed for the first time a sheet of folded paper on the pillow, with her handwriting across the front:

Julian~
I know what you did.

From downstairs, the silence was ripped by a low-pitched scream.

Kate. Kate finding Rory. Her screams deepened to a guttural, rhythmic roar like the cries of a doomed animal. Julian would think of that sound later, would replay it over and over in the long nights to come, feeling again the shivered rise of hair on his arms and the back of his neck, the near-release of his bladder, checked at the last moment to fester hot and agitated in his groin.

He bent to the pillow, plucked up the note with the very tips of his fingers, folded it into quivery squares that he tucked inside his pocket. He couldn't look at Celia, couldn't stroke her hair, couldn't touch her skin even to smooth her eyelids closed. She was gone. What was left of her terrified him.

He backed out of the room, toward the sound of Kate's unending screams.

What were they fighting about? the sheriff wanted to know.

Kate and Julian stared at him blankly, hunched side by side

under blue woolen blankets in the back of a bright white ambulance.

They didn't turn their heads to look at each other.

Sir? Do you know what might have set this off?

The question filled the space like water. Julian could hardly breathe.

Much later, Julian pulled up in front of Kate's house. A sheet of snow drifted through the beams of the headlights.

She sat beside him, sedated, silent, staring through the light at the dark cluster of pines beside the road. Her expression in profile was impossible to read.

He got out of the car, pulled her overnight bag from the trunk and started to carry it up the driveway to the front door. But she stepped out, blocking his path. She took the bag from his hand.

Julian shoved his hands into his pockets.

"Do you—" He cleared his throat. "Will I come by tomorrow?"

Her gaze shifted vaguely to his face.

She turned and went up the walk, a small lone figure, hunched and careful like an old woman. She opened the door and went inside without looking back.

One hour previously: 3:33 p.m.

"I don't know if I want to share you anymore."

The words bubbled up Rory's throat and formed on his lips and burst into the room. For a moment he felt a wild relief at hearing them. Finally, the truth was out. He couldn't take it back, play it off, retreat or rephrase. He'd said what he wanted to say, for better or worse.

Then he turned, following Celia's gaze, and felt the relief ebb away.

Eric was in the kitchen.

Outside, a thick icicle fell past the kitchen window and embedded itself in the snowbank with a tiny hiss. Its falling seemed to open a fissure in the floor of the room, widening to a chasm, with Rory and Celia on one side and Eric teetering on the other.

The color drained from Eric's face. He was looking not at Rory but at Celia, his eyes flickering in place.

"It's just something we say," Celia said in her unhurried way. "It doesn't mean anything."

But her neck was reddened from Rory's stubbled cheek and a sexual musk hung thick in the air. Celia's denial dropped into the silence like a rock into the sea.

Rory opened his mouth and closed it without speaking. This was the day he had long dreaded—the day it all would end. He'd thought it would have been Eric to break free, to become restless or demanding or—and Rory was ashamed of how often he'd wished for this—to become unstable and pull himself away from Celia for her own good. They had talked about it more than once.

"I want her to be happy," Eric had said. "If I really go off the rails, man, make sure she kicks me to the curb."

"You're not going to do that," Rory said. "You're fine now. Everything's under control."

"Am I? Sometimes..."

He'd never finished the sentence, but Rory had seen his fist contract, the strange prick of light in Eric's eyes that made Rory feel as if he were being sighted through the scope of a rifle.

Same as he was seeing now.

Eric crossed the room slowly, his feet scraping along the floor, head thrust out ahead of him until he was right in front of Celia. He lowered his nose to her hair and inhaled, ran the knuckle of his first finger over her lip. He took her face between his hands and kissed her openmouthed, his shoulders bowed and tense, thumbs pressing dents into the skin under her jaw.

"You smell like him," he said against her lips.

With one hand he shoved her away. Celia stumbled back. Her head banged hard against the wall. Her eyes widened, fixed on Eric, one hand moving slowly up to the back of her head.

"You're a cheap girl, baby. A carnival prize. My dad always said you were worthless, and you know what? He was right."

Rage erupted in Rory's chest and flared down his limbs. In three strides he had covered the distance, clenched Eric's shirt in his fist and dragged him away from Celia. A dull red light suffused his vision. The blood howled in his ears.

"It's okay," Celia said. Her voice floated over him, barely penetrating the roar of his own heartbeat. "Rory, I'm okay."

Eric pushed himself free. He looked Rory full in the face, a crescent of white showing at the bottom of his irises, two hard lines from his nose to the corners of his mouth.

"You don't want to share," he said. "*You* don't."

He spread his arms wide. Rory had the sensation that he was watching Eric fall from a great height, like he'd lost his grip on Eric and could only stand helplessly by as his friend's body slipped farther and farther away, plummeting toward the earth. Eric's voice vibrated as if he were yelling, but Rory had to strain to hear him.

"This is mine, brother," Eric said, smacking the door with his palm—the door that they had removed and painted and rehung together, with sweetly oiled hinges and a new brass knob. "This is my kitchen. This is my wall. This is my table. These are my goddamn pots and pans." He grabbed a wooden spoon and banged it against the pots that were hanging on their rack over the kitchen island. The rack Rory had built. "My dishes, my fridge, my oven, my girl."

He dug into the pocket of his jeans and pulled out a jagged human tooth. He slammed it down on the counter and jabbed at it with his forefinger.

"My fight," he said.

A wave of dizzying grief swept over Rory. It was gone. Everything they had was gone, as swiftly as that. A stranger was looking through Eric's eyes, and Rory couldn't find a single word to say to him.

"So when you say you don't want to share," Eric said, "I don't know what the fuck you're talking about."

"No one's sharing." Celia's voice was so quiet after Eric's that it seemed to be coming from another room. "This isn't about that."

Eric swayed on his feet as his head swiveled around. He looked at Celia as if he'd just remembered she was there.

"I'm not—" she began.

"You're a slut, honey, is what you are."

Celia looked back at him, unsurprised. Not shocked as Rory was at the ugly word, but shaking her head as if she'd heard him use it before and was only objecting to the context.

The weight of Rory's anger pressed at the top of his head. His fists hung at his sides like two large stones.

"You fucking prick. Say it again."

"He's drunk, Rory, just—"

"Don't you defend me." Eric's voice rang through the kitchen, shooting upward, a high-pitched, vibrating trumpet of words. "I'm the only honest person in this room. Defend yourself."

He edged toward her, his chin jutting upward like a pointed finger.

"You're the problem here. You've got us coming and going,

don't you, baby. You're the common denominator for every goddamn problem we have, and you know why that is? It's because you're selfish." He wiped his mouth with the back of his hand. "You're the problem. You're the one who can't let her pussy get dry."

Rory started forward, his head swimming with disoriented outrage. A gag line raced through his mind: *Who are you, and what have you done with Eric?*

Celia held out her hand to stop him. Her arm was stiff and trembling, but her voice sounded groggy, as if she were just waking from a thick sleep.

"Rory, don't, it's okay—"

"Don't you defend me!" Eric's face was plummy with rage. "You're a witch, goddamn you, fucking with people's heads."

"I'm sorry," Celia said. "We'll talk about it. Rory, don't—"

"What did I fucking say." Eric's eyes were wild; his eyebrows jerked up his forehead. He rushed at her, his hands stretched open. He caught her by the shoulders and slammed her against the wall.

This time Celia's cry was more pain than surprise, a bleat of distress as if from a small animal. It severed the last thread of restraint holding Rory in place. He sprang across the space, hauled Eric upright, drew back and swung hard for his jaw. The blow landed with a wooden snap, and Eric careened backward. His flailing arms swept the dishes off the counter as he fell. They tumbled to the floor with a deafening crash.

Rory charged after him. The weight in his arms had suddenly lifted, and his fist rose and fell as though rebounding from a single impulse. He couldn't feel the impact of the blows or hear the thud of Eric's head against the floor. The explosive force of his fury held him in a state of suspended, almost orgasmic release.

From a distance came the wail of Celia's voice.

"Rory! Rory! Stop stop *stop!*"

She was on him now, her arms wrapped around his chest, head tucked between his shoulder blades trying to pull him off.

"Please, Rory! Rory!"

He staggered to his feet, legs splayed, reaching with one hand for the countertop to steady himself. The blood rang in his ears. His hand throbbed with pain, but he felt it only dully, a twinge that warned of some deeper injury he might discover later.

Eric crawled to his knees. Blood dripped from his nose and lips, landing with thick wet plops on the pine floorboards they had refinished together only weeks before. After a moment, he struggled to his feet, shrugging off Celia's hand. He lurched from the room, feet clattering through the broken crockery on the floor. His footsteps thundered up the stairs and went quiet.

Celia whispered his name, like she had when they were children and she was at his bedroom door, scared of a thunderstorm or just afraid to be alone in the darkness. Her face was greenly pale, her eyes huge and glassy with shock.

His anger drained away. In its place came an agonizing guilt. Why hadn't he chosen another time to talk to her, bitten his tongue and waited for his need for her to subside? He had spoken at exactly the wrong time, and now everything they'd dreamed of and worked for was gone.

A tide of nausea rocked him. He rushed across the room and vomited in the kitchen sink.

Above them, a thump of boots in the hallway. A door opening. Something heavy hitting the floor.

"It will be okay," Celia said behind him.

Rory splashed his face with cold water and dried himself with a dishcloth. He leaned against the sink, dragging deep breaths into his lungs.

He turned to face her.

"It will, it will be okay." Her gray lips barely moved over the syllables. "Right?"

He pulled her into his arms, swayed her back and forth as he stroked her hair. At the back of her head was an egg-shaped knot that brought another twinge of sickness up his throat.

"No," he said. "This is over."

From behind him came a loud mechanical click. Celia's body stiffened in his arms. He felt the air leave her body in a rush.

Eric was in the doorway. His face was smeared with blood and his left eye had begun to swell shut. Dimly he registered the flatness of Eric's expression, that uncanny glint in his eye.

By the time Rory saw the gun, it was pointed straight at him.

In the second it took for Eric to pull the trigger, Rory remembered a story they had watched on TV years before. A woman was relating the experience of being shot, describing how she was able to trace the wavering spiral of the bullet on its trajectory. She knew she was being shot, she said, because she could see the bullet's nose heading straight for her, during which time she had an entire conversation with herself about how it couldn't be happening.

A lively debate had followed in Eric's living room, with Rory arguing strenuously against the possibility of such a thing and Eric in strident support of the science behind it.

"It could happen," Eric had said. "The human brain is a trip, my friend, never doubt it."

Now, as a tiny puff of smoke popped from the gun, Rory realized Eric had been right. The space between trigger and impact widened to a cosmic expanse. In it was their whole story. Action and reaction, decision and responsibility. An accumulation of events leading finally to the only possible outcome.

And he thought, with a tiny inner shrug to concede a lifelong argument:

That bullet is definitely wobbling.

Finally, impact. The world tipped abruptly sideways and upside down. Time recoiled. Rory landed half inside the pantry and lay staring at the ceiling, disoriented, trying to puzzle it out: How had Eric punched him from clear across the room?

That couldn't happen. It must be a dream. All of it, the whole surreal series of events. He must be really in his bed back home, waiting in a twilight sleep for the scent of pancakes and bacon to come wafting under his door, for Celia's childlike voice to call him down. He could hear her now: "Wake up, Rory! Rory, wake up..." Soon he would get out of bed and shuffle downstairs, and they would all sit down at his mother's yellow Formica table for breakfast. Later he and Celia would take the Wasatch Trail alongside Bear Creek, where Eric would be waiting with an extra fishing rod and three peanut butter sandwiches, and Celia would stretch out on a sunny rock with a book and a can of ginger ale, smiling gently at her story, at the sunshine, and at them.

The weight was pouring from his body. He felt the rushing tow of some thick watery force that had caught him in its current and was bearing him steadily upward.

From somewhere below him came a silvery ringing, like the Christmas bells on Mike Bonner's horses as they pulled a load of tourists up the streets of Telluride under a bowl of glittering stars. He lay back in the bed of the wagon, his body rocking gently, a slow coldness seeping into his limbs. Someone was calling his name, but he was too entranced by the star-field to answer.

A milky light came into his eyes. Through it he could see that the stars were moving. Swirling past his eyes, like the jar of fireflies he'd set at Celia's feet on some long-ago camping trip. The insects rose like sparks around their faces. He moved closer, ran his thumb over her eyelids and upturned brow, her lower lip, the slim column of her throat. Her eyes held his, unblinking, points of light skating across their surface. Then she was running down the hill with the jar in her hand, spilling the last of the fireflies in a sparkling trail behind her.

He could see them now. So many of them, a shower of darting white lights so thick they had coalesced into a single pulsing orb. Its warmth beckoned him like a friendly sun.

Celia, it's beautiful. Come with me...

The gun fell at Eric's feet with a heavy thud. His hand, his whole arm was suddenly light, as if it could float up from his body like a balloon, tethered at the shoulder. The sound of the gunshot rang in his ears.

He closed his eyes. Blinked open, disbelieving the scene in front of him.

Celia was on the ground next to Rory. Glancing up, screaming something Eric couldn't hear. Her face was horribly twisted, her lips snapping open and shut. Her hands were slick with blood. There was blood on her jeans and bare feet. The end of her braid was a paintbrush, dipped in red. She bent over Rory, her mouth on his, and their faces were bloody now, too, and here she was trying to lift him with both arms around his chest, but his head and arms drooped heavily back to the floor, as from a far-off distance he heard her voice rebounding to his ears like an echo:

Ror-reeeee...

Over and over, like it was the only word she knew or had ever known.

Eric clapped his hands over his ears and rushed from the

kitchen, across the great room and out the other side. He burst through the door and slammed it behind him.

Here it was quiet. White. The world was a vacuum, devoid of every color and every sound but the rasping, drowning gulps of air that clawed at his throat. The flakes were floating straight down from the sky, spinning past the smudged shape of the hotel behind him and the ravine below.

A movement from the corner of his eye. His stomach lurched. It was his father, through the window. Inside the Blackbird Hotel! His face was bloody, the way it had been on the night Rory swung on him and knocked out a tooth. He remembered the way Rory had rushed forward, impatient with Eric, a huge unstoppable force while Eric stood with his knees locked, stunned and humiliated in front of Celia. His father had replaced that tooth afterward, but the false one never quite matched, so that when he smiled, the tooth gleamed whitely inside his left cheek, drawing Eric's eye like a beacon.

That was Eric's fight to finish, but Rory had taken it away. He'd always said that Eric would settle things with his dad in his own time; one day he would feel the power surging through his arm and he'd let it fly and would never be beaten again. None of that had happened, because of Rory.

A ghostly pain stabbed in his jaw. He saw Rory's face again, demented with rage and righteousness, his arm flying up and down like an overwound toy. The sickening snap of bone. The pulpy rhythms of impact.

The figure in the window raised a hand to his face, and Eric realized with a shudder that he was staring at his own reflection.

The silence bloomed around him.

What had Rory said, at the end? Standing with his arms around Celia, then turning, his gaze locked on the gun. A quick spin to push Celia behind him. And then the bullet struck and Rory fell, his eyes wide-open all the way down, not even surprised but with a look of bemused resignation on his face like he and Eric had been arguing about music and he'd finally surrendered the point.

Rory must have known they were coming to this. Celia's personality was too fluid ever to hold up her end of the three-legged table they had built. It had been up to Rory and Eric to find a balance between them, and Rory must have realized from the start that it didn't exist.

This is over, Rory had said, and that was true. They had finished it, both of them, all of them, together.

The door opened. A shaft of warm light burst through the snow, turning the snowflakes a pale gold. Celia came out and stood on the step. Her sweater was splotched with circles of poppy-red blood, and her bare feet left two crimson stains in the snow. Ribbons of steam rose from the hot wet blood on her cheek and hair and her bloody fingers, curved around the butt of the gun. She came down the steps. Her feet crunched in the snow, leaving a trail of pinkened footprints behind her. As she reached him, she started to shake. Violent tremors tore through her body and tightened her neck so that the cords stood out like rope beneath her jaw. He waited for her to raise her arms, wrap them around her body to warm herself and stop that awful trembling. But she just stood there with her arms straight down at her sides like she'd forgotten how to use them.

He took an automatic step toward her, as if he still could offer comfort.

"Celia," he said.

The gun swung up, weaving at the end of her arm. At the businesslike clack of the hammer, he felt the numbness split by a first blade of fear.

"Why?" she said. "Oh, God..."

She raised her face to his. The two halves had come undone, with one half drooping and inanimate as if after a stroke, the other drawn back from her teeth in a horrible grimace.

"He was going to leave us, Cee."

"No."

"He was breaking us—he was pulling it all apart."

She shook her head, a loose little series of shakes, swaying on her feet.

"He didn't want this anymore, you heard him. Look at me—look what he did. It was supposed to be the three of us, it was supposed to be the Blackbird. I was protecting us. I was trying to save us. Cee, you believe me?"

She had stopped listening. She frowned, in that strange way she had of staring right through him and out the other side. The shivers stopped abruptly. Her head swiveled toward the hotel, as if she'd heard a faint sound in the distance.

"We have to catch up with him." She swiped at her face with the back of her hand, leaving a streak of blood on her cheek. "We have to hurry."

Fear crackled at the nape of his neck. He turned to where she was looking, half expecting to see Rory on his feet, smiling, beckoning with one hand as if at the start of a difficult run. *Come on, man. What are you waiting for? Last one down's a rotten egg...*

Celia looked up at him with wild, faraway eyes.

"It's today," she said. "Imagine. Even when we woke up this morning. Did you know?"

"No, no, listen." He took her face in his hands and kissed her. Her mouth was salty with blood and tears. Hot things, but her lips were very cold. "It was an accident, Cee. I swear. You don't have to do any of this. We can hide him—we can run away."

"From the Blackbird?" she said. "Oh, no. No, we can't do that."

The gun nudged hard against his chest. He dropped his hands and stepped back. His heel struck the rocky half wall at the edge of the property. He glanced back to the ghostly chasm below.

"Celia, don't—"

"But I promised. You didn't want to live alone, you said. You told me this was too big a love to lose. You made me promise to save you from the afterward. And you were right. That's why we have to hurry now and catch him. Just close your eyes, and I'll close mine—"

An icy terror rinsed through his limbs. His voice shook in a peculiar way, as though all the air in him was gone. "I don't want to die, Celia, please."

"Shh, you're not. We're just going to find Rory. You'll see. I know the way from here."

"Celia, Jesus, don't—"

She leaned closer, pulled his head down so her lips were at his ear. The barrel of the gun was a hard little pebble against his chest.

"It's okay," she said. "Count your breaths, like Dr. Paul says. That's the trick. In and out. I'll do it with you, deep, deep breaths."

"Please, Cee."

Her urgent whisper rushed at his ear. Her arm went around him, cold fingers like a talon at the back of his skull.

"Shh…"

"Please! Celia!"

"One…two…shh, three…"

Counting his breaths now. In and out, lungfuls of cold fire, deep as he could hold them. And Celia's chest expanding in time, her breath crackling along the hot tear tracks on his cheek.

"It was him," Eric cried. "All along."

"No, shh, I was only ever helping...I'll help you find him now, shh...seven...eight..."

He counted six more breaths before Celia pulled the trigger.

Eric had known dozens of constellations by heart. Romantic names they had, too, Orion and Pegasus and Andromeda. In the summer, the three of them would lie in the bed of Rory's pickup while Eric pointed out which clusters to look for and how not to be fooled by a passing satellite. He said all stars were ghosts, that you could never really see them. The most distant stars were billions of light-years away and had long since burned out. Only the light remained.

People lived with ghosts every day, Eric said. "Even if the light has to travel only a foot between you and me, what you see around you has already happened. I'm a ghost, even as you see me. We're always operating on separate planes of existence, then and now. We only think we're really together."

Celia never liked the sound of that. She had stretched out her arm and stared at her hand, outlined against the starry sky. There was distance even between her eyes and fingertips.

"How will I ever know where I am?" she said.

She stood now at her bedroom window. Through the snow she thought she could see a faint smear of light from the house across the way, where she and Rory had lived as children. Another family owned the place now. The house looked almost exactly the same as it had in their day, but it felt altogether different. It had moved on without moving at all.

Houses were smarter than people that way. People carried the past inside them; houses simply emptied and refilled again with other lives, maybe with a fresh coat of paint or a new front door, but looking more or less the same on the outside. With people it was the other way around.

She pressed her hand against the window, wondering what would become of the Blackbird after they were gone. Tonight the rooms would be filled with men and women in uniforms, the flashes of photographs, people gathering in the snowy parking lot to whisper about what might have happened inside the hotel. And afterward…

Afterward the Blackbird would look exactly the same.

She turned from the window. Her feet were shot through with the white-hot needles of retreating numbness, but her arms felt as if they'd been severed at the shoulder. She looked without interest at the gun in her hand.

Julian's gun.

It felt like years had passed since Rory first came into the kitchen. She sat down at her desk, staring at the wall as she tried to remember what she had wanted to say to him. It had seemed so important at the time.

Julian. Something to do with Julian.

An image came to mind, of her father and herself at a long-ago carnival. She was standing with a huge mallet in her hand, three rows of holes in front of her out of which the head of a rubber mole would pop up and down. The idea was to smack the head with the mallet before it went back inside the hole. She hadn't been very good at the game but had fallen about laughing as her father teased her: *Choo-eee, that critter gettin' confident, chère, smack him now, soon as he pops him's head outta there…*

Funny, now that she thought of it, how like her father Julian was. Same dark hair, the big lazy smile. But underneath was something cruel. Julian had the same habit of looking down his cheek at her, fixing her with one dark brown eye, smiling in a way that made her unsure what he really was smiling at.

The carnival image shifted. Julian's face, where her father's had been. Julian's voice saying, "Don't let him up."

And Eric, whose face and words stood out in sharp detail: "You're a cheap girl, baby. You're a carnival prize."

Eric had been strange ever since he returned from Alaska. Off his meds, asking for weed, talking too fast and with that prickly, wiry energy around him that hadn't been there when he left. He said he was worried. He talked about the plumber who'd killed his wife, later staring at Rory across the dinner table as Julian drew out the details of Rory's daring rescue of the skier on the cliff. Right after Eric had said that he hadn't skied the Isthmus.

Julian had made sure Eric always had someone to compare himself with.

I've seen a lot of skiers in my day, and I've come to think physical courage is a good measure of the man. You have that...

For a long moment, Celia didn't breathe. The story played out in her head from Julian's point of view. A hundred small interferences. Lifting Rory up, smacking Eric down. Putting distance between them where before there had been none.

Or had the distance been there always? Had Julian, with his uncanny nose for weakness, deliberately exploited their differences in order to drive them apart?

Why would he do that?

She remembered the way he had waited beside the swimming pool, taunting her, insisting that she acknowledge the reasons she always avoided him.

She had thought herself clever, standing in front of him with the water streaming down her body. But didn't it feel good in exactly the way he'd predicted? Wasn't there also that fiendish rush of attraction underneath her annoyance as he turned her around? *Jesus, baby, and I thought I was competitive...*

Well, he was right. He'd thrown down the challenge right

from the beginning, and she took it up without stopping to consider the stakes.

She set the gun on the desk and rubbed absently at the blood on her hands.

What would Rory and Eric want her to do about Julian? Julian hadn't killed them, after all. He had only talked. If she waited, she would kill him, too, and that would be murder.

She thought about Julian, lying dead in the kitchen beside Rory, or outside in the snow with Eric. It would feel wonderful to kill Julian and if they were anywhere else she would do it. But not here, not inside the Blackbird Hotel.

Besides, Rory wouldn't want her to be a murderer. And Eric would have a better idea.

Next to the gun was a pad of paper. Creamy, beautiful pages with a tracing of ivy in silver around the border. Eric had found it at a shop in Vegas and said it reminded him of her.

"You can write me a love letter, Celia," he'd said. "Full of pretty words."

Well, she had tried. But language had never come easy to her, and in the end she'd given up.

She wasn't like Julian, who understood the power of words, who tossed them around as if they were coins from a bottomless purse. He'd spent a lot of them on Celia. He had annoyed her and teased her and fed her ego, dropping thousands and thousands of words—trying in his poisonous, destructive way to give her something she couldn't get from Rory or Eric: his undivided attention.

The afternoon light was fading. In the distance, she could hear the rusty shriek of a crow. There wasn't much time, Julian and Kate would be back soon. What would Rory and Eric want her to do?

The clock sounded downstairs, a chime for the quarter hour.

She reached for the paper, drew it toward her, took up a pen and began to write.

Julian~

I know what you did.

Maybe this was the end you imagined. Maybe it just got out of hand. Or maybe you're like the rest of us, giving and getting the wrong kind of love. I could wait, I guess, and ask you. But it doesn't seem to matter now.

I only wanted to tell you that I was wrong about the sparrow. He looked dead but he wasn't. I can hear him now by the window. He's out there in the snow, singing…

AUGUST 2014

KATE VAUGHN STOOD at the edge of the Ridge, looking down. No blood on the river rocks, no body tangled in the deadfall. Julian must have landed in the steep brown tumble of water and been swept away.

She wrapped her hand around the pine bough as Julian had done, her heart pounding in anger like a cheated child's. She had been watching minutes ago when Julian launched himself from this spot, arms outstretched and reaching through the hazy air as if trying to catch a bird in flight. She'd been watching, too, the night before, from an upstairs window, when Emma flew out the front doors and tripped across the lot to Julian's car, looking over her shoulder the whole way like she thought he was going to chase her down. Kate wondered what had happened between them—whether Emma had seen that ghost she was looking for, or something even more terrifying in Julian that had sent her over the edge.

Kate had been startled herself at the change in him. His face had broadened over the years, his eyes rolling deep in their sockets, alighting ponderously around the room as if dragged along by the turning of his head. It reminded her of the way Eric looked, just before that sudden explosive movement when he heaved himself out of the chairlift and fell into the white-out: haunted, hollow, as though you could scream into his mouth and hear your own voice echoing back.

She gripped the rough branch, scanning the riverbed. On the rocks below, five feet down the embankment, her eye was drawn by a scrap of white paper, too clean to have been there very long. She worked her way down, careful of her new suede boots, until she could pluck the paper from the thorny brush and clamber back to solid ground.

She unfolded the paper and caught her breath.

The note was unsigned. The words went all the way to the bottom and right off the edge of the page. But the handwriting was unmistakable, slanted and generous, with curvy marks like commas where the dots should go.

Kate read the note.

And smiled.

Stupid Celia.

Celia thought what happened was Julian's doing. Julian, playing on Eric's insecurities, convincing him to stop his meds. Julian building Rory up even as he tore Eric down. Julian driving a wedge between the three of them by finding the cracks in their relationship and pounding in the chisel.

Hell, Julian even blamed himself. He was so caught up in his game that he never stopped to notice who was jerking the puppet strings.

Cute little Katie. Always such a sweetheart, taking it down the throat and up the ass for Julian. And the ego of him to think she liked it! That he was her first choice!

The thought of Julian brought a fresh surge of anger. Kate ground her teeth, staring down at the note.

Maybe this was the end you imagined.

Well, it wasn't the end Kate had imagined. What she had in mind involved a fight, maybe, some final and unrecoverable rift between Celia and Rory and Eric—with herself and Rory starting over again, far away from Jawbone Ridge.

She had tried many times before to break him away from Celia. Ever since that afternoon at the Nugget Theatre, when instead of saying hello and taking a seat beside them, she remained slumped under her hood in the back row, staring in a dumb paralysis at the shadowy heads in front of her. Celia had always seemed so vague, unphysical; that faraway look in her eyes had made her seem like a very young old maid. But there she was in a public theater with her feet propped wide apart on the seat backs, both boys turned sideways in their chairs, small sighs and a scuffling sound when the action of the movie lifted away. And Rory—Rory!—kissing Celia, his face only a smudge in the darkness but clearly leaning in and over, dipping in a slow rhythm above her.

It was disgusting. They were practically brother and sister! Yet even with the fury the memory inspired, Kate found herself thinking of that night all the time. Of herself, in Celia's place. Eric's hand between her legs, and Rory—big, golden, beautiful Rory—leaning down to kiss her, her face lifting to his. She had dreamed herself into that chair a thousand times, imagined what it would be like, as in her wide iron bed she let her hand slip down and stroke the fantasy to life.

It should have been easy to do something with the story: *You wouldn't believe what Jenna Martin said about Celia and Rory. So gross! And totally not true, I can't believe she'd even say something like that…* The rumors ignited easily and raced through the school, but by that time Rory and Eric were gone, and Celia, with that peculiar immunity to public opinion, had simply drifted out the end of the corridor and never returned. And her leaving seemed to have little to do with the rumors. Her mind was simply not there.

Kate had tried again. After high school she went straight to college in Vegas, where Rory had been working in his uncle's construction company. Finally, she thought, she'd have him to herself. She imagined a life for them—dating, making love, moving in together. Maybe getting married one day. Kate was a catch. Rory used to tell her so all the time: "Pretty little rich girl, you'll have pretty little children and a house on the hill."

But he was gone before she even got to Vegas. He'd gone back to Celia.

Celia, who never left Jawbone Ridge. Who never even tried.

In a way Kate understood his fascination. She'd been mesmerized like everyone else as Celia—that strange, awkward girl—grew into her strangeness, cultivated it, the way a homely child will sometimes grow into its face and become striking as an adult. Celia was like that. Her kaleidoscopic appeal became more and more surreal as she got older—you almost couldn't believe the way the angles and planes of her face could arrange themselves so beautifully one second and could utterly repel you the next. You had to keep looking, to know which way she was going to be. You hated to miss the shift.

Even Julian, as self-centered and egotistical a man as Kate had ever met, had fallen under her spell. Julian, who was supposed to belong to Kate. Not that she wanted him, exactly, but she sure as hell did not want him loving Celia, along with everyone else.

Or hating her. Really, it was impossible to tell.

She wasn't sorry that Celia was gone.

But Rory…

Big, beautiful Rory McFarland. Dead. His body lying heavy and ungraceful on the floor, his mouth half-open and full of blood. She still could taste the sickness rising up her throat, with no nausea even to warn her—just a complete and terrible emptying, the bitter taste of bile mixed with the tannic scent of his blood. She was sure she could smell it sometimes in the kitchen of the Blackbird Hotel. She would be going about her business and then—a smell, a presence, as if someone were hiding just around the corner, watching her through a crack in the door, and she would suddenly be bitterly cold—not from outside, not the ghostly chill you'd hear about, which turned your breath to fog, but the kind that crept from the pit of your stomach and spread like ice through your limbs.

She'd rush from the room and into the sunlight, backing across the parking lot as if the Blackbird itself was giving chase, and she'd stand there in a shivery sweat with her heart hammering. But the sun never truly warmed her. The cold had settled in her bones.

Kate shuddered.

Maybe it was the Blackbird, warping her perceptions. The hotel had been making Kate definitely twitchy. A warped, freaky little place, with that long row of doors and the gnarled staircase. Alone in the hotel, she had clung to a fragile bravado, fortified by hot swallows of brandy that seared her throat but seemed to freeze once the liquor reached her stomach. She couldn't trust herself, couldn't trust the walls almost, to stay upright, or the doors to stay closed. She'd more than once caught a flash of movement, a shadow pouring from the corner of her eye—

Jesus. Here we go again.

The Blackbird was only a building, a motley construction of timber and brick. There was nothing to be afraid of. But somehow, in the empty rooms of the old hotel, she never could be comfortable. It was like living inside a desiccated corpse.

Her gaze slid uneasily along the ravine.

The smoke had almost died out. The Blackbird was gone, Julian was gone, and, though she'd brought him here with some notion of meting out his share of the guilt, he'd done her one better. He'd burned the damned place to the ground.

A nervous elation swept through her. She could leave now—she was free!

She would travel. She'd get far away. Her mind ticked through the possibilities. What she needed was a change of scenery. Well-lighted corners, where the buildings sat on the desert floor and were sturdy and brand new. The lights of Vegas flickered briefly in her mind, a street where she'd sat in her car outside Rory's apartment, long after Rory had left it…shadows moving behind the curtains…of strangers, living where he used to live… She gave herself a mental shake. Not Vegas, no. She'd go to the other side of the world, Australia or Brazil, someplace where the earth was flat and sunny, where she could get tan and laid and drunk and forgetful, and she'd leave this whole smoldering mess behind.

Carefully she pressed open the note. Its creases were soft, and the paper bore a slight curve as if Julian had been carrying it in his wallet all this time.

She wouldn't be like him, dragging this story around for the rest of her life. It wasn't as if she'd done anything wrong. Committed a crime, for God's sake. She had talked, and that was all, and the rest of it could not be laid at her feet.

She held the note ready to tear apart, her fingers poised at the edge of the page. On impulse, she lifted the paper to her nose.

Even now, Kate could smell her. That smoky-sweet scent of her hair, the warm hint of vanilla on her skin. Celia's face had faded in her mind. She remained as an afterimage, some shy luminosity, a swirl of flaxen hair through a narrow patch of sunlight.

Kate ran her thumb over the paper.

Somewhere, Celia and Rory and Eric were together as

they had been that day at the Palm, when she had stood not far from where she was standing now, looking down at their intertwined limbs and the water stains drying on the rock. Somewhere they were dancing to music only they could hear, while she and Julian, for all that they had longed to be part of the circle, could only stand on the outside and watch.

She thought again of Julian's leap from the ridge, graceful and unguarded, almost joyful, his arms outstretched, then sweeping back like the wings of a diving bird.

Julian flying, then falling…

His body was somewhere down the ravine, a soft torn husk washed up on the river rocks.

Empty. And alone.

The wind sighed, pushing through the leaves and late summer grass. Down the ridge, the last of the smoke had cleared, leaving a strange hollow spot on the skyline where all her life Kate had been seeing the Blackbird.

She folded the note along its familiar creases. The paper curved into her palm like an empty seashell, but it felt heavy somehow, as if the fibers were shot through with lead or steel and would resist if she tried to tear them. She imagined the page ripped to pieces, drifting on the summer breeze. But her fingers refused to carry out the act.

Later, she thought. Later she would rid herself of this. She'd take it far away, to the other side of the world where the paper would be light and irrelevant and easy to destroy. There was such a place. There had to be. She only had to keep moving until she found it.

With the note in her pocket, tapping gently at her thigh, she turned and started down the crumbling road for Jawbone Ridge.

★★★★★

ACKNOWLEDGMENTS

Deepest thanks to my editor, Michelle Meade, who gave me the freedom to find this story and whose wisdom and careful attention helped bring it to life, and to everyone at MIRA who turned it into something beautiful. Thanks as well to Jeff Kleinman, agent and mensch, and to the circle of writers who inspire me every day with their intelligence and generosity. You are all, in all ways, the very best of friends.

THE UNDOING

AVERIL DEAN

Reader's Guide

1. Rory, Eric and Celia view their relationship as a true, big romance. How did you view their relationship? Do you think it could have survived if not for the interference of Julian and Kate?

2. As we learn more about Eric's past, we realize he's long been struggling with a history of abuse and mental health issues. How do you think his emotions and actions are affected by this history?

3. Celia and Rory describe Eric's manic episodes as him being "in the zone." Discuss how their concern for him in these moments is at odds with the exhilaration and desire they feel when he is crackling with dangerous energy. What effect does this have on their relationship?

4. Julian's obsession with Celia is immediate and extreme, and her disinterest in him only intensifies his desire for her. What do you think is the reason for his fixation? In what ways do the other characters play into it—either purposely or unintentionally?

5. Celia refers in her note to all of them loving each other the wrong way. What does she mean by that?

6. Kate, at the end of the novel, is the last one standing—not even the Blackbird escapes a tragic end. Yet, just like Julian, she isn't able to destroy Celia's note. Why do you think that is? What do you think will become of Kate?

7. Why do you think the author chose a backward-moving timeline to tell this story? How did the unusual structure affect your understanding of the characters and their relationships?

The Undoing is a dark and powerful story about the events that bring three stunning characters together, and the jealousies that tear them apart. What was your inspiration for this novel?

A couple of years ago, I read a story called "All Through the House" by Christopher Coake. It has an unusual structure, beginning with the aftermath of a mass murder and tracing back through time to reveal certain key events leading up to the night of the tragedy. The story is beautifully formed and absolutely chilling, since you are seeing the victims almost as ghosts in their own lives. I began toying with the possibilities of that structure, putting it together with this older idea of an unstable—though consensual—romantic triangle. The reverse timeline seemed to offer an interesting way to walk back through the wreckage and discover the forces that had caused this terrible implosion, exploring the relevance of each character's decisions along the way.

The structure of _The Undoing_ is quite unique—a backward-moving timeline where events and emotions are carefully

revealed as we trace the lives of the characters from adulthood all the way back to their teen and childhood years. Can you talk about your experience writing this story, and the difficulties/advantages you found in using reverse-chronology?

In some ways, the structure of The Undoing *really suited my writing style, which is to skip around from one scene to another, getting it all down on the page and then finding the connection points where I can knit the story together. What was difficult was deciding how to maintain the suspense; after all, we know from the beginning that the main characters are going to die, and we know how. The trick was to keep asking why, and to find new answers all the way through. Eventually, with a lot of help from my editor, I settled on this circular framework in which the deadly confrontation happens near the end, where it matters most.*

The characters in this novel are utterly absorbing right from the outset—compelling at some moments, repulsive in others. Were any of them more difficult to write than others?

Only Celia was difficult to write, mainly because what she wants most is to stay in Jawbone Ridge with Rory and Eric; it's a passive desire, much more difficult to express than those of a character like Julian, for instance, who is continually on the make. Celia's passivity frustrated me and made it difficult to forge a connection.

I don't dislike her, though. I have always been drawn to characters who challenge my empathy. Those are the ones who feel most real to me, who surprise me and hold my attention over the months and years it takes to complete a novel. I want to be in conflict with the characters along the way, as they are with each other. I really want to work for that understanding and make the reader work for it, as well. Likable people are easy by definition, but to feel for someone with whom you fundamentally disagree takes a certain amount of perseverance.

The ancient Blackbird Hotel—located in the snowy, mountainside town of Jawbone Ridge that is teetering on the edge of oblivion—easily comes across as a character in and of itself. What drew you to this remote and dilapidated setting, and what helped you bring its walls to life?

The setting was inspired by Jerome, Arizona, a touristy ghost town perched on a steep hillside, held in place by sheer stubbornness and a profusion of two-by-fours. I was intrigued by the idea of living in a home like that and wondered how, over time, it might come to affect the psyche of the residents. Its precarious existence seemed to mirror the inner lives of these characters, who are holding their relationship together in the same way and whose efforts will also ultimately fail. I wanted that failure to feel like a certainty. You just know the town—and the romance—can't survive.

To the town I added the Blackbird Hotel. Actually, I should reverse that. The Blackbird came first, before Jawbone Ridge, before the characters and any inkling of their story. Stephen King refers to the writing process as an excavation, and I agree. Certainly it was true of the Blackbird, which existed in my mind's eye for years before I actually uncovered it, blew the dust out of the rooms and moved my characters inside.

Like *The Undoing*, your previous novel, *Alice Close Your Eyes*, delves into a complex romantic relationship between dark and damaged characters—exploring themes of love and obsession and the question of whether we can ever truly

know another person. Can you discuss the significance of these themes in your writing?

I'm not sure where these preoccupations come from or why writers tend to circle the drain this way. Probably they are an amalgam of experience and observation, childhood terrors and adult infatuation. Whatever the case, for me there is something unbearably poignant about the human desire to know and be known, eternally at odds with the need for privacy and self-protection. We each are separated from one another by the things we keep secret or are unable to express; that distance, no matter how slender, imparts a loneliness to our existence that we never can quite overcome. I'm convinced that this is what lies at the heart of every lover's obsession. We long to connect, and so we imagine connections where none exist. I feel for Julian in that way. He has realized what the other characters only vaguely sense: that he is, and always will be, alone.

Do you read other fiction while you're working on a book, or do you find it distracting? Can you tell us about your writing process?

Most stories begin for me with other works of fiction. When I'm starting work on a new story, I spend a good amount of time watching movies, reading and listening to music. I'm looking for something that generates a particular reaction in me, something that evokes a mood or sparks an interesting line of thought.

From there, I decide where the story begins and jot down some ideas for where it might go. It's all rather nebulous at this point, and utterly disorganized. I actually prefer it that way. Writing can be intimidating, so when I'm starting a new project, I make a concerted effort to take the pressure off. I write the raw stuff longhand, with a cheap pen in a fat spiral notebook. My handwriting is awful, and the pages are covered with angry scratch-outs and incomprehensible notes up the margins, but beginning this way keeps me from having to face a blank computer screen unarmed.

My thought processes are equally messy. I hop from scene to scene, trying not to deny myself any wild idea at this stage, whether or not I understand how it relates to the story. I carry on this way until I've assembled quite a scrapalanche—maybe thirty thousand to forty thousand words. Then I go through the scenes one by one and organize them into a new document, using only the ones that seem to matter to the story.

Beyond this point, it's rare for me to write anything extraneous. I've figured out what the story is about and have developed an understanding of the characters. All that remains is to keep adding material until the book is complete.

With two books under your belt now, what's on the horizon for you? Are you working on a new project?

Yes, I'm just beginning work on a new novel, which is still at such a nascent stage that I'm not completely sure where it will end up. I tend to make several false starts before I really settle on an idea—and with about five of those behind me now, it's safe to say I'm closing in!